The River Horsemen

THE RIVER HORSEMEN

David Williams

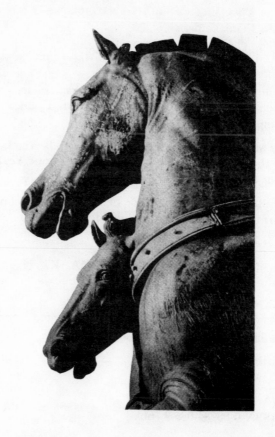

ANANSI   TORONTO

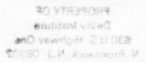
This is a work of fiction. No resemblance is intended to any persons living or dead.

Cover design: Laurel Angeloff
Author photograph: K. Walz

The author acknowledges with thanks the assistance of the Canada Council and the Manitoba Arts Council during the writing of this novel.

"The Magi", from *Collected Poems*, by W.B. Yeats, is reprinted with the kind permission of M.B. Yeats, Anne Yeats and Macmillan London Limited.

Published with the assistance of the Canada Council and the Ontario Arts Council, and printed in Canada for
House of Anansi Press Limited
35 Britain Street
Toronto, Ontario M5A 1R7

Canadian Cataloguing in Publication Data

Williams, David, 1945-
   The river horsemen

(Anansi fiction series ; AF 43)
ISBN 0-88784-086-8 (pbk.)

I. Title.

PS8595.I4762R59   C813'.54   C81-094224-0
PR9199.3.W543R59

1 2 3 4 5 / 87 86 85 84 83 82 81

This book is for Darlene Williams, dreamer
and for Steve Hawrishok and Perry Reilander, voyageurs

CONTENTS

CONTENTS

And I saw when the Lamb opened one of the seals, and I heard, as it were the noise of thunder, one of the four beasts saying, Come and see.

Revelation vi, 1

Now as at all times I can see in the mind's eye,
In their stiff, painted clothes, the pale unsatisfied ones
Appear and disappear in the blue depth of the sky
With all their ancient faces like rain-beaten stones,
And all their helms of silver hovering side by side,
And all their eyes still fixed, hoping to find once more
Being by Calvary's turbulence unsatisfied,
The uncontrollable mystery on the bestial floor.

W.B. Yeats, *The Magi*

FRIDAY

Nick

"Gone," the auctioneer calls above the crack of his hammer. It's the first word I've heard since I got to the rink. Even now I wouldn't know what was bid on if there wasn't printing on that box.

"Now that's what I call a fishy deal," the man reads my mind. "Look at the fellow agree! Yessir. Sockeye at three cents a tin. Somebody feasts tonight!"

But you're supposed to have the cash for a case of it.

Loads of hungry faces here. Not one that I know, save for Mr. Strickert's. I thought David would come, at least. Probably holed up at home with Mama.

The auctioneer plots with one of his helpers. His umpteen gallon hat nods that it sure is too big to be passed. Sure as shootin' too big for this hole he's in. He must be pretty hard up too — or a piss-poor seller — to be gone so far from home.

"Well, they tell me we've finished off the store goods," he says clear enough. "Hell, back home the grasshoppers get more to eat than that. Now I guess we've got to start in on the fixtures."

Mr. Strickert leans against the penalty box, looking beyond disappointment. The bright blank of sky itself seems to weigh down on him. Still he's been man enough never to cry how the sky was falling.

That day his handbills went up, he winked and said, "You'd think I would recall who it was pushed me over the edge like this. Oh, you don't have to look so guilty, none of you. I mean the clerk in that wholesaler's office who still reads Accounts Receivable. Maybe I'd like to thank him for saving me from this business." He laughed a good laugh, not the least bit hollow, and cut another taste from the cheese wheel. A farmer, probably some charge account, stuck out his hand for it. Then everyone in the Red & White laughed. Me too. I used to help David lug those cases from the cellar to the front.

At least all the charge accounts stayed away today. Too embarrassed to buy the guy out with his own money. Not like coming to see Dad off on the train for nothing.

"Bring her up to the podium, boys," the auctioneer says. "Give everyone a look at what you need to make money."

His helpers set the cash register on the table. Its white flag shows 40.00 in the window.

"She's a humdinger," the auctioneer says. He presses one brassy key. The 50.00 flag pops up with a fighting ring. Was it only last week we were listening to Joe Louis take the crown away from James J. Braddock?

The mantel radio sits the next table over. I think of the way it put us right inside of Madison Square Gardens. Dad never had the money for no radio. Now if he weren't sick . . . but aaa! there's bound to be more auctions when Dad is better.

"Well, say now, who'll put up fifty just to put his hand in this here till?"

Folks snicker nervously.

"Lord knows you all could use a till to stash that cash you're hanging onto today. Lord knows as well it's safer than a bank. Ain't that so, Mr Lawless?"

A beefeater's face turns a shade darker red. The man looks like a banker, too.

The auctioneer is much too wise to hurry one last guffaw.

"So who starts the bid at forty?"

But soon he's back in a rush and his words go away.

I look down at the box of goods on this table.

General Wolfe's face gapes at me like a fish under glass. It used to hang on their living room wall. It give me the creeps till David called those dozen man-eaters lolled about the Canuck

Apostles. Then I could see something in the Indian squatting there, his chin in his hand. The Thinker. Yeuhh, those were alright times.

The auctioneer's voice comes clear once more.

"Well okay, we'll start at twenty, folks. Surely there's a one of you here would spot twenty to go into business for himself. Oh, who'll gim — "

The sound of his voice shifts slightly, blurring everything again.

I strain out of the corner of my eye to watch Buddy Cutler cutting up on me from behind. I get my hand back there in time. Then his thumb finds me anyway, giving me a sharp goose. I look at him as if to say, Will you ever grow up? But my eyes must say instead, Am I relieved to see your face! Even a simpering puss like yours.

"What the hell are they trying to get for that piece of junk?" he whispers louder than most folks talk.

"Forty," I say like a human being.

"Shit, it's not worth twenty."

But then his dad is hardly on relief, is he, in that beer parlour business? *Hotel* business, they're always correcting you next door. Still we see what goes in and comes out.

More strangers saunter through the break in the end boards. The Strickerts' brick house stands empty beyond.

So maybe David and I will start off equal again.

The thunderhead swells beyond the elevators. It's out over the lake.

The auctioneer's voice falls away.

And what if I can never catch up to David Strickert? Maybe a real mother gives you a head start for life.

"Sold," the auctioneer speaks sensibly again, "for seventeen fifty."

"What did I tell you?" Buddy digs one thick thumb in my ribs.

"Keep your Christly hands to yourself."

"Aaaa, sore loser. Uke," he adds as an afterthought.

I ignore him, occupying myself with a big box of books. "David Copperfield." "The Adventures of Tom Sawyer." "Treasure Island." All mine and David's favourites. He must be leaving his whole library behind. "The Holy Bible." That's more likely to be somebody's slip-up. I wonder if the box didn't come here by mistake. They say the bailiff's not allowed to clean you out like that.

I check inside the cover to be sure. Nope. Somebody else. Longstreet. Hell, where were they when they named Lacjardin? 1858. Fifty years too soon for this dump.

David Longstreet Strickert   Februrary 26, 1922

Well, I'll be damned. Longstreet's what that "L" is for. The way David's been so ascaired of pussy, I called him Lily. Though you'd think Lily would rub him worse than that maiden name. Mother-fucking only child.

My fingers rise on a maiden bump beneath the lining. *Oi boizha!* A mound of banknotes.

"What have you got there?" Buddy says sharply.

"Nothing. A Christly Bible. What's that on the block?"

"Jars of canning fruit. Pears like her tits."

A thick woman whirls on us, scowling. Then she bids to show us. Her underarm rolls like dough.

There were always cinammon buns on Strickerts' cupboard. The tea towel would be still warm over them after school. Grace made them at noon, before she went back to the store. When she came home at five-thirty she'd say, "Stay to supper. Your father won't miss you tonight, will he? We're having Campfire Sausage." Knowing it would be potatoes and more potatoes at home. The only time we'd get meat in our soup — or fruit, golden juicy oranges — Grace had stuck it in with our order of salt and soap. So at ten after six when Mr Strickert came home, he had only to put his head in at the living room door and say, "Amos 'n Andy at eight, boys." With radio you were spared from having to eat and run.

"Don't tell me *you're* fond of Bibles, Nick," Buddy insists. "Say you were planning to sell them door to door for big bucks. Or have you gone and got religion since the preacher moved in on you?"

"Sure. Why not."

I pretend to be interested in what's on the block.

"So, which is it, fuckhead? Okay, don't tell your old pal Buddy. I know myself there's money in religion, eh?"

It's true. Buddy's got a sixth sense for money. He can smell it like some guys say they smell pussy.

"Damn tootin' there's money in it if Nick Sobchuk's around,"

Buddy says to the next three or four rows of bystanders. "Eh, Nick?"

And gives me that fierce dig in the ribs again. I'd slug him if it weren't for the Bible.

"Piss on you, *putzirrinsky*," I say as soon as the eyes turn away. "I'm not the only one out for money, eh?"

Like the time he bottled his piss and sold it to Colin McComb. The old sot never knew the difference. He got drunk, sitting on the sidewalk in front of the hotel. Buddy lined us up, two cents a bottle, to fill a whole case. With old Colin there, just around the corner, singing them tear-jerking songs.

Again the auctioneer chants some kind of inhuman language.

Marsella said she heard it in the night again, beneath the bed. I didn't believe her. I knew it was a lie when Mother stopped me from looking. She blocked me from behind the stove too. She said it meant someone was going to die. "Aaaa," I said, "in India maybe."

So I told Marsella, "You don't have to act like a *herbooza* any more."

Then Phyllis got her back up like a cat next to water.

"Leave her alone," she said. "She can't help it if she's not as smart as you."

"*Boizha*," I told her, "do you think she's a pumpkin too? Marsella, you can cut out acting like Mother now. She can't praise you from the loony bin."

Something moans. I jump. Turning around, I have to face a flour-skinned woman. Her hair is cut straight, too, across her bony face. And her dress is only two flour sacks sewn together.

I try not to fall.

She's not looking at me. Her eyes have swooned to that singsong gibberish. I swing back on the auctioneer, fighting to hear a single word.

Six. Six. Six something. The bid for a treadle sewing machine. And Grace only bought it last year.

I should be the one to groan. Dad could use heavy-duty needles in it. No more mending shoes by hand. And here I'm letting it pass with probably scads of money at hand.

"Well, I've seen plenty," I say to Buddy. "See you around."

"Me too. Guess I'll come along."

Trust him to catch a glimpse of plenty soon as the next guy.

I try to stare him down. He beats me; I look aside. He's got fuzz, like fur, growing on his ears.

I shiver with that thunderhead passing in front of the sun. Though it's as hot in here as behind the stove.

Aaaa. Just the cat sits back of the stove. Till she's ready to go mousing.

"Let's get out of here then," I say.

For a moment the strange faces blur. Then mix like words in my stomach.

That's stupid. Not a soul here knows me.

I put the Bible up under my arm like the preacher. We push through. The air is hot and smothery. All of a sudden it is breathless still.

"Books," the auctioneer says plain as day. "It's a carton of books."

After awhile, I'm relieved I didn't bolt. Now I can walk through the ring of up-staring faces. Past the shack, through the gap behind goal.

The air is like ice. All those afternoons of breaking in on David there in goal. Aaaa, it's over. Forget it, Dad says. Better to start over.

Through the garden fence I see the Strickerts starting over. With only a table and chairs . . . the stove with soot smeared up its back. Well, no big hairy deal there. The beds are set flat in the grass, nothing under them either.

But I look up and there is Mrs Strickert in the gable window. I nearly drop the Bible.

The thunderhead looms over the house.

Suddenly everything wants to plunge; I can't hold it back. It just goes on plunging and plunging.

Buddy's voice sounds far above me.

"What's wrong with you?"

I puke . . . on pigweed, I think. My guts . . . heave.

"Take your time," Buddy offers his kind of comfort. "At least you've put the shack between your weak guts and the world."

I spit, noticing the weathered boards now on my left. Then heave . . . some more. It tastes enough like salt cod. Relief. The sort just doused in lye.

Buddy comes back from somewhere.

"You ain't finished yet?"

"Ahhgh . . ." I get out at last. "Be glad you don't eat that shit they send from down east."

A little spit rinses my mouth. Lye burns in my throat. Still that meal in the weeds looks the same as on the table.

"What'd you do with that Bible?" Buddy says suddenly.

"I threw it up."

He looks at me accusingly. Then sees the bulge in the bib of my overalls.

"Thought you could fool me, eh? Let's see what we got."

"Are you crazy?"

"Okay, let's go to the other side of the stable."

Maybe a horse will run out and knock him down.

But as we duck across the livery yard, I see that cloud come tumbling by the tops of the elevators. Then it's falling like night.

A blast of wind stiffens us up on the hitching ground.

"It's hail," I say suddenly, feeling the cold in it. I feel sick about what the farmers might have paid us. "Annex look okay to you?"

"Lead on, Macduff."

He'd have to mention that play. Just have to. When he never even read it for class.

We gallop out onto main street, in view of the store. *Oi boizha!* It's the preacher stumping down the boardwalk, still a block away. Maybe too far to see. I take off for the annex.

The elevators light up, white around the edges. Then the thunder swallows us.

Just when the first hail bounces off the ground, we get crouched in the space between the annexes. The stones hit like baseballs on the neck of the elevator, plunging at our feet. We squeeze away from the growing drift.

Strangely, I don't feel all that bad. A little kicked in the stomach. There, it's better with the bib emptied.

In the growing darkness, I let my fingers trace the inside cover of the bible. The lining is double-stitched.

I've gotten a stitch of my own in my stomach. From being cramped. At least my lungs are stopped burning.

Buddy pants and pants with the oddest intake of breath.

"Stop your damn moaning, will you?" I say over my shoulder.

Then I rip the cover off the book.

Many-birds

She's gone. There ain't a single dress left in this closet. Not even a pair of panties on the floor or bed for a sign.

Gone. And I did it to her. I don't know why. It was good the way it was. I knew what to say in the kitchen, drinking a glass of cold water from the well. She'd smile that way and act like she didn't know what I was after. But she knew. Be so goddam nice, too, while holding it away. Now the fort's left empty. Should burn the fucker down.

She was looking for it, fershitsake. She didn't need no man around for chores. She come here off a farm, nothing there but chores. All the men knew it, what she was looking for. The way they talked and laughed outside the poolroom. But she didn't like none of them white guys. She ain't no squaw, like that. Those hoo-ers. She wouldn't do it for no six bottles of beer. I should of let things stand the way they was. Goddam.

That goddam barber. If he was Indian, even. But a bohunk barber. Sneaking up on her in the middle of an afternoon. That bohunk scalper. His next haircut, he trims it himself with his scalp in one hand.

Right on this bed he jumps us from behind. Then he chokes the lights outa me. The last thing I hear's her screaming, before I wake up on the floor. And *him*, looking down on me, holding that razor, almost smiling. He's fighting his hate pisspoor as them guards in the pen used to do. When I raise my head, I see her sitting on the bed. She's up against the wall with a sheet around her, her eyes wild as a mare in a prairie fire. She's looking at me as if I ain't even here.

He looks at me, then at her.

"You fucking squaw breed," he says in a bohunk voice, "I should let your Ind-yun blood run out with his."

I cough, spit up on his rug, and then see hair like crow feathers lying round the floor. My head goes cold.

His mouth jerks, crowing.

"Or maybe," he says, staring just above my eyes, "I should make the two of you look the same."

I hear her voice rising. My head, when my fingers brush it, is just shank bone. I look up at his crotch. The sonuvabitch is too tall to catch before that knife comes down. And he ain't going to turn away right now. But he'll have to gut me, if he plans to turn his back again.

"Ind-yun," he says in a voice that tries to cut like the steel razor, "you get your boar's ass outa here before I send them little pigs to market."

Fershitsake. Why be sent up to the pen again for something like him? So I don't look at him no more. I see her only.

"Agnes," I say.

Her eyes dart off my head like I am the ugliest man alive. Before, it was good to be naked. Her shoulders shake so hard she can't stop it, and the sheet slides down off one of them full tits. I'm already naked for her. The one man in the room.

The bohunk carves pictures in the air with that straightrazor.

"I'll count two, Ind-yun. After that, I cut this bitch another souvenir."

I was powerfully naked, then. Now there's nothing I can do. I get up like a horse, rubbing my neck a little. But she is watching him, not me. I got to watch him too, reaching beside him for my pants. He stands like a gopher, gawking around, only a knife in his hand.

"Take that haircut downtown," he says, "and show how Mikey Betrofsky does it."

The last I see of her, she is sitting with that sheet around her, clean and white.

I opened that window when she closed the curtains. I asked if there wasn't more chores I could do for her.

She laughed. She pulled the curtains across my face. She even shut the window once on my hand. I should have left it that way, fershitsake. Before she left.

Saskatoon. Ain't she got a sister there? Alvie? Elsie? Something like that, without the bohunk handle. Agnes used to bitch, how there was nothing in small towns for a woman like her. Why couldn't she have it more like her sister Elsie?

My feet sound like a drum behind me down the hall. That bohunk ain't waiting, is he? Place so dark, I never should of come in, except the door was still open.

Yesterday.

I got to get outa this sweat-hole, go someplace clean and cool.

I come out the back door into air as steamy as a mare in heat. Yesterday. I should have kept hoeing in the dry dirt of the garden. My belly boils, thinking about it. Like those clouds out there.

I turn the corner by the poolroom. Just three white guys sitting on the steps. I'll get by them easy. They look up through their smoke and spit. Their laughs come after, like the sound of a axe when you see a man chop a long ways off.

"Here comes the world's second greatest lover," one says.

I'd chop his tongue off for that. Fucking king only give up a crown the size of his asshole.

"Hey Many-birds, weren't you good enough, you had to use your head that way?"

"You don't haffa feel bad, that stuff really makes hair grow."

"Fuckyerselves," I say, but one of them stands in the way with a pair of rubber boots.

"Sell you her size," he says. "Real good price. Only been worn by three or four of us."

I got to weasel out of all their hoot and holler. But I walk down the sidewalk like a man, not a goddam gopher. The barber shack is closed, no sign of life. The bastard's even gonna try to beat me to her.

I look away in time from all the glass in the hotel. Then I cut down the path through the trees to the railway station. Platform filled with cream cans. Bright red wagon, CPR on it. I see the face of the guy through the butt-out window. Fat, with a green beak over his eyes. He looks up at me through the glass. I'd like to twist his beak so he couldn't caw.

This morning. Maybe he saw her.

He's got to caw. Was she waiting here to go with all those goddam cream cans? Her ticket would show. Bought inside.

Oily boards in the waiting room, smell of that green shit they use to get rid of whitesmell. Pictures on the walls above the slat-curved benches. Trains coming out of tunnels in the mountains. Last month the king rode a train with his bride through the mountains. But first he rode the train alone to go to her. Once she got clear of that fucking husband.   ·

Greenbeak is clicking away at his machine. He won't look. I wonder if she left me any messages or signs. I watch him through the bars. His machine clicks back at him. He's writing quick. Then he turns around.

"Yes," he says in a click.

I look at him through the bars, like it's me, not him locked in. Like they might send me up to P.A. again if I even ask. Well, let them, the bastards.

"Did she leave me any messages?" I say, jerking my head at his machine.

"Who?" he says, raising his green beak a bit. His face sure enough looks like the inside of a bird's throat.

"Agnes Betrofsky. Did she buy a ticket to Saskatoon this morning?"

"That's CPR information," he says, like a magpie been taught to talk. "What's a guy like you got a right to know for? You got shares in the company or something?"

My guts bunch to think of shares.

"Did she maybe say where she was going?" I ask quick, so's I can breathe again.

"No," he says, looking and looking at my head. "If you want a ticket somewhere, fine, okay. Otherwise observe the sign. Can't you read? It says, NO LOITERING."

A fat prairie chicken like that, I don't know why she'd tell him anything. It won't do no good to ask about the bohunk. I leave Greenbeak's window, looking at the pictures.

"Say," he says suddenly, standing up, "ain't you the Ind-yun the Mounties took away that time on the train? Tell you what, I sure am curious what happened to your head. You can wait here if you tell me about it."

Wait for what? I think. There's only a train out from Saskatoon tonight. She wouldn't be coming back yet.

Greenbeak is over to the window, leaning on his little cage. I stay where I am, not looking at him. Then I look.

"Scalped," I say, just like that. "Indians. They're gonna do lots more of it."

"Bullshit," he says, "you're joking."

I look square at him.

"Do I look like some joker? They scalped me and raped that Mrs Betrofsky. All because I backed her husband, not to let Indians sit in his barbershop. I was working for him. I had to."

"That's crazy," he said. "Why wouldn't they scalp *him*?"

"I warned him. He just got away."

Greenbeak looks like he is thinking it over.

"Saskatoon," he says at last. "She took this morning's train, is all I know. A lot of boxes, suitcases. Had to help load 'em on the baggage car."

"What about my boss? He go with her?"

"Nope. He just brought her here and left."

I'm headed for the door.

"Why wouldn't he go too if, like you say, there's going to be more trouble?"

"It's his trouble," I say. "I guess he's got to stick around for the police."

"Well, waiting room is always open to the public," he says, "till after the night train."

But I am going the wrong way every last step up the track. Maybe Walking Horse or somebody can dig up cash for the trip. Then I can catch the morning train. Start my hunt in the morning. I bagged lotsa birds in the morning before, geese and partridge and all.

I am still in cinders an' shit between the rails, running so my teeth click on ties, when I see Thunder Bird's eyes flash out fire. And here's me without so much as a hat.

"Please don't be angry with me, Thunder Bird," I say, "because I am chasing after a white woman. If you saw her, she would make you want to be more proud and fly higher than even you do, great as you are. I don't know, anyway, she might be part Indian like some say. Come with me to see her, and hold off if you can till I get home."

But he don't. Just as I get to the grain sheds, he drops down in fire on the trees by the lake. As quick he flies up with the pieces in his burning claws to Sky. No sooner is Thunder Bird roaring back up than Sky rains stones on me, stinging my bones. I turn to run with my hands over my goddam head. But the stones smash my fingers, hammer my back, skip ahead on the ties, white, white as she was with her back against the wall. I look for a break in the goddam sheds.

Nick

The Bible spatters bills all over hell. Lightning flashes. Then it's raining money. Enough, for once, for Dad to start over.

"Holy Daddy Bigbucks!" Buddy shouts. "We're — " His voice is drowned in the wave of thunder.

But the notes look strange, even in this light.

I pluck one from the edge of the ice.

Confederate
States of   America. $100. Picture of some man and woman I don't know.

The hail batters the wood above us, clicking and chipping at our feet.

I can barely sit with my heels under my hams. Buddy has his fists full of bygones.

"There's thousands," he gloats. "Thousands!" Then the ugliness passes out of his face. "They'll miss all this much, won't they?"

I want to clutch at it like straws. But it's good for nothing, I know.

"You ever hear of confederate money?" I holler spitefully. It's almost worth it to see his look of disappointment.

Then he looks at me like I'm trying to cheat him.

So I leaf through a scatter of the rest. "It's as worthless as yesterday. Look at it for yourself."

Then I spy a single greenback in my part of the *miche*. I wait for Buddy to paw into his heap. He does. It's his nature to prove me wrong. Good for him. Atta boy.

The second his head is turned, I pluck out the Silver Certificate. A United States one. Again some woman I don't know. But that's the guy, their hero, who chopped down the cherry tree. They stare from oval frames at me. I slip it quick in my pocket.

Boizha! There could still be some kind of coin pasted here inside the lining!

"Shit!"

Now Buddy's bills seem to paste themselves against the wall. They cling, then slip down under the raining hailstones. A gust of wind whips into our cranny. Seeing gets washed away for a second. Above us the annex echoes like the storm itself.

"I didn't know," Buddy looks like a sleek drowned cat, "that Strickert was a damnyankee."

"You never know," I shout back. But I do know Mr Strickert came out from Ontario. Prince Edward County. So Grace Longstreet lost a home at least once before that.

Well, nobody ever said you could take it with you.

A face looks in at us from off the trackside. I stuff the telltale Bible in the dirt beneath these studdings.

Without asking, that stranger pushes right in on us. He's strange, all right. He shakes himself like a dog, but he's much too bald to be wet. Damn near as slick as a snooker ball. Sure; the four ball. It's that Indian who hired on as the new barber's apprentice. No wonder he's suddenly so bald.

He squats, looking round. For a minute I wonder if I've landed in "The Death of General Wolfe." The Thinker glares back at my stare. Then he spies his fortune laid conveniently on the ground. You can see he's learned something from the barber. He grabs up a bill; fingers it; lets it drop. So he's already learned the difference between a joker and a king.

Dad could have taught him more than Betrofsky. If the Thinker really wanted to start over. We should be rid, like the States, of kings. That's why it's the best place, Dad says, to start over. Though he won't ever go himself. His folks came from Ukraine. The bolsheviks took away his chance.

The hail begins to lessen. Then sweeps back, hurling rocks by the hundreds. The Thinker rubs his head, his arms, as if the thought could pain him. He's a pretty grim advertisement, all right, for starting over. I should ask him how Betrofsky the barber is doing. That palooka. But it's too loud around here anyway.

East of town the lightning forks. Thunder rumbles a little beneath the hail. Then Buddy bawls so that the Indian jumps like me. His knee jabs into my thigh, shovel-blunt. *Shlockstrocken!* I rub my leg.

Buddy's got my coin cupped in both hands. I catch a gleam of gold.

"Give me that back!" For an instant I'm afraid no one can understand me.

Then Buddy reads my face; shakes his head. The bugger seems to think he found it.

The hail has quit. This sudden silence is almost scary. Only water pitching off the roof.

"Okay," I say soothingly. "Fifty-fifty, Buddy. You know who took the risk to get it."

"Finders kee —" Buddy starts to say. Then notices my face. He appeals to the Thinker. "Okay. You heard him, eh? Fifty-fifty?"

The Thinker looks wise.

I squeeze it with a thumb and forefinger.

Gold isn't nearly as heavy as I thought. But *boizha*, isn't it beautiful! With its gold eagle on the front. Ten dollars. Sewn in, I'll bet, for a rainy day. Something old, something new; something borrowed, you can't feel blue. You bet your life Dad's had too many rainy days. With never a house of brick to relax in. I'll take him some —

A ton of bricks hits me on the cheek. I fall all over somebody.
"Shit," Buddy's voice struggles under me. "Grab the bastard, will you?"

But I lay facedown on the ice. The hail eats the throbbing pain out of my cheek. Footsteps skid and skitter out of hearing. Buddy's not so dumb he'd call for help. I lie at rest.

"Nick," the preacher calls from beside the other annex.

I have to struggle up, casting round for that damn Bible cover. I will make you fishers of men . . . if I find you, you bugger. There. *Boizha!* Stuff it where the sun don't shine.

"Nick? Nick, are you in here?"

Jesus, but his voice grates on me. I wish he'd get lost.

Then I'm looking down and I see everything's snow white. There aren't any words, any names, written down at all. The page is a blank.

Jack

There's not much left of the liveryman's garden; it looks as if the horses had got out and trampled it. In fact, the whole street gives out upon a City of Destruction.

I was standing in the stable doorway, watching the ice bounce high as a man's head, when the lightning cracked behind me. I turned to see a pale mare splinter the planks out of her stall. Then all the beasts were stamping and neighing like the four horses of the Apocalypse, and I was afraid.

But the storm has passed; some of us are spared this once. Yet a time of destruction cometh.

The windows of Strickerts' Red & White are broken *divided like the walls of the Red Sea* great shards of glass left standing in paint-chipped frames *now are His people called to cross unto a Promised Land* and Nick will think I broke my promise when I said God could heal his father *but first we must wander forty years in a desert* God, it doesn't bear thinking about.

Plagues of drought and locusts Think about the poor farmers, their every hope of summer flattened, gone in the twinkling of an eye. This, too, was the year it seemed they would get a crop. Just this morning everything looked so green. And Nick, who left home so hopeful after lunch, what do I tell him next? I know his sisters aren't loving daughters. But Nick idolizes old Nick *so Dagon lies broken and we ate fish on Friday; like an idolater I had to serve fish*

"Nick," I call out in fear and great trembling. He may have crossed to safety between the walls of these elevators. Pray God he may.

"Nick, are you in here?"

Suddenly I can't hold back my tears. I weep. I have not lived up to the promise I gave when I moved in with them.

After I blow my nose, I recall how it was the verse, 'Jesus wept,' that made me believe. I used to quote it as a kid in Sunday School since it was handy; I didn't have to think when it came my turn. Besides, it fooled the teacher and made the Sunday scholars laugh. But then I saw one day that if Jesus wept, why He was with us, He walked where we must walk, He felt what we do feel. And it made me weep likewise to see how He was here to touch people and raise them up; He couldn't bear either to see folks sicken and suffer. So I tried to be like Jesus, though not my will but Thine be done. And I've done what I could to let Him heal the ills of folk, whether they be doubt, fear, loneliness, or sorrow, or if they're blind, lame, halt, and poor in spirit.

Perhaps He may raise us, then, in spirit, since He no longer — at least not yet — sees fit to lead us over Jordan.

Nick

I trace the edges of my bruised cheekbone.

I hate her.

"Goddamn you," I say. *"Shlockdybetrofet."* I'll speak Ukrainian for that if I have to. Go to hell.

Her eyes, like plates, are gone to smash. I knew she'd never face me throwing back at her.

"Nick," she blubbers. "Nickie. You know I never meant to —"

She's never meant anything. That's the trouble with her; it's why she's crazy like that.

"Nick," she wails, "don't hurt yourself worse. It won't help anything, will it? Nick, it won't. Don't, don't." Then her voice relaxes and deepens. "That's better, Nick, better. Let your grief out, now. Just let it out."

The preacher is staring out of troubled eyes at me.

Mother's eyes looked awful again. They were pressing — just pressing — as they had every other time she went over the edge. Now I didn't want to hear her crazy story any more. So of course she'd try to convince me in front of the others.

"They were all thrown down," she said. "They dropped right out of Heaven. It is *so* true, Nick. They all fell down. But only the bad ones fell back in the bush. So they forgot how to talk to people. But the good ones still talk to us. They tell us things. That's how I know it's true. Maybe I don't know nothing by school, Nick. But I do know how you get lost from people. You should listen to *him* sometimes."

The rest of them stare superstitiously at the bed behind the curtain. Mother always keeps the bedspread down to the floor.

"*He* helps us sometimes out," she says. "You must listen, Nick, before it's too late. Not like your father. *He* could be still forgiving to you."

"Nick," the preacher says, "won't you forgive me? I don't know, sometimes, what happens to my sense. It just gets lost."

But I knew nothing had landed beneath the bed like that. I knew. Preachers and lunatic women, they like to think the worst all the time.

I stare at his weepy eyes.

"I should have spared you the details," he slobbers. "Oh, if I could have cut out my tongue before I told you that."

So I let my eyes tell him we got no serious difference of opinion.

He appears to drop off a ways. Finally he says, sort of hollow, "I'm really sorry, Nick. If there's anything at all I might do. . . ."

So I guess it won't hurt to go along with him.

"Sure, if there's anything at all."

But I know I've searched beneath that bed enough times before. And behind the stove. The only spirits I could come up

with were Puss and Boots. A total of two cats. Unless the sign
outside of town was meant to be a worried hint.

227
LACJARDIN   pop. ~~112~~

if you'd count them blasted curs

Yeuhh. Well, I'd still like to know who in this town had a
better right to worry about some haunts having got in with them.
They should have tried to live with a crazy woman for awhile, let
alone one who was going to get TB. Boy, I'll tell the world we had
bad enough getting in with us, before it was TB too.

A bobcat comes racing round the side of the annex. She brakes
when she sees me, broad paws rolling on stones.
I stare her backward, damping the icy fire in her eye.
She turns away snarling.
It is in that awful snarl that I remember the once-human face.
"Mother," I say sinkingly, "don't tell any more lies about me.
They know about you. They know who's the crazy one. It won't do
a bit of good any more to put the blame on me."

"Well, it's sure as hell not mine," Buddy eyes the preacher
warily.
Then his eyes flare up at me.
"Shit," he says. "You *are* blaming me, aren't you? Well, I wish
he'd knock you down again and put a little sense in you."
"Maybe," I feel myself hesitate now at the edge of nothing,
"you would help me, Jack, to speak to Mother."

She'll have to take back those lies she told. She'll have to quit
trying all the time to drag me down with her.

Jack

He saved others, himself he cannot save

No. No, Brother Giesbrecht, doubt not that God might save him yet. Do not sink into that Slough of Despond!

But Peter Giesbrecht only bows his head. I look down on his grey, wavy locks. I want to take him in my arms and comfort him.

I say, "God cannot mean to take the life of your only son. Maybe the doctors are right about Paul. It could be that his blood is filled with cancer. But God cannot mean for him to die, any more than He meant for Isaac to die on that altar He commanded Abraham to lay him. For perish the thought that He should break His covenant."

A glimmer of light has stolen into Peter Giesbrecht's eyes.

"Now don't you see, Brother Giesbrecht, that His covenant is with thee specially? You who must remember only who you are? For has He not called you to start Gethsemane Bible Institute at a time when your people were called out from their fathers' house unto a land which He has showed thee? And lo, there is famine in the land, but you have not gone down to Egypt, nor have given your wife into the hand of the Egyptians. You have stayed to call up all people who do love the Lord, not Mennonites only, nor those who speak the German tongue, but a new chosen people, called by grace to minister in these last days.

"Oh Peter, don't you see? Surely you have realized that it is your life, more than any other, which helped me remain a prophet of the Lord. In a way you saved me, Peter. The fact that I again was chosen. So don't you see? You need only choose yourself to confirm Him in his covenant, and your little Paul will be saved. Oh, He would prove you in it, Peter, and us in you, like the time He proved Abraham on the mount of Jehovah-jireh. For think you He now regards us less than He did little Isaac on that day?"

I look out the school window at the bracing of our great signboard by the highway's edge. There it proclaims to all passersby, but most of all to Love, that 'All things work together for good to them that love God, to them who are the called according to his purpose.' Rom. 8:28 Now I feel the faintest stirring in me that I, who deeply love the Lord, may be called upon again to make all things *work*.

Love, Saskatchewan! What a name for a town with Biblefounded beliefs. God could not have found one better for the founding of His inter-denominational school. I knew it before I got here. After all, I grew up pretty near this bush country. True, I've seen God rear His seedlings anywhere; but the tallest trees grow most often in the forest, far from towns and cities.

When my father wrote me in Ontario to say, Jack, they have a place prepared for you, I knew God had not forgotten a poor country boy. 'For those He did predestinate, He also called, and whom He called, He justified, and whom He justified, He also glorified.' And how should I doubt any promise so great as that? Especially when a man of Brother Giesbrecht's stature had called me? So I came in the fall with new life in my soul.

Brother Giesbrecht's face, like an outcropping of our northern rock, is washed by tears. Hesistantly he looks me in the eye.

"God sees you," I say. "Maybe He will even see fit to use this humble servant one more time. Will you not let me try to help you?"

Brother Giesbrecht's rasping accent is softened by an ultimate gentleness.

"Don't you think, Jack, that God has spoken clearly enough?"

"No." My own voice reflects his sorrow, as a mirror should give him back to himself. But I must keep alive in him the miracle of God's promise. "The example of our Lord is clear enough in His earthly ministry, isn't it? Jesus wept, but He also went out and did something about it. Why, two thirds of His career was spent in healing the sick! I can't accept the idea that God puts these afflictions on us to make us better Christians. Christ was the best Christian, and He wouldn't accept less than total deliverance of the human soul, both of mind and body. For our God is a good God, and the devil is a bad devil. Surely you see eye to eye with me on that? God helps them who'll help Him fool the devil."

"Dear Jack," Brother Giesbrecht's chest heaves like a sea of sorrow, "remember our Saviour died. That's why He was born. And He wasn't as old as I when they put Him on the cross. So you see, I have no special claim on my — my young son, Paul."

"Peter," I grasp his arm, "you don't think God wanted more than one crucifixion, do you? You don't believe He gave us His religion to put up with just the failures of life? He meant us to have life, Peter — to have it abundantly. Why, he meant us to have it in the living Christ."

Brother Giesbrecht only looks at me.

"We must be patient, Brother Cann. There are some things we cannot know."

"But why? Didn't our Saviour come here to be the Light of the World? Would you suppose *He* would set darkness in our paths?"

"But surely, Jack, you recall the end of that verse? 'I know that my redeemer liveth, and that he shall stand at the latter day upon the earth. And though after my skin worms destroy this body, yet in my flesh shall I see God.' And I know," Brother Giesbrecht's voice trembles only slightly, "I shall one day see my living son, Paul, clothed in His glory."

But little Paul died. Bright-eyed, blessed little Paul. He died, not even reaching the age of accountability, on Christmas morning.

Then how my heart went out to the Giesbrechts. All that nativity week Dorcas Giesbrecht had to cheat her grief. She stitched up her sorrow in our poor Bible students' clothing. Such faith amazed and even heartened me. But I wept for that woman in her Christmas of the year of our Lord, nineteen hundred and thirty. And for her husband in his folly *who saved others, but his son, his very own son he would not save*

Poor Nick. How my heart goes out to him. *I would* But there was nothing I could do to save his father. Time was when I cured so much worse than pneumonia. And now I couldn't even spare him knowledge of his father lying choked beneath a bed. Oh, the hospital told me they found him so! What agonies he must have known in those final moments, drow . . . — his lungs filling with that self-made fluid. How he must have fought!

I don't blame Nick for hitting me. Naturally he'd strike out at the bearer of news so grievous to him. I believe he hoped, with his fists, to make a liar out of me. Flesh hoping ever to make a fool of the Word. But he is emptied at last of hate. And now he awaits the filling of love which surely must follow.

When those Indians see how desperately he seeks a mother's love, why, the bowels of their compassion will be opened unto him. Then he will board the train and go, in that deep hurt, to tie up again the broken cord of life.

So have I wanted to go myself unto a world that was broken, to reach out and touch folks and tell them of the love of the Man from Galilee. At times I was anointed, too, with the fullness of the Spirit, with the strength and glorious health of God. For I in His name have raised up multitudes. So will He raise up again His hallowed Fool. All things must work together for good to them who will love Him as ever.

Nick

I wake up, wringing with sweat. I feel how strongly the dream wants me back. But if I give in to its pull, I'll go over the edge.

I stare at the shadows moving over the wall, trying to firm them up in my mind, trying just to hold them where they are.

Suddenly they've taken the shape of the Bunna place. The yard looks so empty now, sheds tumbled down, windows boarded up, grass growing belly high to the door.

If the Rangers hadn't lost Bill with his cut Achilles tendon last spring, they'd have won the Stanley Cup. Then we could have given a shit in Lacjardin for all the stubblejumpers from Nisooskan. Those guys thought they were so shit hot anyways. But Bill let us down.

Boizha, how many times were we let down? By the both of them?

"If you don't make her go," Bill said on that last day in the poolroom, "then you better go yourself, eh?"

"Hell," Bun said, "if the going's even going any more. Sometimes I'm scared to death to go back to New York and find the Gardens as deep in drifted dirt as our farm. You ever have a nightmare like that? Trying to skate in dirt to your knees?"

"Well, goodbye," Bill said briskly, but holding out his hand to every one of us. I was trying not to bawl, thinking how they wouldn't be ours any more. Never again would Foster Hewitt rasp from coast to coast, "New York may be a powerhouse, but it imports its power from Lacjardin, Saskatchewan."

"Goodbye," we said, and I saw on all our faces the feeling of loss before they had even pulled out on us.

We went indoors where their '36 Buick was waiting, blackly gleaming. You could see from the sidewalk that the back seat we'd all ridden on was piled with clothing, dishes, boots, shin pads, even their skates. It was true then. We were losing them forever.

At last Maxie Cooper said it for all of us.

"Don't forget, when you win the Stanley Cup, you come from Lacjardin, Sask."

Bill and Bun smiled sadly, and then looked square at every one of us. Maybe Maxie was right; maybe we couldn't lose them.

They drove off down the road, waving—

— and then the road was frozen over, or maybe it was the lake; we were skating, anyway, three on two at goal, and I could feel the hairy fronds touch up under the ice before the crack funnelled after us, and then there was nothing for a moment, or maybe less than nothing rushing everywhere around us. . . .

That's crazy. I'm in some muddy ditch. There's the Bunna place over there, off the road. I'm all right. I slipped in the mud, is all, trying to look around. I can't — I won't look back any more.

Jack

We walk up the hill side by side, Nick and I, and he's quiet now, I think his father's death is starting to be for him. He is surmounting life's supreme difficulty: to remember a loved one even as he was, and then to dismiss him.

Mrs Cozens wept and wept when I arranged for her to look after the children. Her husband's death last year is still, I suppose, too much with her. But people die and you have to let them go. You let go, or you go down to Sheol with them. Selah.

This mud on the roadway would get us down too, if we were not careful. It would be so easy to backslide were we not called to struggle onward, yea ever upward. But oh how difficult it has become to gain even this low hilltop!

The house there in the bluff looks no better nor worse than it did in the wintertime. Except it was never meant to be a winter habitation. The owners who abandoned it were hockey players or such; they suffered it merely in the summer. They never had to sit about the kitchen with snow sifting like flour around their feet. We stuffed rags in every nook and cranny, but to no avail. Even on a clear day the light of afternoon seemed to stripe our wall like the bars of a cage, a prison. Eventually the sun itself partitioned us, cold walls of purest crystal between.

We were sitting around Crystal's family's table on our first Christmas eve with one another Her sister Else and husband Henry Rempel, lately arrived, were seated opposite. Little Abe sat, in his excitement kicking the table leg, next to Crystal. Even her wild brother Thom, the one who ran away to be a cowboy, was home for Christmas. Now the moment supper was over, he pushed back from the table, all set, I would imagine, to sneak a smoke in the barn. But his mother hastened, as it were, to close the door before the horse got out.

"Father," she urged, "isn't it time to read the Christmas story?"

I could see her hold, with her hope alone, her doubting son Thomas.

Jake Hildebrandt looked up from a platter licked clean. No feature could have been more rounded nor more indefinite than the long cherub face which shone in that plate. Only his ears appeared to stand for anything at all. And they stuck far outside the circumference of his shining dish.

His eyes, in rising, evaded ours, even those of his eighty-three year old mother seated on his right hand. Her features, unlike his, seemed pinched from that platter and then kiln-fired. There was nonetheless in both, I thought, the same unbreakable quality, or perhaps the like capacity to hold much.

"Yes mother," Jake answered flatly, somewhat as a dish would answer *but never the dish who ran away with the spoon* I would have feared for him a little, that his wife might scour him after dinner, save he found at once his place in the well-thumbed Bible and began to read. And then another voice took hold of him. I don't mean just the German of Luther's Bible. He read in calm, steady tones like a man in whom serenity dwelt. The words, so memorable in the King's English, did not now seem strange to me. Their meaning dwelt at once in my heart.

And it came to pass in those days, that there went out a decree from Caesar Augustus, that all the world should be taxed. And this taxing was first made when Cyrenius was governor of Syria. And all went to be taxed, every one into his own city. And Joseph also went up from Galilee, out of the city of Nazareth, into Judaea, unto the city of David, which is called Bethlehem; because he was of the house and lineage of David; to be taxed with Mary his espoused wife, being great with child. And so it was, that, while they were there, the days were accomplished that she should be delivered. And she brought forth her firstborn son, and wrapped him in swaddling clothes, and laid him in a manger; because there was no room for them in the inn.

I caught Crystal looking shyly sidewise at me, and my heart pounded so, I feared they would hear it for a blasphemy. But I took it only for a promise.

The words of the story seemed suddenly to engulf the room in light, and I was there with Crystal around that blessed manger. My very bowels twitched out to entwine with hers, and then the child was ours, and the glory of the Lord shone round about. And the shepherds who arrived were come to White Fox, Saskatchewan, and a multitude of the heavenly host sang round about the house, and praised God in the sparkling cold of twenty-five below.

Crystal looked again at me and instantly she shone bright as the lamp of heaven. I seemed to see her from the eye of the belly, even deeply from the seat of my affections.

Glory to God in the highest, and on earth peace, good will toward men!

But my daddy, when I made known to him my intentions, showed less than good will towards these people. He said, "Son, you are a-setting out on the devil's work. You know she has not been properly saved and you know it says in scripture that a believer shall not be unequally yoked together with an unbeliever. Son, I think the devil is laying in wait for you to wreck your ministry."

I was shocked and grieved by my daddy's doubting word. I assured him in Christian humility it wasn't so. For in that radiant moment a voice had spoken unto me, "Jack Cann, take unto you this woman, this Crystal; make her to shine with my light and I will cause you to shine with Mine."

And it came to pass even as it was spoken. The Word which was from the beginning came to be with us; and the Word was made flesh, was for an ailing humanity made glorified. So we did glory in the Lord in spite of all our difficulties.

I'll never know why my Crystal, who was faithful, forsook me. She was never timorous nor mistrustful, not she who stood by me through doubt, dirt, and depression, through even drouth and despair, to see our God work His miracles. Oh, I suppose I'd have had to be a fool not to see how difficult it was for her, night after night, as God transformed the lives of others, while, day by day, it was all we could do to keep both body and soul together. But I thought we did at least cleave together through all our tribulations — before I found out she was cleaving to another. Then for a time the light went out of my life.

I must have fallen asleep In those weary days when I should have been waiting and watching, surely I was entered into an evil sleep. So must one have come to her who said, Will thou not be content to dwell with me if I give thee many delights? Then my faithful wife, unable to wake me from my faithless sleep, and finding no other near to succour her, must have given herself in lonely whoredom to that seducer.

Now the prophet Hosea, whom God called to be wed with a whore, now he was sent to preach by example unto Israel. But I — perhaps I can never preach again because of the evil of my sleeping.

God forgive me for my folly. At least I've retraced my steps to this place. So may I help this boy even now to escape the tempter. Together we might surmount the Hill Difficulty.

Many-birds

I told the long-necked guy and the kid they better get off the Reserve by dark.

The long-necked one give me such a hangdog look, still hanging on, we oughta got a rope and finished the job.

Trouble with stretching that neck is it'd come at you, afterwards, even round corners. I never seen the like. He kept honking like a goose in a fog.

Finally I couldn't keep my old man out of it. He's to the door before I know it. Wheezing like a winded horse. So I know he's come galloping from stud in her bedroom.

Puffed-up old fucker. Leaving a spread snatch in there. Like he's the only chief here. I'll go take over. If he wants to talk to Goose Neck so bad. I'll show the old cunt what a goose is all about. Old women are best anyway. They got to worry how each time might be the last. Can't afford to hold nothing back.

"Well my son," the old man says with that dog-grin of his, always grinning, "have you traded 'em our scalps now too? Or will they be happy with just that little one in your pants? I hope for our sakes you didn't lose that one, too, for her!"

And then wheezes away like a broken-down old horse. Blowing at us. That lovely stink. Fucking lucky old bastard. He ain't the only one who gets it for nothing.

"I never lost it," the kid whines. "I mean, he never traded a thing for it. He just lambasted me one."

And *just has* to touch his purple cheek where I got him. It shines through all the fuzz. Poor little crybaby Fuzzy Nuts.

Now Goose Neck cries, "He took the boy's savings, mister. Say, I'm sorry; we should have introduced ourselves. I'm Jack Cann. This is Nick Sobchuk, from the poolroom in Lacjardin."

The old man grins and nods like a horse in the wind.

"Many-birds. Edward Many-birds. Some looks at him, though, and calls me Many-More birds."

And cackles like a goddam hen. After he just about made it up to crow.

"You fellows are looking in the wrong place," I say. "For the wrong man."

"How many bald-headed Indians you got out here, Many-birds?"

Goose Neck really starts to grate on me.

"For the last time," I eye him carefully, "fuck off."

"It was you," the kid accuses me. "I got a witness."

My old man eyes me. And sees his only son sent up the river again. Then he goddam grins his face off. Thinking he could screw her, maybe, in the grass. No fear of me stumbling on top of 'em. Always crowing how his bedroom's too small for him, he can't turn around.

"Thunder Bird is *my* witness," I say, "I never stole this kid's money." It was the other kid's money. Saw him give it.

"You're a liar."

Somebody oughta teach this kid to respect the old ones. Before somebody hurts him bad.

Goose Neck says, "It was all his summer savings, Mr Manybirds. Picking beer bottles; trapping gophers. It's awfully important. His dad just died; his mother's sick with TB in Saskatoon; and he's got to get the train fare to go tell her. Won't you let us look around here for it? How much, Nick, did you say it was?"

"Uh — He got five dollars of mine."

Fuzzy Nuts sees my surprise. What can he be up to? He stole the ten himself, fershitsake.

"Come on in and look around," I say quickly. "I got nothing to hide."

Goose Neck is trying to figure me out.

"Will you let us search your pockets, too?"

Aaaagh. Crawly feeling of that neck poking round in my pants.

"It's no use," the kid says, quick as me. "He'll have it too well hid by now."

He only lost his father, anyway. The lucky bastard. I lost a woman. But Thunder Bird give me the money to go see her again.

And then I see it, almost like another flash from Thunder Bird's eyes.

"Sorry we can't help you *out*. But I know a guy who can. Old Fine-day there. Just down the road by the lake, half a mile. He's used to helping people. He helped my father a lot."

The old man is wheezing and cackling and crowing all at once. He won't think to ask for my money tonight. Too busy being cocky about the whole situation.

Goose Neck and the kid should be gone for good. That old turd, Fine-day will scare the shit outa them with all his fear. So I'll be on the train like that king in the morning. To be with the woman I love.

I got to remember to smoke some tobacco to Thunder Bird. And ask for his blessing that things will stay so easy as this.

Jack

That face. Now why should I imagine that I've seen that face before?

I know what it was: a nightmare, the like of which you'd not imagine.

I dreamed (I have tried for so long to forget it) that I was in this very old house and I didn't want to be there. It was terribly run-down and everywhere there were odours of decay. But that wasn't the reason I wanted to be out; there was some other presence, some awful thing lurking just around the corner. It was waiting out of sight in every room that I entered. Before I could leave, though, I had to do something, I wasn't sure what. And then I came into a room with a skeleton in the corner. I saw at once the breastplate lying there, so I began the work of girting up its ribs. Then I took the helmet of salvation with its wings of peace and I crowned with God's own glory that slack jaw, heir of all mankind's sinsickness. And in those bony fingers I was about to place a staff, Aaron's rod it must have been, when the front door opened, I heard it echo, and I waited, paralyzed, for some awful thing.

But there was no terrible principality or power which rushed into the room; it was that Indian with his face painted up in shocking stripes of purple, green, some black. He came near to me, and I was going to warn him about the hidden danger, when he gives me the strangest look and opens his mouth. His front teeth are all filed to a point, sharp as wolf's teeth, and he stands there grinning. I guess I'm as surprised as he when I pop my fingers in my mouth and show teeth just as filed and just as sharp as his. His bony jaw goes clack and he hightails it out the door. I hear the front door slam, and then I know I'm alone again with the terrible thing, I won't get out.

Later, I think, the house must be the world and it is filled with every kind of disease and decay. My job, then, is to put on the whole armour of God, to dress up corruptible with incorruption, mortal clothing itself in immortality. But then the devil comes bursting in, he's going to stop me from doing the work of the Lord. Suddenly, by God's grace alone, I am enabled to fool him, and I drive him off. But I am left here alone, God having gone out with the devil. And now doubt assails me that not even God's armour can keep the awful thing from coming.

Only now, in this latter hour, is my own folly made apparent to me. All along I have had in my bosom a key to unlock the doors of the dungeon! Instantly my beleaguered imagination takes hold of the Gospel's promise.

Fine-day

White men . . . coming up to my door. . . .

So long ago they came and my father went away. . . .

". . . . to the Sand Hills," my mother said, "where nothing can be any more . . . but shadows."

"Maybe shadows . . ."

". . . . are only shadows," she said, "nothing more than a dream."

So I had no spirit myself . . . for anything . . . though my heart still flutters with their knocking . . . if I could only hide there under my bed, like my boy could do when he was so little.

"Mr Fine-day."

He turns to catch me in the window. I shrink away from his stare.

"Mr Fine-day, won't you help us please?"

They're going to mock me before they kill me.

"Have pity, Mr Fine-day, on this boy whose father has just died."

Hi! Don't make me suffer that again!

Still he shades his eyes to peer in at my window . . . a shadow? . . . or a dream?

"Maybe if you could help us just to get our money back from Many-birds. This boy has got to see his mother, Mr Fine-day."

So Many-birds . . . these men are really come. . . !

But what can I do? I couldn't get my own wife back from that one. . . .

"I can't help you." I shake my head at shadows straining to see from the dark of my memory . . . the window is empty. I hear footsteps going off the porch . . . safe again.

The door creaks, swinging open.

"Could I have a drink of water?"

A boy stands there, staring from under his rough beak of cap. His eyes look almost glassy. . . .

. . . . his lips were blistered, too, from that fever. . . .

"Wait."

My cup slops all over the floor . . . I hand it out. . . .

. . . . but I could not save him from going to the Sand Hills. . . .

"Suffer the little children . . ."

Why? Why must they?

. . . . oh, I didn't see that white man forcing his way in here again . . . like some dream that won't go away. . . .

"God bless you, Mr Fine-day, for your kindness to Nick."

My breath comes in short gasps . . . I don't know where to look. . . .

"No."

I must not get mixed up with anyone again . . . but the boy's eyes will not stop looking for help. What can I do? . . . what good have Indians ever been to white men?

Nick

We're going to hit.

This is it.

The ground bursts like fire in my brain. When my neck snaps, the redness begins to go away. It goes in a wavering, distant line toward nothing.

I wake up on the floor. I am clawing madly to take another breath. Something choked lies beside me, all wrapped up in sheets. I fight like a wildcat to get out.

Shlockstrocken!

I touch my banged head, then feel what I've hit. *Boizha*, bedsprings! So I *have* landed under the bed with it!

But when I jump up into a moonlit room, I see that that was crazy.

I have to force myself to look at the thing lying under the bed. Then I can think clearly again.

HIS EYE IS ON THE SPARROW. It's just that godawful drawing I stuffed away last night so I could go to sleep.

The thought of it makes me shiver.

I drag sheets up on the bed, rolling inside the rumpled-up mess. I blow to get heated up.

Now I don't dare to sleep any more. To fall asleep. Sleep is crazy.

She was lying down when we walked in, her hair swirling like foam over the dark blue chesterfield. *Boizha,* she's come home to get me! And they wouldn't even warn me. But when I tried to stare back at those accusing eyes, there was nothing there. Her face was as empty as a looking glass out of reach.

Only then did I notice that the radio was on.

"— in the glare of a rising sun. Miss Earhart is thought to have overshot Howland Island, a mere sand spit rising two feet out of the water for one and one-half miles. Her aeroplane, its load of fuel consumed on the two thousand mile hop from New Guinea, is believed to have come down and to be adrift on the equator. Two radio hams from Los Angeles report hearing her distress signal. Others claim to have heard the voice of Miss Earhart herself.

"The USS *Itasca,* nearest the scene, is now steaming into the area to attempt a rescue. As one official of the *Itasca* says, 'We remain hopeful that Miss Earhart will soon be sighted afloat.'

"This has been another news bulletin from the wires of the Canadian Press. We return you now to the program *Hawaiian Nights.*"

Then the solemn, deep voice was lost in a crash of waves. I knew they were coming and still I jumped. Almost at once the sound of ukeleles and woman singers drowned out an endless ocean.

"It's her husband, isn't it, that we have to feel sorry for?"

Still I couldn't see any lips to speak, or any ears to hear, within that shining blank framed by her hair.

I began to feel so sorry for myself, I couldn't stand it. Finally I thought I knew what the trouble was. It was the sound of that radio and we'd never got one and why should that make me so sad?

Then I was choking back the tears, scalding, salty tears that I hadn't cried since I was a kid — I'd sworn I wouldn't any more, no matter what she did in her worst crazy fits — so I knew it wasn't just the radio now. It had to be the way she wouldn't even look at me.

"'His eye is on the sparrow,' Nick," she finished up. "It's the promise God gave to us. He cares for our smallest and our deepest hurts."

But I looked at that blood-red eye going down between two mountains, and at the red and yellow chalk swirled madly for a lake, and I knew that the bird on the pine-branch was as good as lost.

"You only want to take us down with you!" I said hotly. "*You*, you're drownding in your own self-pity!"

But when she raised her head to look at me, I saw my own face staring out of that flat, polished surface.

Suddenly I see the flat sea tilt toward us and it's wide as the world, we can't avoid it any longer, we're going in! I brace myself, feeling the steepness of our descent, and at the last instant the nose of the aeroplane comes up. Sheets of spray wash over the glass.

I fight beneath the water for air. My lungs are choking. A gargle floats in the green water and is gone. My last cry went with it.

Then the bubble pops. My eyes open on a fierce sun beating down. It is bloodred at noon. I've gotten out somehow on the downed wings of my craft. The current is turning me around in a slow circle.

I don't know why I know that a search for me is underway. I look up again at that sun like a maddened eye in the sky. And then I feel how awfully alone I am.

Jack's voice says out of the midst of the eye, "Nick, are you all right?"

My eyes open on the sun shining through the window.

Boizha! Help has come in the nick of time!

SATURDAY

Fine-day

My arms flap . . . and lift. I feel so . . . wonderfully light again.

When I was young, I remember, I could do this every night.

Still my palms beat the air and I go up and up . . . I might not stop. . . .

. . . . wires? crisscrossing my way . . . I fear I won't get over. My arms grow weak as grass. I look to one side . . . another face . . . whose? with arms veed out in this same flap and fall.

I strain to see, but before I wake, I know . . . I've lost it again.

My room is bright. I lie here panting a little. Something tells me to get out. Then I remember. . . .

I'm lying on my wooden table, naked as the day my mother bore me . . . when something out of the darkness . . . the bread knife . . . touches my throat. It slices just once, grinding through the neck bone, and my head drops off. An awful blackness rushes out . . . but something tells me I still have to clean the skull, like scooping out a cow's belly. As I work, a long grey rope begins to slide down in the slop . . . and my eyes sink in, but watch as the knife carves meat from my thigh. Bones crack . . . sinews tearing away from the joint . . . and then both legs just pop out. My arms are stacking them to one side when suddenly they turn on one another, hacking and gouging like they were only legs. The pain is awful, I know I can't stand any more, but then it seems as if all four limbs are just being clasped together like a bundle of sticks. So I am more than pained when I feel my hands and feet trimmed with one sharp chop.

I can taste that blackness now, where my mouth should be . . . and still that awful knife is gouging, this time in my trunk. Guts sprawl, the whole barrel splitting up from groin to chest . . . and yet I do not feel light, feel instead so lumpen-hearted. Maybe I will lose it all this time, have my heart skinned like an onion . . . but those tireless hands turn instead to bone, carving and carving till every rib parts, every joint is scraped dull white. And nothing is lost, least of all the pain like fire in these bones. . . .

I sit up on my bunk . . . arms played out . . . my arms still joined to my shoulders. Just a dream of dying, though you could never stop living . . . so wouldn't they ever let you forget your troubles, not even in death? Suddenly I feel cold fingers walking on my spine, my neck hairs lifting like a horse's tail. You Spirit Helpers, were you my carvers, like that? Is that why it doesn't show? And were you also the ones who made my mother cut her wrists . . . for thinking she could ever forget you?

It troubles me to think this is the bed she lay in . . . her blood lapping like a lake around her thighs . . . still a river really rising. . . .

I land on both feet on the floor, the shock like lightning to old bones . . . but how could I help her after my father died? I could hardly help myself, barely managed to save my own wrists from the bread knife . . . laying there on the table . . . blood-drinking blade. No! I will not look at that.

. . . . something pounds at the back of my head . . . if only to turn it. My eyes flick over . . . manage not to look quite on it . . . still an awful blackness rising in my throat . . . got to get out of here. . . .

All right you Spirits, I say to myself, then I won't forget since you force me . . . must remember what it is to live in company. Only this time, when the troubles come of it . . . his blood be upon your . . . Spirits. . . .

Jack

Naturally I spoke to Gaudreau about the fare to Saskatoon. But he floored me when he said there wasn't a cent, that this was all bought on borrowed money.

"Hazel will never have anything more in this life," he said. Then he added softly, "You know, Jack, we're never going to have that child you thought God would give us."

His face returned to me, meek and gentle like the good man I have taken him to be.

"Jack — I'm sorry. I shouldn't have been so thoughtless. I was thinking only of Hazel. You do remember, though, what you promised when you sold us that set of books?"

My eyes followed his to the embossed, leatherbound encyclopedia, *The Life of the Healer.*

"Now I know how poor you've been, and I'm not asking for my money back. When I made the purchase, it could have even been my faith at fault. I don't know — maybe I was hoping to buy from God some children to read them. But would you think it a second fault of my faith to bestow them on that poor child and his family? I know it would make Hazel feel better, since we realize now we have no right to try to adopt a boy. Not with her condition as bad as it is."

"No," I said uncertainly, "no, I don't think it would be a lessening of your faith."

But I am uneasy after that; I can't help myself. It has nothing, when it comes, to do with Nick's polite refusal of the books.

"But you could still come for them, couldn't you?" Emil says. "Once you're settled again?"

"Could be," Nick says. He reaches for the last slice of buttered toast and spreads syrup like he bought the pail himself. Isn't it odd, though, and wonderful, how he helps to ease my uneasiness? I guess it's the way he makes himself at home like that. In spite of aught that's happened, there is here a gathering and a closeness around this table of which he is the centre.

It calls to mind those five youngsters sitting to table in our shack in the bush, with Mama wondering where our next meal was coming from or worrying the Lord how He'd provide, but every one of us kids shouldering against the other and eating as innocent as hogs along a trough. Our family was too poor, as the saying goes, to paint and too proud to whitewash. All the poor called us poor. I'll never forget how my daddy would write home from his schoolhouse meetings. He said folks had decided if the Lord would keep Reverend Cann humble, why they would help to keep him poor. I was next to youngest then and didn't even know what trouble was.

So Emil and Hazel must feel this refreshing childness too, breaking in on the routine of their trouble. They are watching Nick like he is the child they never had. I see the bittersweet joy in that wasted woman's eyes, and I wish I could restore her hope. I admit she received again the gift of sight, but her total healing, by any standard, was a failure. It's clear, the way her muscles have now fallen in on themselves, that she can't have much time remaining.

"Maybe God will see fit to restore you through a different vessel," I say gently. "It was never your faith that was at fault. You've had enough to move mountains."

She did, too. I'll never forget her ready look in the tent meeting that once, with my laying on of hands. She reminded me of more than my younger self in my affliction. Maybe she had heard how I was struck down with a like disease in my teens. Maybe she knew God had freed me from my paralysis so I could walk, and He had loosed my tongue so I could talk. So might there not be a better comfort which this poor, decaying woman might take hold of? Some greater gesture for these blighted eyes that I might never meet again?

I say without, I hope, any pausing, "No, it was never you, Hazel my dear, who fell short of miracles. It was only the lack of this weak, doubting Thomas. You never needed me, you know, to bring His healing touch; you need only to seek it yourself, alone. Your faith is still the loveliest of miracles."

Then she is broken-faced and crying and I never should have stood up making speeches.

"Jack," she twists her mouth around to me, "Jack, God be with you and keep watch over you in the Valley of the Shadow."

She is that kind of woman, to be always thinking of others before herself.

Fine-day

The white-man-who-speaks-for-the-Grandfather looks right at me. He's not the one who was so much against Sun Dances . . . so I ought to find again my lost man's tongue.

"I need what-you-have-instead-of-horses," I say. But this shameful tongue limps, wounded by the word it doesn't know.

"You mean tractor?" His voice speaks as clearly as our Warriors used to do. . . .

I have to keep my feet from shifting. I plant them firmly on his stoop . . . look away at those trees beyond his shoulder . . . dark . . . wet . . . I look down again at my feet.

"I can't let you have it. You haven't cleared land like Stan Smoke-a-day. It's only for farmers, old fellow."

I hear him. He is not unkind . . . but I heard Many-birds took it to hunt ducks. He ran its head under water . . . so it would likely run away worse from me.

"What did you want it for?" he calls after me.

I have to face him again.

"Haul wood," I say into the grass.

"Harold Cuthand isn't going to do it for you this year?"

I wouldn't know how he knows so much about me. Because he's Boss, I guess. I shake my head.

"Well, I hate to turn you down. Fresh air would do you good. Look here, do you think you could learn how to drive it yourself?"

I hold his eyes just long enough.

"Well, come on down to the shed, then."

He walks ahead. One leg is stiff . . . I turn my eyes away.

Horse-with-wheels sits in the stable beside the barn. Maybe we shouldn't wake him.

Boss climbs on his green back, touches him here and there, and gets off. Horse won't wake. I breathe again.

"Here. You have to start it up here."

I start to follow, but that big wheel has me spooked. Boss bends over the belly wheel. He spins it. Horse coughs . . . Boss rolls it again.

Hi! I'm shot in the head! Oh, I hit myself on that timber. Still the gunfire speaks to the roof. Smoke belches out of Horse-with-wheels's mouth. I could never be on a thing like that . . . so you have no right, old man, to laugh like Harold Cuthand at Many-birds.

Boss crowds past me. I follow gratefully. I want to go home. If I said right now. . . .

"Come on up," Boss says.

Wind sucks out of my belly. Still Horse doesn't move when I step on his tail.

Boss touches Horse's penis, a sharp kick backwards. I cling for my life. We stop. Horse snorts and snorts.

"No, get right up here."

I shut my eyes, then feel Boss hauling me up.

He is talking, wants me to touch Horse's penis too. But my heart is in my mouth. Boss hits my hand and we jerk forward, rolling slowly. I am holding the rein-wheel with no trouble.

"See, it's not so hard, is it? Turn like this. You see? And now like this."

Could I be boss, then of Horse? My heart pounds almost as loud as his. Still I refuse to touch his lower penis, fearing to get in the way of that cunt-like thing where he slides around. But Boss forces the penis there. Horse grinds his teeth.

"Fifth will do for hauling wood," Boss says. "Get Gus Brown at the store to fill it with oil. I've got none left or I would. Remember to do that. It's important."

He takes out his leather pouch and counts four pieces of money for me to take. Then I have to ride Horse off alone. Alone is not so bad, though, much safer than any People around. And then I can hardly believe that this is really me. Horse obeys me, the Sun beams warmly on my back, and the wind brings smells of grass and trees to me, so that I move through one great yellow lake of light. My heart sparkles . . . I can't bear such happiness.

Sure enough we roll into shadows, clouds hiding the Sun. My spirit plunges. I fight Horse to follow the road, but he's going to each side. I fear I will lose him; I can't go on myself like this, a speck in the midst of nothing . . . yet wasn't I glad in the old days to keep this empty circle around me? But now the Nothing seems to open and I feel the bush along the road plunge past on my way into blankness.

I yank Horse's fake penis; he actually stops. But he is mad, for his voice goes on louder than ever. I leap off his back . . . knives stick in my ankle. I almost go down. Then I wait, bent over, for the Spirits to let me be. . . .

I look around. Horse stands where he is. I limp to one side of the road, buttons sticking, bladder bursting. Then all my buttons spray, but not my piss. Suddenly it does, spraying that tall weed along the ditch. I try to turn aside. The piss pinches off, burning, before I get it going again, and then the last of the ice is drained away.

The Sun is back. I climb, relieved, onto Horse's back. The way he waited . . . well, maybe I will get us there after all.

But I am scared when I pull into Many-birds' yard. She is in that house . . . I ought not come too close. I stop Horse some distance away, here beside their wagon. And then I see I am already come too close . . . must try to forget . . . the knife-edge of memory.

But now the only place for me is at their house. I limp toward her windows. At least Horse makes a lot of noise to warn her. Then I find I have been hoping with every step . . . hoping for what? I only brought her a sorrow that she gave back to me . . . like Many-birds in there rooting deep . . . her heels hooked into his back. So can I not walk up to this door without cutting myself up?

I hesitate outside Maggie's new house . . . but after so long, they can't hurt me if I don't hurt myself.

Sudden voices rise as I climb the stoop, and then the door bangs out on my bony ankle. *Hi!* How can you ever know what will hurt you? *Hi hi!*

"Fuck off," Many-birds is yelling, "you can both fuck right off!"

The white boy stoops beside me.

"Boysha! I'm sorry. Are you all right?"

I step . . . wince . . . but I must not be carved again into bones. I try to nod.

The white man flaps like a chicken flock out of the house. Many-birds is following, younger, somehow . . . but old too. And bald.

"What!" he stops when he sees me. "What the fuck are you doing here? You come to take the old cunt home at last?"

But there was never any way to answer that one.

"Well, God's blessing on you, Mr Fine-day," says the white man. "I have prayed his spirit would move you."

I am startled . . . is this the one who knows my thoughts. . .?

Still I don't dare to point at Horse. But everyone looks toward his coughing anyway. The white man looks back at me.

"You came for Nick? Well, praise be! Let's get the blessed thing hitched."

"Fuckyerselves, I ain't going after no woman on no goddamned tractor. I'm going in style like that ex-King. No woman of mine rides round in a wagon, fershitsake."

"You take it yourselves," I say to the man and boy.

"We haven't got the money for gas," says the boy.

I hold out my hand.

"Thanks anyway, old fella. That wouldn't get us to the highway."

I would spare her if I could . . . spare me, really. But now I know that I will have to speak to Maggie.

"Hey, where the fuck you think you're going, old man?"

I limp past Many-birds to where she is eating at the table . . . my Maggie no longer . . . so big and fat. Someone sits beside her . . . an older Many-birds, fat as her. Of course. This one was his son, not hers. In those days she was still my wife.

Still my thoughts turn to her.

Maggie? I should not have been the one to stop us being . . . who we were. . . .

But I can't tell her . . . my tongue sits limp. I try to smile but my knees grow weak, chest all hollow.

She gives me an unforgetting look. Then all those years without her seem to fall away. . . .

"Maggie," I say. "That boy . . ." her eyes fall to her lap, ". . . needs our help. . . ."

She is going to cry. But she won't look at me . . . she must think. . . .

Maggie, do not make me remember it after so long!

"What can I do?" she says softly . . . her voice was always soft like that. So this much, at least, has not changed.

"Get young Many-birds to give them their money back."

"Bullshit!" the scalped Warrior yanks his pockets out by their ears. "What money, fershitsake? I didn't take . . ."

"He did too!" the white man thunders . . . "Did too," the four walls echo back.

Edward Many-birds laughs his old disgusting laugh. It sounds like buzzards choking on meat.

The boy only looks at Maggie. She looks once at Edward, warns him with her eyes like she did that time with me. And he obeys her, swearing now at his son, fearing really to lose her. Then he gets up and goes purposefully toward a back bedroom.

"Bugger off!" young Many-birds runs after him. "Fershitsake, leave that pillow alone!"

Above their uproar Maggie speaks in Cree to me.

"How have you been keeping?"

"Keeping okay," I smile nervously . . . and then I know why I have been keeping away. I can't be myself with her. I would've had to do away with myself . . . if she did come back to me . . . I couldn't be putting up a show for her any more. . . .

Edward is back already, pretending to be Weesakayjack, wearing a trickster's smile, just the sort of thing to make her itch for him. Now he is holding up one yellow piece of the sun. Back in the doorway his boy looks like a thunderhead.

". . . stool pigeon . . . slit your throat one day," he is mumbling just enough so his father won't hear all of it. Edward ignores him, busy as he is making a show for Maggie.

"My son the jailbird would like you to have this back. Would you care to take him with it? My old woman and me like it quiet around here."

So he lets me know what she thinks of me yet for losing our only son . . . Many-birds always mocking. . . .

Still the white boy has pocketed his money. He'd never understand if I told him he has helped me too. For I might go home and be myself, now that I've helped like the dream wanted me to do.

"We'll have to make a dash for that train," the white man says suddenly, then turns to me. "Do you think you might take us back to town?"

Just the thought of the place wakens young Many-birds.

"How do you bastards know Fuzzy Nuts didn't steal that money himself?"

But we are going out the door . . . I have not looked again at Maggie.

"You ask him, goddamn it! Just ask him!"

Man and boy look at one another.

"Nick?"

The boy says nothing.

"Nick? Whose gold piece is that?"

"Not his, that's for sure."

"It's sure as fuck not his either."

"Whatever you say, Thinker. But where did you get it?"

"Nick, didn't you say you had just five dollars? Did you . . ."

But the boy is looking sharply at Many-birds. Suddenly he sees what I do too.

"Naaa . . . ah, let him come, if he wants."

"On the train? With his fare paid for by the Lord knows who?"

The boy turns suddenly to me.

"Will you take the tractor? I'll buy all the gas."

The white man looks helplessly at me, like I could do something more. . . .

"You take it," I say. My heart has quickened, but I wouldn't dare to go.

Dumbly the white man shakes his head.

"He'd only steal your tractor too."

Then Many-birds is laughing and laughing, like another Weesakayjack.

"It's his tractor about as much as that old cunt is . . . what everyone rides . . . hey, Grandfather?" he says in Cree to me. "My other Father. Sharing her cunt with the prick who made me, hey?"

But I know I am no father . . . could not have been. Maggie stares over the tops of her breasts. She would never try to stop me from feeling bad . . . now somehow I will have to stop young Many-birds from pushing in like me . . . but I begin to feel as if I am in that dream again where black stuff floods what's left of my throat . . .

. . . . I fight to hold it down . . . I can't . . . Many-birds is driving so fiercely I spit it out with every bounce. So I'm not dreaming, I'm being carried back where it's unsafe for me to go . . . still I must hold on, remember to tell them oil when we stop . . . if we stop. . . .

. . . . we are stopped. Horse goes right to sleep. . . .

I open my eyes. We are beside Carnegie store. Horse has been entered by that long hose . . . I look away.

"Oil," I say the strange word to Many-birds. "Boss said give it some of that stuff." . . . giving them whatever I can myself to stop the trouble from coming. . . .

Many-birds leans back from Horse's saddle.

"Give me the money."

The boy shakes his head.

"I got to pay for gas and oil, fershitsake. You think I'd run away when I can drive?"

The boy is still suspicious. Only when I hold out the coins that Boss gave me does he finally let go. Then I feel strangely better for him . . . for me too. . . .

Many-birds grins as wide as Weesakayjack, putting the money in his pocket. And goes indoors with the storekeeper. . . .

Once we are on our way again, I know where the place is that's not safe for me to go . . . where it's going to happen . . . the place I cut my own throat. Still I can't help sliding down into this corner now, putting myself in my dead son's place. My face is scorched like his was . . . and then I feel the strangest satisfaction when my chest and legs begin to burn . . . head rattles on the wall . . . at least his was cradled in his mother's lap . . . until, with my teeth clicking next to breaking, I feel a deadly joy that this is finally happening. . . .

. . . . but why, when I danced with the stake through my chest, was I not allowed to die if I couldn't save him? . . . why, when it was all my fault anyway? . . . or when the Sun Dance failed to work, why wouldn't the police take me to jail for making it, like they first said they would? Maybe someone would have even killed me in that place. But nothing happened to me, just to my son who was slowly burning up. Finally we decided, his mother and me, that we would take him by wagon to the white man's medicine. We wrapped him in an old buffalo robe and Maggie sat with him while I drove the team. It was a bright, fine day, such as this, but he died along the way . . . died here in this clattering, metal-hammered wagon . . . before we ever got to Melfort. I stopped our horses and we sat in the silence . . . just sat here with that boy in Magie's arms . . . in the flattened, final silence. . . .

"Did you check that oil like you were supposed to?" someone is saying.

Many-birds sits with his head down, now that Horse is quiet. Then I'm sure I smell something like an overheated gun barrel.

"Fucking government," says Many-birds. "Fucking white fucking meddling fucking fuckers!"

"Hold on," the white man says suddenly.

"Fucking hoo-er of an old tractor like that," Many-birds blusters as if death herself wouldn't stop him. "Sucking off that money when she meant to die in the middle of it."

The boy turns to look at me . . . smiles right at me. . . .

But anything I ever touched dried up and died. All my life I had to go on living like that. . . .

Many-birds

By now, the city will be filled with people getting up. Horses clopping past her window. Maybe trolley bells clanging by. She will be out of bed to start the day. I hope. I goddam got to hope. The worst would be that scalping barber getting to her first. Then she wouldn't be up. Fershitsake. I got to get into Saskatoon.

Fucking hoo-er of a tractor. I could have been there by now on the train.

Fucking white fucking meddling fucking fuck fuckers. When Thunder Bird had already coughed up the money like that. You'd think at least an old Indian would have more respect for a Power like Thunder Bird. The godless old bugger. He can go bugger himself with that tractor. The way he's shitting himself about what Boss is going to say. But then that guy always has something to say. Let him speak up to Thunder Bird if he dares. Me, I ain't meant to ride that heap of junk. I got me another ride.

So then these assholes had to get in with me. Nothing but assholes, including the cocksucker driving us to St. Louie. Stops for us back there by the tractor and acts like he's taking us to see the King. Fuck him and his St. Louie sports day. Begging us to stay for it tomorrow like there ain't no better place to be. Chuckwagon races. I wouldn't get into no goddam wagons if I stayed, fershitsake. I'd get into their goddam women. No real women would stay around these horseshit dumps anyway, unless they give 'em cars to ride in.

Fershitsake. One more asshole in this car than I counted on. Me. I'm riding in a car meant for the two of us. I could be there this afternoon. She'd have me for sure. And here I sit crying about horseshit.

Hell, I won't wait no more for some guy who thinks he's King Shit of Turd Island. I'll drive myself like that stud King up through the gates of her castle. And as my baggage truck pants behind, I'll run up that castle stoop and grab the woman I love.

I gawk over the front seat into the mirror. The dopey bastard ain't looking back a-tall. Now and then he yaps like a goddam coyote to the boy and the old man. I look across to Rubberneck's open window and wish I could roll it up on his throat.

"Cloud of dust," I say. "Could be someone coming to find out about that tractor."

The birdass is stupid enough to twist his neck around. The minute his eyes are gone, I reach forward to choke off the coyote's bark.

Jack

I got to him just in time. His arms were about to close around Mr Carriere's head, and then we'd all have been dead. He's an utter maniac, is this son of Apollyon. The devil's own fool.

What surprises me is that I guessed he would do it. I could see it in his eyes, like he is demon possessed and it must break out somewhere, even unto wrestling in the King's Highway with the driver of a speeding car.

I myself have never wrestled so ferociously with the devil before. I have always believed that the only enemies of mankind were Satanically inspired: that fear, sin, disease and death were but the works of his destructive power. But I'll be blamed if the watch you have to put on him doesn't come nigh itself to destroying you.

Still I fooled the fiend. I got him from behind by the chin, just as he was about to do as much to our driver. Then I forced a hand over his mouth and gagged him, though he nearly bit my middle finger off. He fought like all the furies, kicking his feet against the door until it flew open, and I guess that was the first our benefactor knew something was wrong. He hit the brakes so hard, we fell between the seats onto the floor, and it was like trying to bind the jaw of a rabid wolf. Foam came oozing between my fingers, covering the blood, and I could sense the faces peering down, like King Darius looking into the lion's den.

"What's going on?" I could hear Mr Carriere asking them. But I must not let the old man give us away.

"Epilepsy," I gargle through teeth as clenched as the demon's under me. "Taken a fit. Tongue. Got his tongue."

The Indian claws at me like a wildcat. Surely I am no more a Daniel, not if the Lord won't close the lion's mouth. My finger is about to crunch at the second joint. Not a single tooth missing. Surely the devil is his own dentist too, the way they are all so tongued and ridged with fire. But thank Heaven the foam continues to bubble over my hand, and Many-birds yowls down in his throat like the real thing.

"Poor devil," Mr Carriere says. He is opening his door, coming round to help.

I take the opportunity then to smite the devil's cheek. I knuckle hard into his wisdom teeth. The jaw pops open. Once I get my fingers out, I tap it shut again, just one light rap on his rounded chin. He is lying quiet by the time our driver looms across the running board.

"He's unconscious," I say as if he were sleeping. "It's the way the fit usually leaves him."

Mr Carriere regards him more kindly than me, perhaps not having now to risk those closed eyes. But it's a mockery, asking him to show pity for the devil like that. I don't like to see him make a fool of himself that way.

"We should maybe get him to a doctor," our companion says more guardedly now. "Unless he'd need a priest instead."

I take the liberty God has given me.

"He'll be all right. They don't often show after-effects when they wake up."

Old Fine-day looks concerned. I know he knows what I have done.

At last he says, "You did okay fer 'im."

"My brother used to have epilepsy. It isn't much if you're acquainted with seizures."

Surely I have known them, one way or the other, all my life. My eldest brother, Timothy, took terrible fits. I remember my father having to stick the wooden spoon in his mouth and hold his tongue like a leash while he rolled on the floor. For years after he found out I could heal, Timothy was too proud to let the grace of God cure him through me. For I had been seized by a different power — God's Power. The devil had seized Tim and made a fool out of him. But God gripped me and made a Fool who healed fools. Tim resisted my kind of folly till he nearly died; then he came, like a brother unto Joseph down in Egypt

"Sacred blood!" Mr Carriere says. "What have you done to your hand?"

Father forgive them

But I shrug it off, denying their fussing while we lay Many-birds out on the seat. Mr Carriere hasn't said more. Now I see him come from the trunk with a metal box in hand. TRAVELER'S EMERGENCY KIT, it says in red letters.

"Hold out your hand," he says.

Father forgive them though I knew they meant to do it. Timothy was hoping to build a stairway up to heaven, starting with just slats nailed to the trunk of a poplar tree. Thelma was up there with him, when I came in sight, helping to figure what you did after you had arrived at the treetop.

"Don't you know about Babel?" I rebuked them in their foolish little perch.

Yet they invited me up, kindly, I thought.

Tim said, "I've figured out a way," just as I clambered up the last rung. He had a hammer in one hand and some nails in the other. The next thing I knew he'd clasped my wrist to the branch and he was spiking the palm to the wood.

"Timothy!" Thelma sounded alarmed. But he only looked at her a certain way and then she helped to hold the other hand.

The pain was more than I could bear. I cried out at last in my agony.

Our daddy was shocked speechless when he came running. The hammer claw galled my handbones and I was speechless too. But even with the nail beginning to draw, I would not revile them. I said only, 'Father, forgive them, for they know not what they do.' Then I was freed from my torment, though I saw I could not now be free of my tormenters' hate. For they hated the truth in me.

Many-birds appears to eye me with the same hateful gleam. I don't know how long he has been awake and watching out the open car door. He sees he has lost the battle. But he cannot see I would be more than a conqueror through him who loved us. Then he sees me looking at him. So he stares no more at me.

I survey instead these last windings of gauze which our Samaritan wraps round my fingers. I wriggle them in their thick graveclothes, praying they might rise to work a healing ministry again.

After a bit Many-birds touches gingerly his mouth and chin. Fine-day notices and starts to talk to him in Indian. Now he sounds like the one preaching sermons. Nick is watching him and me both with a real catgrin.

"You took quite a spell," Mr Carriere says when he discovers Many-birds is awake. "Is there anything we could get you?" He talks, I notice, without quite eyeing anyone, as if the look into another man's face would be too much for him. But he's determined to be of help, to give of himself the only way he dares. I think how if a Catholic's faith can work like that with just a smattering of Scripture, then there must be other ways to Heaven besides our own.

Over the rest of our way into St. Louie, I see the devil's fool is now departed. I know from experience he will be back; he's only hatching out more of his folly. But for the moment the man Many-birds sits peacefully empty.

Our friend, who has work to do at the Sports Grounds, stops to let us off at the B/A station. I get out, not looking at the black girders of the bridge or at the width of the river below. Then I see that our Samaritan means still to wait for us.

"Go on," I say. "You'll be late for your duties."

He looks past me, sort of. "It would be lonesome not to know a soul in a town. You try to get help. I'll wait to find out."

This man, I realize, is truly a Christian. He puts me to holy shame.

I make certain Many-birds comes with us into the garage. I don't aim to leave him there to have another fit. Bite the hand that feeds you; rob the pocket that befriends you; it's the kind of Satanic world there'd be without some salt of the earth.

A tall, gaunt man stands up behind the counter. He looks at us when we come in, gives us a sort of red-eyed glance, but doesn't speak. His long, thin hands play continually about his mouth, and then I hear he is whistling through his teeth and fingers, a quiet tuneless whistle which is lost in the loops of fanbelts overhanging him.

I ask if there's anyone here could give us a smidgeon of help down the road a ways. He hardly takes his fingers from his lips to say, "No," really short, but not mean, and he's whistling again up through those belts.

"Well, do you repair motors at all in this shop? We've got a John Deere AR seized up on us."

The whistle falters into "Yuh" before the fingers are up and covering his mouth again. I notice how he doesn't look anywhere but out the window, and it comes to me suddenly that maybe he has a stutter, or he's shy of people, so this is his only way to fool the world.

"We've got to get to Saskatoon, but we don't have any money. Would you do the work on credit?"

Another quick "No" escapes his toneless playing. But he doesn't act like our request offends him. There is only seeming indifference in that long, bony face. I think how once I might have brought him all alive into the world.

"Is there anyone else, then, in town who might help us?"

"Se-se-se-se. Expect so. Se-se-se-se-se."

Nick says, "Been nice chatting with you. See you around."

"Se-se-se. Expect so. Se-se-se-se."

The three of us, excepting Many-birds, can't help but laugh when we get out into the street.

"We should have asked," Nick says, "if he knew Turkey in the Straw."

"Se-se-se. Expect so. Se-se-se-se-se," the whistling escapes me.

It is the loudest I have laughed in many months. But I think of that poor man in there, how long it's probably taken him to manufacture any mask at all, and I hope we haven't punctured it in our brief stop. Because he must have heard us hoot like that.

I turn back to let him know I understand. If not to speak it and so embarrass him, at least to let him tell us what he thinks of us — that we are fools too. But the door is locked. I see him through the glass stand belly to the counter. His hands beat like birdwings on its surface. When he spies me, they fly up again around his mouth.

"Aren't you open?" I shout through the plate window.

He shakes his head once, not looking. The last I see of him, he is still playing piper to that host of fanbelts which seem, somehow, like rats stood up on their hind legs behind him.

Mr Carriere is an older man, weighted, it appears, with years and wisdom.

"Alf is a little queer," is all he says. "If anyone might of given you credit, it would of been him."

We find, with much searching, that this is true. Our friend takes us all over town, but no garage or businessman will credit us. We are done, it seems; and I don't know how that poor boy will get in time to see his mother.

"Might as well stop in here," Mr Carriere says. "It's the least I can do."

We pull up to the curb before a grocery store. The sign over the window reads, "A.M. Lacoste. Free Delivery." Well, I think, you can't fool me, Mr Lacoste. There's nothing save God's grace which is truly free.

But it isn't what I think at all. Mr Carriere walks down a creaky aisle and starts back with four tins of something and a white box of crackers. Sardines is what they are. Sardines in oil. I'm about to say we haven't got a cent when he lays the works on the counter and rings down some silver. Those tins, I know, are at least a nickel apiece.

"We can't let you do this," I begin to say, but he fends my words away with swimming hands. He never quite looks at us when he gives them over. This ordinary, thickset man just hands them out like he is playing Santa in the Sunday School Concert. It's kind of like he takes for granted he is the hander, not the giver.

"The Lord bless . . ." I say automatically. I stop when I remember the time Mama shouted and rejoiced over a hamper of groceries left inside our door. My next eldest brother, Vernon and I said privately that it was only Mrs Wilson from across the road. We could spot her basket. Then I realize how totally ungracious I can be. "The Virgin keep you and intercede for you," I say, somewhat uncertain of the phrases. It is only a little thing to say to a man who truly believes.

And I'm blessed if it doesn't fit somehow. Though I couldn't say how.

"I've got to get along to the Sports Grounds," Mr Carriere says, somewhere amiddle the four of us. "You be sure and stop, now, if there's anything else I can do. I've got to go, you understand. They're waiting."

"No man could have done more," I say in farewell. "No man would."

We go out of Lacoste's store and wave as he turns in a billow of dust, back down the way we came. It is not so hot like it was yesterday, before the hail. The wind flaps at our clothes and licks the sweat. But it is still a limp feeling, being set adrift like this in a strange town.

"I guess the one place we haven't tried is the elevators," I say after a couple of minutes. "I wonder if there's anyone there can help us undo Many-birds' mistake."

"Where *is* Many-birds?" I say suddenly, looking around.

"He went back in the store," Nick says. "He'll be swiping pork chops or something. I saw him wrinkling his nose over just sardines."

"If he steals anything, he's on his own. We'd be well rid of him."

But Many-birds ambles out to rejoin us. It's not edibles he's stolen, it's a hat. A brand new tweed cap. It sits low over his ears so you just see an edge to his baldness. He's got his chin well up to see from under that proud peak. Then I see him, indomitable in his colossal vanity.

"Don't come near us! We'll not be party to your crimes."

"F—yerself," he spits at me. "I paid fer dis hat."

"So you wrecked his tractor," Nick says, "to get yourself a hat. Why, you cheap son of a -----!"

Then it comes to me like an answer to forgotten prayer. The Lord won't let us be permanently fooled: Nick has a Yankee dollar that he found behind the elevator. I am washed over with relief; the train fare can't be more than a dollar from here.

"Nick," I blurt, "we're taking that dollar you showed me and we're putting you on the next train to Saskatoon."

Many-birds swings sharply on him, as if he's sizing up an unexpected rival. Then I see we're never exempt from playing the devil's fool.

"Swell," Nick says, giving Many-birds an equal eye before he scowls at me. "I don't suppose you've got Wells Fargo handy to get us to the station?"

My only hope is to try to undo my folly. "We'll march you there at once. We'll wait in the station together."

Nick spits in the dust.

"And what do I do then? Rent a room in the best hotel?"

Will not wisdom prevail for once?

Suddenly Nick turns on me.

"*Shlockdybetrofet*! You're not dropping me on my own in the middle of nowhere!"

Then all is vanity

Fine-day touches him lightly on both shoulders.

"I'm stayin' wid you," he says, "I'll help you get to where you're goin'."

Father forgive them I have to go along in silence. So we traipse toward those elevators standing head and shoulders above the town. Indians, I imagine, have always travelled in tribes.

I consider walking out myself to the Sports Grounds to see if there's aught our Samaritan might yet do for us. But I know he spent his entire mite on us already. Were he to take us, even with Nick's dollar for gas, we'd still be worried all the way to Saskatoon about Many-birds stealing the car or something. It wouldn't be fair to the man or to the folks who are counting on him at the Sports Day. Let alone fair to Nick's — *vanity*

We go down back alleys past junkyards fenced with chicken wire. The stench is awful. Slop rots in the dust where pigs wallow, and the chickens fluff up showerbaths in the midst of all. Rusted tin cans fester like sores on people's skins. Then the doorway to the Chinaman's kitchen gives out black as cancer with flies, and for a minute my stomach runs liquid at the backdoor of people's lives. *All, all is vanity*

There is no one in the office of the Pool elevator. We walk across the catwalk to the main elevator, step into the dusty gloom above the pit. I look away out the truckdoor into sunlight and I see the motes of dust lean like yellow planks on space. The agent isn't back in the bay window of the weighscale. He is either home for lunch or he is gone up the lift.

We sit in the shade of the catwalk, eating our meagre lunch *of loaves and fishes* The Pool man isn't back within the hour. As it turns out, the buyer at the second elevator is willing to talk with us. He is a very nervous man, eyes squinting and winking so fast you'd think they were warning you about his mouth. The mouth is sharp, almost hawk-beaked, except his face is rounded with eyes as big as owls'. An owl who's got his days switched with his nights. I guess that's it; those eyes aren't really warning you; he'd just as soon fold his wings and drop on you like a stone. No, he's been forced into daylight, and he blinks a lot because light is bad for his doings.

He sits in his bare-walled office, only a barely-clothed calendar woman behind him, and he drums stubby fingers on an oaken desk, shifting that neckless head toward each of us. We sit uncomfortably on a bench backed by the wall. I can see the smoke-stack of the donkey engine through the window. Fine-day is getting our story across, feeding it into that hawkbeak, doing a tired, sad job of it. I would take that tractor myself in pawn, if I could. Pawn, not buy. We've got to have a chance to get it back again.

"Well, I can't do that," the buyer says after Fine-day sums it up again. He leans back in his armed swivel chair and his face tilts up. His eyes make his very features wink.

"Even if you were grain farmers — and you're not —" his eyes bat swiftly, "I could buy only by the bushel from you. This elevator's not in the broken-down tractor business, you know."

I lean away from the wall, feeling like a reprieved man somehow *we won't have to deal with the merchants of Vanity Fair*

"Now don't get me wrong," his eyes hover to hold me just where I am. "I still operate a bit of merchandising myself, you understand. Strictly on the side. My question is, what will you buy from me?"

"Truth," I blurt, unable to hold my tongue. "We prefer to deal only in the truth."

The eyes dilate until I am imprisoned there in hate. I see myself, a martyr for Truth's sake, shine out of his glowing pupils. *But I will do him no reverence, I will not honour his wares*

"I'd like t' buy a ride on your train t' Sas-katoon."

Many-birds takes away that stare, letting me slide out of my confinement.

"Why? What's your hurry, fella? You got some young squaw up the stump? Or did one fly the roost on you?"

His voice is calmly indifferent. The eyes blink once, then twice, adding Many-birds up.

"She took off on you, eh? Well, I got no say on the railroad. They just stop here to shunt my box cars around. But would you want to go like some hobo after her, Romeo? No, I didn't think so."

He swings his feet up onto the desk, the swivel chair creaking back.

"I got me a canoe tied up along the river. I might trade it for a tractor. Hell of a lot more romantic, you know, the next time you lay eyes — or whatever — on that little piece of tail."

"F---yerself and yer canoe."

"That might be a bit delicate, Romeo." The buyer blinks impassively. "You ever try it in a canoe? They got a place in Saskatoon that rents 'em to itchy-assed young guys like you. They paddle their young ladies around on that moonlit river, and you better believe it's a balancing act."

"If I get one," Many-birds says to the floorboards, "I'll rent it

w'en I get dere. I ain't haulin' no boatload a assholes wid me every-
w'ere."

"Sure," the man says, bland as can be. "If they even rent to
young brown bucks. They're mighty particular. They won't rent
to me no more. Another white guy and me took a canoe one time
on a Sunday afternoon, and this guy got to showing off for some
dames on shore. Well, we tipped her and did we ever feel stupid
dragging our butts in to the bank, good suits just a-dripping.
There was a crowd of dames around, and the boatman told us in
front of them not to come back again. 'We don't rent to guys like
you,' was what he said. But if you took this canoe in there yourself,
why you'd be in with the best of them. Your own private loveseat
up and down the length of the city. Just picture yourself drifting
along under the stars, and all them lights like diamonds on shore."

Many-birds gives way visibly to vanity.

"We need cash," I interrupt quickly. "We don't need any
canoe. The rest of us aren't going rutting."

The buyer can barely put a face on his manipulation. He des-
pises me.

"I don't need a tractor myself, mister. I ain't going farming. Not
with crops the way they been these last few years."

"A tractor costs more dan a canoe," Fine-day says abruptly. At
least he is on my side.

"It ain't worth much without a motor, though, is it? It's only
scrap iron."

"We can't trade their tractor for a canoe," I say. "It's not
right."

"Okay," he says, blinking so hard his lips flutter with his
eyelids. "Though I don't see why. Canoes are how they travelled
before we ever come here. But suit yourself. Was you planning to
walk?"

"We'll take dat f---ing canoe," Many-birds says.

"You know you're the only one of your crew talking sense,
Romeo? The river's right there for the using. You only got to get
on it to go courting."

"It's upriver," I say. "We'd paddle our arms off."

"There's a northeast wind blowing right behind you today.
Going as fast southwest as your pretty butts could be. You'd get
there sometime tomorrow, four of you paddling like the voyageurs
did."

Fine-day brightens like his name. I can feel he's going to
commit us.

"Give us a way, den, to get our tractor back."

"And guarantee the use of my canoe for nothing? I can't make the same trade twice, you know. The Hudson Bay Company never got where it is through dealings like that. Besides, I might have it fixed by then."

He grins, finally relaxed, as if it's all settled now. I think how it's a shame tractors didn't have faith like people; then they could be healed too, the Lord willing and providing.

Fine-day stares at the floor. He is safely glum again.

The buyer looks at his watch, glances cunningly at Many-birds. "Well, I don't want to waste any more of your friend's time."

Now he stands behind his desk, seeming to dismiss us. For just a moment I smell through the window the dirt and grain rot from the annex.

"Would you consider renting your canoe?" Nick says suddenly.

The buyer goes to blinking again. He's just seen a mouse run out of the stubble.

"Sure I would kid. Cost you a buck a day though. And I'd have to keep the tractor as collateral."

I look at Fine-day, then at Nick.

"Isn't there something else we can do? Nick, are you sure you won't take that train?"

"I'm not going anywhere alone."

"Let's see dat canoe," Fine-day quivers with excitement. I just don't understand it. He's the one who a moment ago saw how surely we would be ensnared by this man.

"Let's see the colour of your money first. I'll also need directions to where Dear John is."

Nick pulls a crumpled dollar bill from his pocket.

"We got enough to pay for it through tomorrow noon."

"Sure, kid. It's a dollar and a quarter, though, for any day that's not prepaid."

"This dollar is worth a quarter more than ours, isn't it?"

"Not here, it ain't. It says 'One Dollar' clear as can be."

"You crook," I hear myself saying. "We don't want anything to do with your wares."

"Sure," he says. "Just ask your friends. I hope you haven't cost them extra. Where'd you say that tractor's sitting, boys?"

And so he takes us out *to do to us according to their law* on a
steep and winding trail to the river. But when we step through the
brush I cannot look at it *I am much stounded by it how deeply it
flows I know I've seen it before I know too I've always been saved
from those horrible black waters but now I cannot withhold
myself I am drawn willy-nilly to the water's edge now as we pan
out along the shore everything turns murky, uncanny, and a gust
of sudden wind rushes over the face of the water I grow chill as the
depths knowing I cannot I must not brave those billows then
luckily I awaken*

"No," I am shouting, "no, I will not — "

"Sure," the buyer says, putting the paddle he is holding into
the canoe. The craft sits like some green bird upon the water, its
tail lifting and stirring . . . upon that dark and swirling water.
"Sure enough," he undercuts me with the current, "you couldn't
get me to paddle either. Not if the rest of them would let me ride for
free."

Nick

We inch around the bend and St. Louie bridge is gone. Then I
can't prevent the sinking feeling that I got last night in Gaudreau's
house from coming back again.

My money's wasted on this bobbing, useless boat. We're going
nowhere fast. I flail once more with my paddle. The current slides
by. I can't find anything to dig against.

"Shlockstrocken!"

I suck on my pinched finger, jammed against the side. Just
then the river plucks my oar away.

The canoe lurches. I grab the crosspiece, not to fall out.

"Fershitsake!" Many-birds yells. The canoe lunges again. I
see Jack in front holding on with both hands.

Many-birds' head shines bald. Now his sleeve is wet to the
shoulder. He whirls on me, eyes glaring.

"You swim fer dat goddamn hat, Fuzzy Nuts."

Two paddles clack behind. The old man holds one up,
dripping, beside me.

"Pass it up to him," he says vaguely.

Thinker takes it, feints to club me, then jabs Jack instead in the back. My fists unclench.

"Sweep out more," the old man says. "We'll miss it."

But he talks so quiet, you hardly notice. Then I see Jack's paddle lying in the water. We're sailors, all right. *Boizha*, I'd as soon walk as be cooped up here with them on the *Bounty*.

Many-birds doesn't do what he's asked. He just stares around at me, stranger than usual.

The canoe tilts again.

"Fuck yuh," Many-birds mutters. "I'll use yours."

He lunges for my hat; I roll away; his hand flies by. The canoe teeters. We hang on nervously. Jack looks like he's shit.

"See?" I say accusingly. "You see what you do when you jack around? You'll drown us all, you wise ass."

"Gimme dat hat, den, Fuzzy Nuts."

A floppy felt hat comes over my shoulder. Captain Bligh avoiding the mutiny.

Many-birds scoops it right in the river; holds it under water.

"You think I want yer lice, you old fucker?"

A paddle appears in the air beside me.

Many-birds jams the hat, water and all, down over his ears.

"Thanks," I say sarcastically to old Captain Bligh, Hiawatha, whoever he is back there.

I don't feel like paddling any more.

Stop feeling sorry for yourself.

Tell it to your old man. My ass is smarting on this floor. Just to have my feet on solid ground again!

"Make a crossin' here," grunts Hiawatha.

We edge out of the outside current. Crawling inside the bend.

Just eighty more miles of this hell. Around the block in eighty days.

An island starts to come by. Tropical paradise. Sand. And a few low bushes.

Anything is better than this floating unrest.

I look again at that cove grown over with skinny red willows. A pretty girl sits with her feet in the water. Her mouth is open, singing like crazy. I look away in time from eyes glittering like emeralds. I glance to see if Jack has seen. He hasn't.

"The moment she drownded," Mother says, "she turned into a spirit."

"Anna," Dad says, forbidding.

"I seen her since," Mother looks only at us kids. "She'll try to hold your head under water too."

"Go outside," Dad says to us, though it is forty below.

The ice, I know, is frozen. Mother has been let out of the Asylum for Christmas.

From the porch we hear Dad say, "Anna, don't tell them stories like that no more."

"But I saw her."

"One of the reasons they made a revolution in Old Country," Dad answers after a time, "was to have sanity for once. Not to live by old wives' tales."

"She come from the river up the bank. She sang outside my window."

"That was in North Battleford. You see what I say. You'll only make Marsella sick again."

I can hear Mother crying, then.

She cries again in the night, as soon as their bedsprings stop squeaking. She takes a furious pounding like that every first night she comes home.

The canoe scrapes and we jolt stockstill. We're between the shore and a low sandbank, flocked with gulls. The water riffles yellow-brown over ribs of sand.

"Went d' wrong way," the old boy says apologetically.

"Fershitsake," Many-birds says. "You was born out d' wrong end, old man."

We get out in water to our ankles. Jack leads the canoe like a lamb to the slaughter. I'm so glad to be on solid ground, I let right go of the boat. My next step is off the shelf, over my head. Water pops inside my ears, as cold and sharp as ice-picks.

"Chr—bllist!" the water gets in my mouth again.

Through a curtain I see the paddle Fine-day holds out. I clutch it; he hauls me in.

Laying here, I feel like a damn drowned dog.

I'm scared to go back on the river. *Boizha*, I might end up like Jack. I'm not going to stay on some birdshit sandbar for the rest of my life.

"Now you're like me," Fine-day says quietly. "One of d' River People." When I don't laugh he says, "You okay?"

"Fershitsake, he could have tried t' fish out my nice hat when he went down."

Many-birds sounds happy, though.

I climb back in the cramped canoe. And sit in water again, between these sucked-in ribs. Fine-day shoves us afloat. He sinks our back end jumping on. We totter. I hate this water slapping so unsteady beneath us. I hate our narrow quarters, nowhere to turn to.

Mother is sitting on a chair by the window. We troop past her with our school books. She continues to watch the Bauer kids going up the sidestreet. I see Helmut's tassled red toque disappear. All of us in school say his mother dresses him.

"Hi Mom," Phyllis says. "What did you bake for us? Something sure smells good."

Mother turns around, smiles. A white cloth muffles the pan beside her.

"Shh," she says. "Baby's sleeping."

Eugene's rump bulges out of the cradle.

"Buns," Mother whisks her cloth away like a magician doing tricks.

"Oh boy," Iris says. "Did you make them with cinnamon, Mom?" Rosie reaches with her. They might as well be Siamese twins.

"No. Molasses."

"Oh Mom, you said once we could have cinnamon."

The buns are still warm.

Mother lets on her surprise isn't spoiled.

"Marsella peed in school today. The pee come right past me, picking up sawdust down the aisle."

"I did not," Marsella says harshly. She sits in the Grade One row, though she is a year older than me. Her hair is wild. She won't comb it, or let it be combed.

Mother laughs with the rest of us.

"Nick's the only one," she says proudly, "who didn't have to wear a diaper past two."

"Ahhh Nickie," the twins and Marsella say.

"Past two what? Grade Two?" Phyllis says. She's got the tits to make her sassy.

I enjoy their laughter, getting myself a glass of water. A few drops off the dipper spill on the floor.

"Nick!" Mother says. "Goddamn you!"

She is out of her chair and shaking me by my right arm. Now I spill half the glass.

"You *geetko!*" she slaps my face.

Then I lose my temper and throw the rest at her.

She looks at me a split second as if she's sorry.

"I wish Helmut was my son, not you."

While she is pulling my hair and pushing me around, I think, Why did it have to be Helmut passing by just then? Why did it have to be a *paunya?*

Then she is yelling, baby Eugene is screaming, and I break away, slamming through the hallway, four steps down to the poolroom.

"Don't you come back in my house," Mother screeches at the booker, holding the door open just a crack.

I barely miss the soft drink cases. I've slept down here when I've had to. With just a coat on the old, unused table. It would be warmer if the felt wasn't stripped off.

"What's the matter?" Dad says. No one is in the barber's chair. He is mending bootsoles over the last. All the pool players are standing with their cues butt-ended on the floor.

"Spilled some water," I say, determined down here not to spill more of it. She's crazy. I wish she would go crazy again and leave us alone. Still I feel hollow from her wild unfairness.

"You deserve it?" Dad says.

I shake my head, looking hard at the scores on the chalkboards.

"Let's go talk to her," he says gently.

When we come into the kitchen, Eugene is up and sitting in Mother's lap. The girls all sit on the cot or in chairs, avoiding my eyes. Except Marsella. She is grinning wickedly.

"What happened?" Dad says directly to Mother.

"He called me *geetko* and threw water in my face."

"Is this true?" Dad asks the girls. They don't look up.

Marsella says, "He hit her too."

Then Phyllis says, "She shook him and slapped him for no reason."

"It's not the right way to bring up children," Dad says.

Maybe I won't peep through the curtain any more when Phyllis is undressing.

"I'm not strong like you," Mother says. "I don't know nothing by children."

"Women can be strong too. My mother had fourteen children. She was up in three hours after every one of them, working. Except the last. He was a fat baby. She stayed ten hours in bed that time."

"Why didn't you marry your mother? You don't care," Mother's voice whitens before it starts to fail, "nothing for me."

"Anna, don't speak that way. Not in front of the children. You know it wasn't my mother, anyways. It was most women who were that way. I've told you about the time in Duck Lake, crossing the tracks, when I saw a big lady squat down between the rails. When I come up to her, she had a baby dropped in the back of her skirt, like a bloody shit. Then she bit the cord with her teeth before she smeared him off. She was no squaw, Anna, but a Ukrainian woman. Mrs Manchuk. She walked away with the baby inside her dress. She was strong, a real good worker."

Mother looks as if she would retreat, if she could, back into the plaster.

She doesn't speak again. Not that evening, nor for two awful, awful weeks. At last Dad gets her a ride back to North Battleford.

We pull up in the mud along the bank. Many-birds is over his ankles in ooze.

"Goddamn gotta piss," he says, blowing a fart back at the boat.

I have to prod Jack, then, to get him over the bow. I don't want to go over the side.

My trousers cling wet, still, against my legs. I step on a stone to save my running shoes from the filth. They squelch with me along the bank.

I am turning back to the boat when five little ducklings file up towards me. They are all alone in the world, it seems.

Peepeepeep, they say.

But it wasn't my fault, I say. How can you possibly blame me?

Fine-day

The River trembles lightly at bearing such a boat as this . . . so unlike our birch barks she once cradled in her silver stroking arms . . . Mother of the People . . . your River People were not lost utterly. One of them is now returned to you. . . .

She flies at me like the sunlight winking off her waves . . . pours under me, through me like the current of olden-times, waking olden-time memories . . . so that I half expect to reach around another reach and find my boyhood self paddling down to meet us. . . .

. . . . whenever my father put me in the canoe, I remember, my mother was as skittish as a mare cut off in floodwater from her colt. She really hated water. She was Blackfoot, not one of the River People. I don't think she once let herself feel like the rest of us. What she must have felt, then, when my father took me out here! . . . he always took me along . . . save for that last time . . . and taught me to hold a paddle like this one while I sat still between his knees. We would go out to where the fish were caught inside our weirs and I remember him slapping their ugly heads across a thwart such as this. Whenever the pile got too high, one would always flop over and rainbow down into the water. My father would look back at me and smile. "That one was the River's son. She wouldn't go on without him." But the rest belonged to the People. We would come back riding low in the water, bearing our catch to add to that of the band. Those days, there were always long racks of pike and pickerel and tulibee drying under the sun. River fed us and the Sun kept us warm.

So why do I remember another time? . . . one winter when there weren't many fish, and the ground was bare of windbreaking snow . . . the air as cold as knives . . . the time we surprised a herd of buffalo in a hollow above the River and, fanning out, caught them between two horns of the People and ran them, before they knew it, off a cutbank as steep and sharp as that one over there. The first ones bellowed abruptly and the rest, plunging after familiar wool and withers, fell in a silence broken only by the snapping of necks and legs and backs at the bottom. By the time we climbed down, only a few were left kicking. . . . One, a rearguard young bull, was trying to haul himself off on two broken legs that suddenly buckled. The men, along with my father, stepped carefully among

all those jerking hooves, sticking knives into hides that would
warm our legs, into meat that would warm our bellies. But my ears
would not stop hearing those dying moans. . . . I heard them still,
the following summer, when my father fell in the killing at the
half-breed troubles . . . and I remembered with sadness the pile of
drying bones beneath the cutbank. . . .

Think of something else. River never meant to bring you such
a sadness . . . you did it yourself . . . now don't respect her so little. . . .

Mother . . . and then I remember something from only this
afternoon . . . those pelicans I saw back there . . . we used to say they
were River People too, that's why we never ate them . . . the way
their bellies sagged so heavy today on the sandbar, you must still be
feeding them pretty good. When we came by, they could barely
flap up off the water. . . .

. . . . and then River brings to mind a glorious time, one
morning long ago, when my father pointed through the spirit mist
hanging above River. In the midst of that whiteness I saw only the
sun's yellow stain like a great goldeye swimming above us . . .
suddenly shadows loomed . . . with one great flap of wings . . . a
thousand pelicans burst out of the fog, bills at the ready, beating
up toward that great yellow fish. . . . We were so near beneath them,
I could see the scabs on those grey gulping pouches . . . passing on
in that eerie light like creatures from another world. . . .

"Soon you should be going, my son," Father said then. "To
seek your vision." And he touched his hand to my head.

So one day we left camp, climbing toward some hills. My
father built me a brush shelter and then went home. For nine days I
waited . . . had nothing to eat . . . and then one night I dreamed I
was flying. . . .

I was back in camp. I walked out of my father's lodge, and my
arms went out and began to beat. Suddenly I was rising straight
up. I thought, Why has no one done this before? I must tell my
father.

Then I was high enough to reach full out. I let my feet drop
behind, my arms neither shaking nor tired, but I knew I had to beat
on like this, or fall. I looked beneath me at our green grass world.
River flowed into that shining haze. Then my heart flamed bright
as the Sun . . . I could look directly into his Eye.

I beat upward after that, soaring . . . suddenly I was settling in
a bright clearing. I knew it was as high as I could fly.

I noticed right off the girl with shining hair . . . she was west of me in the meadow . . . while I came at her from the north. She was combing her tresses down to her waist. At every stroke the light flew at me, but I could stare right into it. I stepped close to her . . . she turned her head and smiled at me, then flew up. I knew I could not follow.

But someone was behind me. He didn't tell me that he was, I only knew his thoughts.

Stay here, he was thinking. Wait on this side   she will come back tomorrow

He was about my age, I think, but he was feathered. So I lay and slept . . . suddenly it was another day. She was already sitting there like before. I approached a little closer . . . she turned and smiled, and flew up again. It happened this way twice more. But on that fourth day I finally heard him thinking once more.

She is the Sun's Spirit   take her gently by her arms and stop her from combing

So at last I caught her and held her beside me. Her face was as lovely as the River with the Sun above it.

Why have you caught me what do you hope to do with me

I would like to make you my wife you are prettier than any girl I ever saw

But I was only ten years old.

All right though it cannot be forever

She sat down on some grass at my feet, then lay back.

What do you think of this

She had pulled one bow painted blue out of her side . . . I did not know what to say.

The one behind me thought, Its name is Soaring Hawk's Bow.

So I said its name.

Yes now what is this one

I looked at a yellow bow . . . then waited for my Helper again.

Double Runner's Bow

That's right

And I was very pleased since Double Runner was my father's name.

These are to be your sons' names   first I'll give you Soaring Hawk then you will have Double Runner   now I cannot stay but I will send Helpers to teach you to make the Sun Dance I'm really boss of that though

I woke up just after the Sun was rising. I looked out over our green grass world. I could see my father's lodge far away there, beside River. I felt he would live forever. . . .

. . . . and then, not long after, my father died. . . . I didn't even know how I could be any more . . . still I kept having this beautiful dream. My heart, so heavy when I was awake, swooped and soared. But I never saw that clearing or that girl again. . . .

My mother moved with a Woods Cree, named Iron Cap, to his reserve. We left the River for his place on the lake. At least my old friend Pelican was there with plenty of fish. There was also one new face . . . Muskrat. Iron Cap had got a taste for white bread so he was hot to skin Muskrat.

Still this woods of his wasn't the River . . . and I felt I could never get used to a square log house. . . .

One day my mother just left for the Sand Hills . . . she cut her wrists. . . .

Iron Cap was okay. He let me stay.

The next winter he froze in the bush . . . it was snowing bad when he went out to check his trap line . . . so I lived alone in that house . . . my house.

Then one summer, many years later, I went with some people down South. We took horses. It was to a big Sun Dance. In that camp it was like the old days. . . .

The moment I saw Maggie I knew she was the girl with the shining hair, my dream come true. I waited till the Sun Dance was over to speak to her. Of all things, it turned out she was part Soto . . . but she went for me in a big way too.

I brought her proudly back to my little log house. The next spring, when we had a son . . . my only child . . . I could not bring myself to name him Soaring Hawk. My father hadn't lived now for twenty years, so his name should come first, I believed, and I could still call my second son Soaring Hawk. . . .

Right off, I asked my brother-in-law Thunder Child to give him the name of Double Runner. Thunder Child, who was up from down South for a visit, hadn't forgot the old ways.

"You haven't made enough gifts of print to the Spirits."

I remembered what my mother said . . . the Spirits hadn't helped my father any . . . but then my childhood vision had given me my child, hadn't she?

So I took horses to Prince Albert, the closest place, and got lots of cloth.

"Now you can name him," I told Thunder Child when I had hung all the cloth out in the bush . . . yet I dare not tell my wife's brother about my vision. Maggie must know nothing of her son's true name.

Thunder Child smoked East, then all the way around. He blew smoke to Sky and to Earth before he started singing. I was glad he had so many Power Songs. I had none. When he quit at four, I knew that four was a good number for us. Four would make my father's spirit and me and my two sons have power for a long time to come.

Thunder Child held up my infant son.

"Your name is Double Runner."

In that moment my father's name came to life again. Double Runner . . . *alive* . . . *here* . . . as we passed the child from arm to arm. He was kissed by everyone.

One man said, "I hope you will hunt well when you grow up."

Another said, "I hope you will have lots of horses."

One old woman said, "I hope you will *steal* lots of horses."

And looked closely at me . . . she didn't have to. I meant to raise him the old way. . . .

He wouldn't even be two before I took him in my birch canoe. Maggie was worried like my mother had been . . . I saw it in her eyes . . . but she was woman enough to keep silent. I set him between my knees and skimmed out over the water.

I could feel his little head against my belly. I dipped my paddle. His face tipped back, his eyes sparkled like drops from the blade. I grinned. He laughed out loud. My belly tingled all around him . . . he looked just like me at that age, going everywhere with my father . . . and so the life I thought was lost was given back to me. I would make the old willow weirs again and teach him to be a fisherman like Pelican and . . . oh, I would have him know all the old ways. . . .

That night Maggie teased me before she would open to me.

"Maybe I should be the one to get on top. You've turned out to be such a good mama for Double Runner."

And squealed with delight when I nipped her a good one on the nipple. Afterwards we lay flank to flank, she running her heel up and down my calf and ankle.

"You're really a good father," she murmured into my throat.

"I just hope I give you lots more children to make us so happy as this."

I grinned into the darkness.

"You want to try again before we go to sleep?"

"*Hi!* Don't I even slow you down? Go to sleep, old rutting moose, unless you're planning to get up with him in the morning."

But I lay there after she was breathing deeply, feeling, for the first time since we had met, my old sadness. I don't know what it was . . . maybe only a dawning sense of loss.

It would be years yet before I thought, When did I stop having that dream? Was it when I first went to bed with Maggie? Maybe a man wasn't supposed to lie in love with his Spirit Helper. Maybe the Great Spirit was punishing us for it, and we would never have that son named Soaring Hawk. I decided it was time to seek my Dream Helper to find out the truth. And I would take Double Runner with me to teach him the way of visions. . . .

"You understand," I said to Maggie. "I know you're used to it pretty often. But we've got to give it up for our son's sake." I was still careful not to say which son.

So she really undid me when she said, "You don't have to feel bad for me, Fine-day. I only do it because you want to. Don't you think I can see we're not going to have any more kids now?"

Now it was there stronger than ever, the old sense of hopeless loss . . . and when I looked at her, I couldn't remember any more what my Dream Girl had looked like. So I went away sadly, praying that my Spirit Helper would show herself again to a foolish man. . . .

But when my son and I built two separate brush shelters on a hill overlooking the lake, and I began to teach him how to go about it, I wondered through the empty nights if I were teaching him anything of value. Clearly Double Runner would not tell me if he were having visions, or he would lose them . . . and yet I sensed this misnaming had doomed us both to a dreamless sleep. . . .

Then my son got sick . . . like all the white men dying that fall from the fire cough . . . and he died too, though I made a blue bow called Soaring Hawk's Bow and put it in his hands and gave him that name . . . I touched his fiery head . . . he stirred . . . but he was never to wake up again. . . .

Maggie cried for days afterwards. I would see her and she would stop . . . she would try to cheer me up but it was no use . . .

better to hug a rock . . . at least a rock is firm . . . until I saw, in time, she was turning bitter. Then I thought again of our unborn son Soaring Hawk . . . Double Runner, I should say . . . and decided to risk telling her.

"We could try to make another," I began carefully to try her out.

She looked down over her breasts.

"Why not," I said.

"Because I hate myself," she whispered. "I hate my body that made him to die."

So I knew at last why my Dream Girl would not come back to me. I had to make Maggie know who she was if I hoped to ever hold her again.

"Did you never wonder why I changed our son's name to Soaring Hawk? I knew you before in dreams, Maggie. You said our first son would be Soaring Hawk. After that we would have Double Runner . . . only I renamed him for my father's sake."

Her face changed slightly, as if she were just waking up. . . .

"We still have one son coming, Maggie. So don't say bad things about your woman's body."

She gave me a funny look.

"What's wrong? You don't think that I. . . ?"

She didn't answer . . . but her eyes were clearly blaming me. . . .

And then I knew I should have never said a thing. I never should have blabbed my Helper's secrets like that. . . .

Now I had no choice any more but to be quiet . . . Maggie was quiet too . . . For days we said nothing. But it wasn't doing any good now . . . it was too late for that . . . I could feel her going steadily away.

Still she cooked the wild rice I brought in . . . we ate together . . . but the food she prepared was not made with me in mind. . . .

"What can I do?" I said at last.

She glanced at me. Only her eyes spoke of my betrayal.

"I'm going out this afternoon."

And she left me sitting at our window. She took the road up from the lake. . . .

. . . . next day she went away again . . . then every afternoon after that. . . .

Now when we were together, she wasn't with me any more. . . .

One day she said simply, "Many-birds has asked me to live with him."

I was afraid I wasn't going to stop her . . . but I had to try.

"That joker? Who let his wife die when his son was born?" Then realized what I had said.

Maggie buttoned her coat.

"At least he doesn't make me hate myself."

She stopped in the doorway. I could see she still had tears for me . . . she wasn't going to say the worst that could be said. I got up, thinking I might yet hold on to her. . . .

"Goodbye," she said, backing away. "I'm really sorry for you."

. . . and then my old fear was waked in me. . . .

Nick

The river swerves around a bend in these hills and sweeps on, urgent, unavoidable. A sullen light shows on its face. I wrench at the water with my useless cue stick. Each stroke ahead is worth two back.

The lineup has passed by the head table. Cousin Pollyanna and the groom wait for latecomers and we wait for the newlyweds to start the dance upstairs. The band waits by the door to strike up for any last presenters. Already Pollyanna's got two hundred dollars in donations. I wouldn't mind sticking my hand in that pot. *Boizha*, the way her groom simpers, she might appreciate more than a hand. But I have my eye on a browneyed number still eating *holubchi* and turkey at a sidetable.

Uncle Oofer comes along the wall with a pitcher, pouring. He's got his white lightning cut with whisky, so the Mounties could waste a trip tonight from Melfort.

"Nick," he says to Dad, "I'm counting on you still to hold up the pride of Gronlid. The boys from Brooksby are here."

A lot of men down the wall laugh harshly.

Dad is for once cleanshaven. But he still looks whitefaced, compared to farmers with their leather jaws. Only he looks more comfortable than them in his old wedding suit. Most of their wrists hang down, sharp as pigsfeet, out of those shiny black sleeves.

"You're the one doing the driving," Dad shrugs.

"Oh," Uncle Oofer looks around, for once his chest near as big as Dad's, "didn't Anna tell you? I decided you're staying till tomorrow. We got a spare bedroom after tonight."

He sends a mischievous glance the way of the bride and groom. We men laugh, glittering-eyed, at one another.

"Nick," a stubble-chinned man says when Uncle Oofer passes out of hearing, "what's the story about the boys from Brooksby?"

Mother's eyes are downcast. She sits alone at the table across from us.

"Nothing much." But Dad can't hide his pride.

"Tell it," I prime him. The homebrew foams like gasoline in my nose. Uncle Oofer should give it to us straight. Not to cut it with ginger ale like this.

The men drink and gather closer. Some move up to the table with their blacksuited backs to Mother.

"Well, I used to go around in the old days," Dad says, "to the wakes in every parish. Oofer and me and a couple others, since moved away, went to them all. That's how me and Oofer married two sisters from Brooksby."

"Is that all?" a man six-foot sitting down, great stuckout ears, says in a hurt voice. With so many marble patches in his varnished skin, no wonder he's never found a woman to marry him.

"'Course not," Dad says. "Hello there, Angelina," to a wide-hipped woman in a flowerprint dress. She comes toward Dad like a prancing dray horse.

"Nick, are you telling stories about us again?"

"No, a little after that, Angelina. When I went away to Brooksby."

"Oh. Do you mind if I listen in? I always wanted to find out where you went wrong."

Dad grins sort of sheepishly. I never knew he had a past with her.

Some man stands up to give her his chair. A couple of more stout women scamper in like thunder. They're grimacing like mongrel hounds.

Angelina's all right.

Dad is well into the story when I notice Mother wandering around the room. Some little girls had started out sitting beside her. Now they've moved over here. I wish they'd have brought the big-titted browneyed girl with them.

" — remember it was teams you were drinking in in those days. So when one of your boys missed a *klishik*, maybe worse, passed *out*," — we guffaw and titter in our expectancy — "you had to carry his part of the load."

Mother is back by the kitchen window, talking to a woman in a blue dress. Her face is intent.

" — so finally there's only Oofer left with me. Andrew is lying back in the wheat, feet up on the bench. We can hear Metro throwing up on the sprouts outside the granary door."

The gust of our laughter turns every head in the room. Mother is talking now to some lady with a plate in her hands. The lady is turned partways towards the kitchen; Mother's mouth is straining to make itself heard.

" — finally the third guy on the other side goes over backwards, but his feet spill the whole *klishik* of his homebrew.

"'Pour that man a drink,' I say."

The plate-bearing woman bolts through the door into the kitchen. The sudden sound of a fiddle saws through the ceiling. Mother looks away through the roof.

"Hey Oofer," a bullet-headed man brays at Uncle coming up the wall, "don't fall down now."

We hold our tumblers gladly to the enamel pitcher.

"Bottoms up," Uncle Oofer says, drinking out of the pitcher.

"*Nesdyrovya*," we say in chorus, slugging back with Dad.

Uncle Oofer lands lightly in the lap of Angelina.

The fatter women are squealing with pleasure.

"That's just how Oofer went down and out on me," Dad says. "As soon as he found some woman to catch him."

Mother has stopped Aunty Mary by the stairway. Aunty shakes her head, lifting her skirt, and clambers up toward the swell of music. A slight stir, a shuffle of feet up there, but as yet no stamping.

" — so their head man pours out eight *klishiks*, four in front of him, four in front of me. 'Drink up, boy,' he says."

Mother stands by the double door giving out on the skating rink. It will be pitch black in there, lonesomer than at home where no one comes to visit. If only she knew better how to talk to people. Not to tell those crazy old stories that nobody cares about —

"Finally the head man says, 'Well I never seen a drinker like you, boy. So because you're company, I give up.'"

The feet hit the floor upstairs. Our room sways with the sound. I'm in a hurry to get up there and find that browneyed girl. But nobody seems to have heard the music. Dad's last word is still hanging in the thumping air.

"Remember, he called me 'Boy.' Well, I show him, I think.

"'Pour me one more, mister.'

"And that's the last thing I remember."

The men are grinning, almost ready to own to the music. The women still have eyes only for Dad.

"Their head man said next day that I knocked myself out, hitting my head on the table."

The roar from our party rebounds off the roof. For a moment the paperboard seems to bounce and buckle with just our shout.

Now Mother stands off the edge of the group. Her face is drawn and white. She tries in vain to make herself heard.

"What's that, Anna?" Dad says, when at last he sees her. "Ready to polka?"

Her voice scrapes up through that crashing overhead like fingernails sliding across a blackboard. "I — you're starting *over*, are you, with them old stories?"

We enter a stretch of puddle river. The sand, scoured by wind and water, humps from shore to shore.

"Can't see no channel," Fine-day mumbles. "Have t' walk along d' bank."

"Can't see no fucking river, you mean. Why, old man, wouldn't you dry up too like dat?"

The water creeps in sheets across the floor.

Mother is swishing the mop when we get home. We invade the room, throwing down our schoolbooks.

She doesn't look up. Her eyes, anyways, are snailed again inside her head. Her face is grey as shell.

She's gotten so awful low again. She's only been home from Battleford for two weeks this time. They said there was nothing wrong; only a little depressed.

She doesn't care to be home with us. She only swishes the mop over the floor, flinging suds toward the door. I see she is backing, side to side, toward the corner beyond the cot.

I go down into the poolroom. Right away my nose bristles with the heady mansmell of chewing tobacco. Dad keeps it racked in a column back of the counter. Copenhagen snuff; a red cardboard tin with a silver top.

It's so much more homey down here. Nights when I was little and lying in bed, I could feel mother's presence through the curtain, sour and gritted as her teeth, and I would listen to the smack of a break out here — the pleasant sound of snooker balls running, the comfortable chat of men — and I'd wish I could live out here, that I wouldn't have to go back to the smell of her harshly scrubbed floors any more.

Dad's clipping hair right now. Old Noah Andersen. Been building a boat for ten years is why they call him Noah.

Dad motions me to sweep up the clippings. I get the broom and pan.

The hair on the floor is rust-red. Poor Dad is already salt-and-pepper grey, though he's younger. He's had a hard life, playing houseman for his cousin Steve's poolroom, owning a sawmill up north of Gronlid, things like that. I remember the sawmill. Remember the day, sort of, that he went broke. Mother just said, "It serves you right." She never had no sympathy for him. But he made us a living at barbering and shoemaking ever since. He could still make his living at pool if anyone would play him for money. Down here, nobody's crazy.

At least the better ones will listen to Dad, or ask his advice how to make a shot. Even the bad ones ask him to umpire whenever there's an argument. Lately he's got them all going on pocket billiards, so much tougher than on the shoebox American table. Some of the older ones prefer to see none but British games. But Dad tells how many games Cochran, the world champ, is good at. Ones like golf, and baseball, and 14.1 continuous. That shuts the limeys up.

"Nick," Dad says when I'm finished, "I want you to make me a sign. Print it in big letters that these palookas can read. NO SPITTING."

Ed Turl who is about to make a shot — with a pool cue for a change — looks up surprised.

"You meaning me, Nick?"

"If the shoe fits, wear it."

"You mean," Bill Dietz says, "if the shoe fits, it's because someone rammed it up Turl's ass where it belonged."

He grins his catching grin. He's a good shit; even Ed Turl can't mind him.

"I mean," Dad says, "I'm not going to stand in here all day in juice soaked through *my* shoes."

Which puts an end to it. Just the plump sound for a time of balls banking, and a carom clicked and running.

I get the coal scoop from the booker and walk around, scraping snoose off the floorboards. It doesn't smell sweet in the pan.

Later, I get a Coke out of the watercooler. I don't bother to put five cents in the till. I earned it.

I make the sign in bright red crayon, adding "!!" Then I try to scratch one exclamation point off. Merle Guttormson scratches on the table. He lets a dozen of them off, all blue.

By supper time, I have my red-letter sign all finished. Dad locks the door and we go back between the empty tables.

Pop sits at the supper table awhile, letting his *borscht* cool off. He's got his shoes drawn up on the clawfoot of the table, resting his feet and his belly both.

"Cows shit in their stalls," he says to me. "Not humans. You shouldn't have to clean up after them."

Mother looks as if her head has been jerked back by a string.

"I clean up after you. I clean up after all of youse, all the time."

Her lips seem to have tasted vinegar.

"You don't know what I'm talking about," Dad says in a soothing voice. "You don't see what it's like out there."

"You don't know nothing by housework," her voice rises strangely. "You don't know nothing at all."

Then the string releases her; her chin drops, cutting into the bony hollow of her neck.

None of us has lifted another spoon. None of us feels like eating now.

Dad leads her over to the bedroom.

"Anna," we can hear him saying strokingly. "Anna. Anna. Anna."

But we know she is off the rails again.

Dad, when he comes out from behind the curtain, sits without looking at his *borscht*.

"I don't know," he says after the longest time. "She won't

listen to anything I say. She never would. She doesn't want a husband to tell for her, I guess."

The girls, except for Marsella, are looking down at the table.

"I think sometimes she blames me," Dad says to no one in particular. "She blames me for making her sick in her mind."

Jack

That horrible dream will live before my eyes. I bare my teeth at the devil; he whirls and runs out; and God is gone out with him.

God, how have you gone the way of Baalim?

For He hears not my cry; I, even I only, who have remained a prophet of the Lord.

Someone touches my shoulder; I start awake.

An angel bends over me. A womanly angel. When I was a boy I imagined them so, and I refused to be disabused of my notion, even when I learned as a man that they were all male-named.

My angel watches over me 'neath this juniper tree. So the Lord is with me.

"Get up," she says, "and eat."

There is a radiance in her look that impels me to my feet. *The first time ever I looked on her face, I heard anew the voice of God* He said, "Jack Cann, take unto you this woman, this Crystal; make her to shine with my light and I will cause you to shine with mine."

She was seated in the midst of my classroom, in the beer parlour of this old hotel which our school had taken over. And didn't Christ's ministry start with the miracle of wine at Cana? That occasion, as I recall, was already a wedding.

So to that class I came, I saw, and I was conquered. Crystal sat — I seem to recall her sitting, always placed and placid — more beautiful than beauteous. It was as if she were a vision of something: on her lips there played a most mysterious smile, some holy secret, almost. Somewhere there is even a painting, I have heard, of some woman with the like smile. But I sensed at once this was only a face which a shy girl put on, innocent of the confusion it might breed in the world. She meant nothing by it, save to meet the world on acceptable terms. But to eyes that were any more worldly it could have signified anything, from coyness to contempt. In that instant I knew I wanted to save her from all such eyes.

I detained her after class, meaning to warn her directly of the danger of her deportment. But the instant I looked into those demurely lidded pupils, the voice of God hit me like a thunderclap.

"I love you," I said.

She looked at me as if the thunder bolt had unnerved her every limb. Or perhaps as a large-eyed doe would look, uncertain of the way to bolt. Her smile vanished behind a veil of sudden cloud.

"I'm sorry," I said. "God told me to say that. I didn't mean to startle you. Only now that it's said, I do feel it. Your name is Crystal, isn't it? I truly do love you, Crystal."

And I did. Love at first sight, the love of God. My very insides turned outward to her.

She looked swiftly, then her glance evaded me. And her lips persisted unsmiling and unspeaking, as if in concentrated thought. But a flame rose on her throat and over her chin, like the flaming tongues of Pentecost. I knew then I need not tell her of the ways of the world; she was to be given into my highest care.

Yet was I tempted, there and then in our shabby beer parlour-classroom, to take her in my arms. I longed to see the brown wainscotting of the room shine round about with the glory of His Love. For here was the love of God revealed to us in Love, Saskatchewan, Canada! Then I considered the ways of the world — and of women — and concluded to refrain. Yet love's refrain I could have sung forever.

God moves in mysterious ways His wonders to perform. I met Crystal the rest of that fall, but in the classroom. I spoke to her only with twenty other students about. But the more I spoke, the more her smile played for me upon those lips. I was inspired to teach Personal Evangelism in the light of that personal glance. For the more I catechized them in a series of questions to put to unsaved souls, and the more my students answered with the proper scriptures leading unto salvation, the more I saw in Crystal's face how far she was being won unto me.

That fall I took but one liberty — in view of our school's forbidding of converse between the sexes — of addressing my intended through her class essays. I poured out my deepest passions, in hints and in guiding questions, in the margins of her thought.

Crystal's response, when it came at last in early December, was securely trusting. "Would you come home for Christmas and meet my parents?'' she wrote between the lines of her remarkable study of why the Witnesses winked on the day of Jesus' birth. I took it now as a fundamental confession of her faith.

What surprised me greatly, in next securing permission from the school, was to learn that Crystal wasn't even saved. At first Brother Dueck, the Dean of Men, was quite opposed to my going at all to her home.

"Brother Cann,'' he said, "our people have never rushed into things like this. Don't you think you should pray earnestly some more, and wait upon the Lord to know for certain?''

I looked at Brother Dueck's stout chest, immovable as a stump, and it surprised me less that he should counsel waiting.

"Why, Brother Dueck? Do you imagine God sometimes doesn't know for certain?''

He only smiled heavily, the way he did at his own ponderous jokes in the men's residence on the third floor.

So I spread my heart upon the desk of President Peter Giesbrecht. I told Peter everything, excepting God's covenant to restore my gift of healing. And this godliest of men, for all his stone-grey looks, proved to have a heart as compassionate as our Saviour.

"You're convinced, Jack, that this is of God?''

"Peter, I feel His hand upon me as I stand in this room.''

"Then I give you, personally, my blessing. I think I would still like, though, to know of your young lady's heart. For her sake, you understand. But tell me Jack. How would you know that she is so certain as you?''

"Well — of course, I don't know that much about her feelings. I have written her, chastely, circumspectly. Naturally, her modesty has led her so far as to an invitation only . . .''

"Don't you agree we should try to fathom her heart a little further? In such a matter as this, where she must be your student through the rest of the winter — you see what appearance of evil we must avoid? I think it best, don't you, that Sister Friesen, not you nor I, should be the one to speak to her? And then, if we are satisfied, I will write to her parents.''

I couldn't blame him for his circumspection. I have lived in the world, and know the gossip of the godly, let alone of the ungodly. Peter Giesbrecht is a good and honourable man. I just wish he hadn't waited on the Lord when little Paul had so little time for waiting.

Crystal, throughout our period of trial, said or wrote nothing more to me. For my part, I taught Evangelism and False Cults as they had never been taught before. I made the errors of Mecca and Rome to live before my students' eyes. We left not a stone unturned in the Kingdom Hall and in the Mormon Tabernacle. And though I kept my own counsel on the sheepishness of the Mennonite flock, I prayed in my heart that they would forsake their meek self-sacrifice, exacted not by our Lord but by the devil. Then I knew I had not failed when, on the Christmas examination, my class brought down the folly of false faith to the devil's inspiration.

Brother Dueck brought me his hand-signed permission on the eve of Christmas recess. With it, he brought the required letter of invitation from Crystal's parents. I read the flourishes of its feminine hand. The letter was hardly as forthright as Jacob's offer from his Uncle Laban. I was invited to her home, at the discretion of the elders of the school, for Christmas week.

Then I realized the depth of my unkindness. Jacob had laboured fourteen years, bilked by his Uncle Laban, for the hand of his beloved. Lord, I prayed in the quiet of my heart, save me from the likes of people like me. Make me ever more humbly grateful.

I was thankful to God, too, during this time for keeping Crystal and I in our separate orbits, shining as with the steady light of planets. Our lives were as open to all as the nighttime sky. Glory be to God on High!

Then Brother Dueck said something which brought me down to earth again.

"Last night — Sister Friesen — the young lady — uhmm — she admitted, Brother Cann, that she didn't know the will of the Lord."

We stood in the hall of the washroom next to Brother Dueck's office. The chain within the little cubicle was drawn, and the rush of water flushed my mind away.

"She — "

Brother Dueck stared steadily, but also sorrowfully, at me from beneath those lion-maned brows. There was not a twinkle of a joke in his look.

"At first — she told us she did know what God willed. That's why Brother Giesbrecht wrote her parents. But last night, when Sister Friesen questioned her one last time — "

He stopped, waiting for me, it seemed, to supply his conclusion.

" — Crystal Hildebrandt admitted she didn't even know the Lord."

My mind raced in avoidance of his pursuing eyes. But his mouth had not yet left the trail.

" — parents — when a child is sent — taken their faith for granted, I suppose, as the means of her salvation."

The trail ahead, his eyes pronounced decisively, will be strewn with burning coals should you proceed.

So, as the Scriptures taught me, I heaped coals of burning fire on his head.

"Fear not, Brother Dueck. I realize that the salvation of a soul is no joking matter. But surely the Lord can't mean for us, with such long faces, to be the instruments of Crystal's redemption. I admit I was unprepared for what you've told me. I'm also confident of what the Lord meant in what He told me."

I had to admit, however, that I pondered these things in my heart, and wondered how the Lord was going to work.

It was the morning but one before Christmas. Crystal and I had arrived in a sleigh last night with students bound for Nipawin. Now I sat, the only man among the women, in the cellar kitchen of the Hildebrandt house. Well, almost the only man. Little Abe was with us too. He was knee-up on the bench, reaching for the scraps of dough his mother sliced for the *rollkuchen*.

"Can't you wait?" she smiled at him.

"How can I?" Abe paused to stuff the rolled pastry in his mouth. He gobbled it down till I feared he would choke. Then he grinned across the corner of the table. "Mr Cann ate all the old *rollkuchen* for breakfast. So what's there left for me to eat?"

Crystal reached for him and smothered his squeal in her breast.

"Oh you!" she said, nipping gently his ear. Then she caught the hunger in my eyes and she blushed clear down into her blouse. I admired her so: much taller and more rounded than her mother. Already, it seemed to me, she was her father's daughter.

"I'm making it for your sister," Mrs Hildebrandt said fondly. "She hasn't had any since last summer. So I thought I'd make some for Christmas. I'm glad Mr Cann likes it too."

"Das nützt nichts," I replied happily.

Crystal choked on a mouthful of swallowed laughter. Then her smile rounded, though it failed to ravage, that tender, soulful chin.

Mrs Hildebrandt stared at her, then at me, confounded. I noticed the old grandma, in her chair by the heater, look at me most strangely.

Abe said, "If you didn't like 'em, why'd you eat so many?"

"They were delicious," I said. "I love their crispness overspread with syrup."

"But you just said — "

Crystal's suppressed laughter had infected the older women, and I sat, mortified, in the midst of their epidemic. Later, when the sick were cured, Crystal quietly explained.

"I only had a chance to teach him 'good' and 'bad.' You were supposed to say," she looked shyly toward me, "*sehr Gute.* You got them" — and then her lips began to quiver — "mixed up." Then she was giggling again, and both women with her.

I had to laugh in their joy of my foolishness. The old grandma, after one cackle more than the rest, sat smiling at me until she raised her apron and, with its corner, dried her eyes.

I greatly rejoiced in my role now as Fool. I wished I knew more German to garble. But by way of apology to Mrs Hildebrandt I said, "Thank God I've been blessed with better pupils than Crystal has been given."

The mother said something in German to her daughter. Crystal blushed again, and looked down at the red-check oilcloth. Old Grandma, dressed in black, looked at me with all the warmth of a coal Booker.

Little Abe cocked his head like a squirrel and said, "I bet you don't know the best place to find a Christmas Tree. My dad and me and Thom are going out this afternoon. Would you like to come?"

He reached for more dough without taking his glittering eyes off me.

"Sure. But do you know, Abe," I said confidentially, meaning to make the women listen more carefully, "that your sister has already taught me something about Christmas I didn't know?"

"What's that?"

Crystal, in her seemly modesty, appeared about to hide from all eyes.

"Well, she wrote a paper for me on why the Witnesses — you know? — don't celebrate our Saviour's birth the way we do. Did you know, for example, that they don't give Christmas presents to anyone?"

The seed of rebellion was sprouting in Abe's eyes. So I hastened to explain the reason.

"It's because the custom of gift-giving began with the Magi. But they gave to Christ, not to anyone else. So the Witnesses think our custom is a mockery. As for Christmas trees, I learned from your sister that it was an old pagan custom, probably from the German tribes, in worship of the sun or something."

The look on the boy's face made me bite my tongue. I had meant, mostly, to praise his sister. Little Abe's eyes, so hopeful, now seemed like broken panes of glass.

"Mom — " he said, but his voice trailed hopelessly away.

Mrs Hildebrandt looked only at her son. She didn't stop trimming the pastry, but neither did she leave the boy uncomforted and untouched. She caressed him with her eyes.

"I'm sure, dear, that Mr Cann didn't mean to say it's what he believes. He was only telling us how other people think. And if our German people started it, you don't think it could be all bad, do you?" Then she let go her hold on him and spoke quietly to me. "I'm sure God doesn't mean us to refuse the Earth He gave us, does He? Somehow, whenever my men have brought the Tree into our house, I have felt it too is holy; it has sanctified my home. Haven't you felt that way, Mr Cann?"

I could only nod in acceptance of her reproof. Crystal seemed not to be with us any more, but to have sent her spirit unto another room.

"Besides," Mrs Hildebrandt added, "it was a fruit tree which led to our fall, not a pine. Isn't that so? Eve would not have given Adam a pine cone to eat."

"Yes," I said gently, for the sake of the boy. "I only meant to show how we could learn from other faiths." But in my heart I felt the woman had proven more than was necessary.

Later, when Crystal and I walked down to the cowbarn to see how milking was coming, I asked what her mother had said to her in German.

"She thinks — " Crystal blushed again, "you're cute." But she kept her eyes upon the icy path before us.

At noon, little Abe couldn't sit still enough to eat his borscht. I was adding more cow's cream to the delicious winey broth, so heavy with beets and peas and carrots, when he said, "Thom, could I ride Flight this afternoon to find the Christmas Tree?

Don't you think he should be there too, like all the cattle and the horses were around Jesus' manger? Do you think if we left right — "

"Whoa boy, whoa!" Thom said in a wolfish grin, showing stumps and pits of broken molars. He had a way, too, of speaking out of the side of his mouth as if to lengthen his lean, brown visage. "Sometimes you run off wilder than a little bull dogie. Or even one a them other kinda bulls that killed them three miners down in Estevan." His eyes, for just an instant, flicked to his mother, then back to the boy.

The mother observed her son as narrowly as she had me this morning. But she bided a time for her boy.

"Yep," Thom continued casually, "I rode them rods clear over from Central Butte to see what was going on. The radio said there was going to be trouble and they sure wasn't strayed on that one."

Mrs Hildebrandt looked to her husband who was inspecting his soup so minutely.

"Should we Mennonites," she began softly, "not remain apart from worldly affairs, Thom? As Christians, are we not called to higher things?"

"Than what?" Thom said shortly. "Higher than to keep kids from starving? Or to see that working men get a decent wage?" He leaned forward to the table and suddenly his whole supercilious mask slid below his eyes, from off his jut of chin. "Mom, you don't know what it's like down there in the world. We live up here in isolation, sheltered by this bush. We don't even have the drouth they do in the south. We can look out for ourselves just fine where we are. But I don't call it being a Christian to let others suffer in our own homeland."

Again Mrs Hildebrandt appealed to her husband whose eyes busied themselves below. His face, though, looked longer than usual.

"Thom, you know all about how we came to this country, how we suffered in our old homeland. You don't think we want others to go through what we did, do you? I don't really remember it, of course, I was only a baby, but Grandma has told you what she went through. The last winter of the famine in Russia — " she stopped to ask her mother-in-law something in German. The old lady nodded, looking only in her bowl too. " — almost forty years ago, it was, we could have died too. We almost did. Your father remembers how the Mongols broke into his father's barn, don't you, Father? See? They stole from our people who have never done them any harm. They took the last bit of flour your father's family had, hidden away under the laying hens' nests, and left them to die. They didn't know what they were doing; they were starving too. Your grandfather forgave them before he died. Oh yes, as swollen as he was with starvation, and weeping for a family he feared would follow after him, he prayed for the thieves who had killed him. Don't you think that was a Christian way to respond to the suffering of others?"

Thom held her eye, but his thoughts seemed to waver.

"Thank God, Thom, that we were brought by God alive out of Russia. You were born in this land, too, because the government of Canada promised we'd never have, again, to suffer from such lawlessness. Of course, suffering by the law never occurred to our people. But we were willing, when the time came, for that too. Don't you remember how, in the Great War, your father — " for a moment Jake glanced at her shyly, then away in confusion " — was sent, because of the law, to the CO camp? And we had to bear our burdens, regardless, while we awaited his return? And what about all the Mennonites who in the last eight years have fled again from famines in Moscow and the land beside the Urals? Don't you think maybe God has called us, as Christians, to suffer as He did on earth?"

Thom looked at her in silent, but evident surprise. His re-gathered thoughts found tongue, however, before I could.

"Mom, if you'd seen the way the Mounties fired their guns at us, and me there just for the — principle of it, but the rest of them there for their bread and butter, I'm not so sure you'd say we should remain separate. When they drove us back over a vacant lot, you know, some of the men found washers the size of coppers and hurled all they could. I helped too, with only my throwing arm, to fight off repeating rifles. And a guy named Nick Nargan jumped on top of the fire engine they were using to hose us down, and shouted 'Shoot me! Shoot me!' And they did. I got the guy that did it with a washer right between the eyes."

"Thom!" Mrs Hildebrandt cried out as if in physical pain. "Not before little ones!" Then, as if she despaired of her woman's voice, she said, "Thom, how could you so break with the traditions of your fathers? Not just to fight like a hooligan, but to offer violence to anyone. Father, won't you say — "

"Mom," Thom retorted in equal earnest, "don't you see there are times when you've got to try to change this world? Not just try to run away from it?"

Into the painful quiet which punctuated this question, I said, "I agree with Thom. I believe God means us to have more abundant life in Christ, not to suffer the stings and defeats of an outrageous fortune."

"But surely," Mrs Hildebrandt said in deepest hurt, "you, Mr Cann, as a minister of the gospel, would not deny Christ's words, 'Love your enemies, bless them that curse you, do good to them that hate you.' We ought not to be fighting people in the streets to show our love, had we? Thom, I know how keenly you feel the pain of others. But tell me you didn't — "

"Mother, do you want me to lie to you? Sure, I did. A fella has to do what he can about this world."

"Yes," I said softly now. "But the means are also important, Thom. Maybe your mother's right about that. We ought to try to ease people's suffering, not provoke more of it."

I looked to Crystal. She sat unmoving, but her spirit was gone from me. Outside this hedge of Brother Giesbrecht's principles, I nevertheless summoned my courage for a dash I felt I had to make.

"I believe we Christians have been called to acts like those of Christ and the apostles. I believe we can alleviate the misery of those who only believe. God wants to give us His power to work miracles. Now little Paul Giesbrecht, last year, he need not have died had we but dared to believe. For God doesn't stand for disease and bitterness. He — "

"Do you mean to say, Mr Cann, that Christ suffered in vain?"

The hushed words were like a slap in my face. But Mrs Hildebrandt never even bothered to look at me. Her eyes tried only to hold and cradle her wayward son. Still the soul in her eyes was suffused by sorrow.

I could but hold my tongue. And yet I misliked this woman's theology. No wonder, I thought, you Mennonites have been called upon to suffer.

Jake looked up from his unfinished meal. He avoided all eyes upon him.

"I — " he said. "Would anyone like to come for the Christmas Tree?"

"I would! I would!" Abe kicked over his chair in an instant revival of his spirits. The clatter of wood upon scrubbed linoleum broke the spell which had fallen on the gathering. The joy of Christmas, not the gloom of Good Friday, returned in glowing measure.

"Sure, I'll mosey out with you," Thom said in obvious affection for both his father and his brother. "Abe, we'll leave Flight to doze away in his barn. He's gettin' too old to flounder in snow up to his withers, don't you think?"

Crystal smiled her curious smile.

"Would you — " she said to me, then stopped.

"Wouldn't miss it." With lightened heart, I returned her smile.

Then Crystal wasn't sitting for once. I had an overwhelming sense of her tall, swelling womanhood, dressed in her father's trousers, there beside me.

"Oh," Jake said. "Is there slop for the hogs?"

"Yes," his wife said with her eyes upon her bowl of soup.

I went with the men.

"Don't leave without me," Crystal said to our backs upon the stairs. I looked down upon her heightened colour.

Jake carried the slop pails. I offered to take one; he gently refused on grounds of balance.

The air sparkled with ice crystals. Two sun dogs stood to the south in the sallow noonday light.

"Change of weather," Thom said indifferently.

The hogs grunted and grovelled beneath a sudden waterfall of peelings.

"Come on back to the pasture," Jake said with a kindly nod of his head.

The stock huddled together in their warmth of winter wool. They stood, heads lowered, facing us like sausages already in a can.

"Do you see the roan one second from the end?" Jake said gently. "No, the other end, Mr Cann."

"Call me Jack," I offered, following his arm where it pointed.

"She still has her stick," the father said happily to his prodigal son. And to me, "She scratches her back with it."

"Yeah," Abe stamped on the snow like a bull calf. "She holds her stick right up in her mouth and reaches back over her shoulder. She can rub herself clear back to her tail."

I looked in wonder at one of God's creatures.

"I can't," Jake said into the host of wooly faces before us, "eat beef any more."

In his softspoken sentence there awaited the confirmation of a promise. Then I saw as for the first time the man behind the bending roundness.

"Suffer," I said, astonished that such gentleness could be, "the little children to come unto me?"

The man, swallowed up in sheepishness again, could only nod dumbly. But I remembered the tale of the beasts that spake on that blessed birthday morning.

Lord, I prayed in the silence of my heart, forgive me for forgetting the patience of thy creation. Keep me humble, and even teachable, as this thy Lamb.

The brief afternoon was at an end when we trudged out of the bush. The tree swished over the trail we had broken for it. It was a perfect little tree, perhaps the height of Jake or me. Crystal's eyes had sparkled like the silver air when we came upon it. Abe danced in snow above his knees. The tips of three tall spruce, dark as the Magi, had led us to the spot. There, beneath the spreading arms, or perhaps the fluffed-up feathers, of the brooding trees, we espied our waiting quarry.

"Oh, it's too lovely," Crystal said. My look now went deep into her and she shone with my reflected love.

"Oh, poor little tree," Abe cried, suddenly sobered by Thom's axe biting into the bark. Jake was kneeling to hold the lower branches back from the stroke. I held, for the moment of this unearthing, Crystal's mittened hand. "Do you think its Mother will miss it?" Abe asked plaintively.

"Nope," Thom said between heaves of the haft. "Do you think your Mother would be sad if you turned out like this little dogie?"

The tree, so quickly felled, lay there in a sorrowful bundle until Jake raised it with one steady hand. For just an instant through Crystal's mitten I felt that power of old tingle in my arm. The stinging fire of the Lord. Then it was gone. But my heart leaped up in memory of the rainbow in the sky. God's covenant renewed with me. Even in those crystals of ice!

That evening the tree was dressed fit to kill in the little parlour off the parents' bedroom. When the last candle had taken flame, then risen and flickered, a hush fell over the family. The light seemed to have drained, then pooled in every eye and we all looked on the tree in awe.

Abe was the first, with a clap of his hands, to break the spell. "*O Tannenbaum, O Tannenbaum,*" he sang, his fluting melody soon joined by alto voices, then by both tenor and bass together. I relaxed among the unfamiliar words and let Crystal's clear, low voice rise under me. One thing about this Mennonite submissiveness — it should make for perfect harmony!

Then Mrs Hildebrandt broke off the song after just one verse.

"Our guest knows no German," she said. "Those who know the English, sing."

> *O Christmas Tree, O Christmas Tree,*
> *Aflame with lights and splendour.*
> *O Christmas Tree, O Christmas Tree,*
> *Aflame with lights and splendour.*
> *Thy boughs shine forth with candles' glow,*
> *And flash on eager eyes below.*
> *O Christmas Tree, O Christmas Tree,*
> *Aflame with lights and splendour.*

I and everyone else seemed to forget, once the two languages moved together, which was which. We were all drawn toward the brightest star of heaven. I felt the wonderful love in the room, and then the insignificance of all but its gentle harmony. For a moment I could almost imagine we had entered into that holy stable.

> *O Christmas Tree, O Christmas Tree*
> *Thy beauty doth remind us.*
> *O Christmas Tree, O Christmas Tree,*
> *Thy beauty doth remind us.*

In mid-verse, the mother glanced at me. It was a look, what I could see by candlelight, lambent with significance.

> *Tho' hearts are filled with joy and mirth,*
> *We hail today the Saviour's birth.*
> *O Christmas Tree, O Christmas Tree,*
> *Thy beauty doth re-mind me.*

Then the glory of the Lord shone round about and the angels sang as they had to shepherds on the brown Judaean hills. And the heavenlit tree glowed bright, even dazzling, before it dimmed away.

In its place there stood a radiant young woman though she is shorter than Crystal, perhaps even squat. Still there is a cherubic roundness, and the like ineffable light, that so much reminds me —

"There's more bannock," the woman speaks, not unkindly, to me.

I look toward the fire and see cakes baking upon the coals. A cruse of water sits at my feet. Then I notice the boy and men — of course, the Indians I came with — sitting crosslegged, cakes in hand. We are on an island in the midst of the river. The current washes by so darkly under the fading light.

Suddenly I am afraid.

"Who are you?"

The men, especially Many-birds, eye me peculiarly.

"Yvonne Pronto," the shining woman says, as if her name might be anything.

"What are you doing here?"

"I got a camp here," she says simply. "For my kids."

For a moment I doubt whether I can bear it. I see, where I hadn't before, her children seated in the shadows. *Suffer them* My heart quickens when I see her beauty reproduced in them. The eldest, a stripling boy in his teens, seems sturdy, very broad in the shoulders, with dark good looks. But the two girls, younger each by a year, are sparkling copies of their mother. The last one, a cherub boy, gets up just now and passes in front of the fire. He snatches a cake from the coals, tearing it to cool a piece for himself.

"Joseph," the woman rebukes him. "You're supposed to give around first to our visitors!"

Nick dismisses the fault with one raised hand. Fine-day doesn't look up. But Many-birds watches her, his appetite whetted, it seems, for other things.

The woman looks exclusively to me with her apologetic smile.

"He's a good boy, really. He's just too glad of the company, aren't you Joe?"

I know now how deeply blessed that boy is in his mother. I suffer him, in my heart, to come unto me.

Then I remember more is expected.

"I'm ashamed of how much I ate," I try to recall my country manners.

"Don't think nothing of it. A man as big as you are."

Now I discern, from those demurely lidded eyes, how virtuous she also is. *Chaste* When her eyes rise again to mine, I try to pour my whole self into them, to let her know my soul could be the pure mate for hers.

"Hey, whaddabout me?" Many-birds spoils the magic of our moment. "Ain't I a big man too, and where it counts? Not in d' neck?"

The two daughters rise instantly from the log on which they are seated. They stroll innocuously away with Nick and the two brothers. Even they are old enough to judge the folly of some of their elders.

"You have a beautiful family," I say most meaningfully.

"Thank you. They take after their father, I guess."

She smiles pitifully, half of a laugh.

A thought oppresses me. I search her face where she reposes, not four feet off.

"Where is your husband?"

Her eyelashes curl upward as much as her tiny mouth pouts downward. Then her glance brushes by me, dropping to her feet. I watch a vein flutter like a butterfly impaled in her throat.

"There's lots of folks have been good to me," she says as if by rote. "They always look out for us when he's away. Most don't ask nothing for it."

Then I am touched by her naked sorrow. She can't be more than twenty-nine and here she is marked by so much bitter knowledge — bootless suffering, really.

"There's lots," she says superfluously, "that think enough of me."

But I'm the one, my eyes speak to her, who truly loves you.

Not right now, her glance warns me, I don't know how I could suffer it.

She is jealous yet of that good name she keeps for him, protective to the point of hiding thus far into the wilderness. She cannot be expected to know that we are not always called to suffer, nor to flee for long from the world. May she recognize in time — the Lord's own time — what she has been awaiting in this quiet place.

I remember how I went down into a silent cave and lodged there And behold, the word of the Lord came to me, and he said unto me, What doest thou here, Elijah?

And I said, I have been very jealous for the Lord God of hosts: for the children of Israel have forsaken thy covenant, thrown down thine altars, and slain thy prophets with the sword; and I, even I only, am left; and they seek my life, to take it away.

And he said, Go forth, and stand upon the mount before the Lord. And behold, the Lord passed by, and a great and strong wind rent the mountains, and brake in pieces the rocks before the Lord; but the Lord was not in the wind: and after the wind an earthquake; but the Lord was not in the earthquake.

And after the earthquake a fire; but the Lord was not in the fire: and after the fire a still small voice.

And it was so, when I heard it, that I wrapped my face in my mantle, and went out, and stood in the entering in of the cave. And, behold, there came a voice unto me, and said, What doest thou here, Elijah?

Lord, you have brought me here. You know better than I. I may only attend upon the marriage of your Lamb.

So night is fallen over the island. These dark shores are walled in by a shining river.

"Do you want some of this stuff to drink?" my angel speaks with human voice.

It doesn't matter. Once again, the still, small voice has spoken.

I beam, in my turn, upon this chosen woman.

Many-birds

"Why does he keep staring at me like that?" she says in Cree.

"I don't know," I say. "Could be he wants another slug from your jug."

"He spit out the first, soon as he tasted it. I don't trust a man who won't drink."

"Maybe, like me, he just wants into your pants."

"He gives me the shivers."

"*Hai!* Now don't get sick and mess up our night. I'd have to let him doctor you, fershitsake. He's got really strong medicine. Look at him there, ain't that mouth been sucking bad spirits from someone? See 'em? Still goddam foaming on his lips. You should have smelt his breath in the boat. From sucking bad spirits all the time. Awful. Just awful. I couldn't get the fucker to quit breathing down my neck."

"Shut up Many-birds. He'll hear you."

But she is starting to giggle. The old man, I notice, ain't able to hold back a grin either.

"Ah, he don't understand Cree. Just bad spirit talk. Don't tell me you missed what he said over your bannock? Driving 'em out like that. When his eyes were closed. That's the only way to see his kind of spirits."

"Yes," she says, laughing now behind her hand. Her tits go up and down, up and down. Under that goddam shirt.

"Let's make a gift of cloth to his Spirit Helpers. Your shirt. Your panties, too, fershitsake. Spirits like them a lot. They'll all sniff at them. You'll get over your shivers pretty quick, I tell you."

The old man looks scared. The godless old bugger — who's he to give Thunder Bird's children dirty looks?

"*Hai!*" I say suddenly. "I feel my own medicine coming up. It tells me — it says to tell you, Medicine Man is the one making you sick."

I stop and take another sip of homebrew. Toss it off. Ahhhhgh. That burns.

"Wait, now. Yes, I see he's sent something moving into you."

She stops laughing. Eyes are goddamned scared.

"He blew it up between your legs when you shook him awake. But it's gonna be okay; just close your knees on it. It'll give you a good enough time for a skinny white man's."

Her laughter rips from her throat; goddam screaming with laughter. She holds my arms to keep from falling back.

Medicine Man looks at me like I been giving her straight goods. Then he gets up and goes to the canoe. Tips it over; slides under. He's sailing down to the other world, now. So he can die and come alive again. Good, Thunder Bird, you keep an eye on him down there. Let fly a bolt from your eye if he's up to any bad medicine.

I look around. The boy-hunk is off fucking green snatches in the tent. I know I would.

"Well, goodnight, old man," I say, drawing her up on my arm. "Don't forget what your hands are for."

We walk on the sand beside the water. She has her head against my shoulder. I put my hand up higher, against her fat tit. She doesn't push it away.

I be damned, Agnes, but this is one you ain't going to find out about.

I stop on top of a good couch of grass.

"Gabriel would kill me if he found out —"

"Don't let him find out. You think he cares about anything more than what he's screwing right now?"

She is too quiet for awhile.

"My kids are still here. See? Look what they gave me."

She holds her hand out under the moon.

"For my birthday. It's a ring with their initials carved in it. My son Jean Baptiste made it. He wants to be a blacksmith, like that. Don't you think it's nice?"

"Sure," I say. I give a shit. "A woman needs a man around to look after her kids."

She is quiet for just the right time.

I let go her hand, sitting down on the grass. Let her think she makes up her own fucking mind. Then she sits down beside me.

"There," I say when we finally come up for air, "ain't this more fun than being stared at?"

She nods her head, licking still at her lips. Her eyes are closed, like Medicine Man praying to have his belly filled.

I feel inside her shirt, stroking under her tits. Then I bring 'em out in the moonlight. Pretty good; nice, hard nipples. Then she stands up against my face, butting them at me. I suck and bite till she's moaning good enough. Then I jerk down on them little panties.

"Aren't you even going to take your hat off?"

I got to find her crack before she changes her mind.

Ow! She's cracked my hand, fershitsake!

"Gab —" she yelps, flinging round to see —

That fucker Goose Neck! His face is twisted like the belt in his hands. *Crack!* he laces her little ass again.

She howls like a goddam dog.

I'm jerking my trousers off my ankles when I see the fucker is after just her. He belts her again. Then has the balls to say, "You whore. Did you think you wouldn't be seen? Whore, whore! You're weighed in the balance, and found wanting."

Oh sure, she'll want it now. Stupid whore.

He walks off like a prison guard, putting on his belt again.

I watch him go, not believing his medicine could be stronger than Thunder Bird's. But he's gotten clean away with it. Fucker.

I'm left to stare at a crying, moaning woman. That moaning's worth a fuck of a lot to me now, eh?

How come my medicine turns to shit any time a white man's around?

SUNDAY

Nick

The ice cream in the canvas barrel starts to drip. *Boizha,* I see it's running off the teacher's desk. I try to catch Hughene's eye — Hughene Simpson with the freckles and honey-coloured hair, and round red mouth you'd like to stick it into. But Hughene is paying too much mind to all their guff up there to notice.

The congress of IODE don't notice either. They're stuck up stiffer than their Union Jack set on a pole. I suppose Gail Archibald and them in Suck Up Row are swallowing enough hot air, though, never to miss some old ice cream Coronation Special.

Well, they aren't seducing me with a flick and a lick of their royal purple. I give a whore for the Daughters of the Empire.

"Hey sport," I swing round on Many-birds the butter-churn man, "where'd you save up a quarter to get that whore last night?"

His eyes radiate steady heat, like walking from grass onto plowed land.

"You mean she put you on the pogey?"

"Fuckyerself Fuzzy Nuts."

I start to laugh, then am checked by Jack's face lowdown in back, all tense and intent on his paddle swishing along.

Mr Waters sees the ice cream too. He has that same look as when he's reaching to nab you and his fingers burrow beneath your collar bone. "Dumb boy," he breathes, and you feel dumber than dumb as you scrunch down under that thumb. He should pluck on those clavicles up there, play on them like a *cimbala*, just to give us a new tune around here.

Though I suppose the real harmony of those biddies is funny enough. They do their song and dance beneath the bare spot on the wall where horny Eddy used to hang. Long Live His New Majesty who couldn't even hang his picture where his brother would be hanging clean out of his pants.

So maybe Mrs Hardy has left her husband hanging again, too, eh? She's taken over the show as usual. Lady Eleanor, the mayor's wife. We never had a mayor till Harold failed at farming. Then they moved to town and we found out a mayor is the guy who has keys to a school, a curling rink, and a skating rink, places that were never locked before we found ourselves with a mayor. But say, you can't lock ice cream in a duffle bag, in a duffle bag, in a duffle bag. . . !

Still no one notices but Mr Waters and me. I wink at him with his back there to the door of the chemistry lab. Cloak room. His eyes twinkle but his mouth has only the trace of a smile. "Dumb boy," I hear him thinking.

I could shout with laughter.

" — and so, boys and girls," Mrs Hardy starts to blow out at last, "our own boys, you see, will be representing us tomorrow in that colourful procession that will set out from Buckingham Palace through the Mall to Westminster Abbey."

I look at that honey hair across the aisle and think of setting out with that one through a royal maul.

"Just think," Mrs Hardy squeezes in rapture her lean tits between her elbows, "tomorrow we'll be there too, the Dominion of Canada with Australia and New Zealand, along with Rhodesians and East Africans and South Africans and Indians too, why half the world" — the sweep of her arm takes in the half-pink map of the world with a Nielsen chocolate bar beckoning from every corner — "will be there, Britons all to see George VI crowned King of Great Britain and Northern Ireland and of all these splendid Dominions, imperial and august Emperor of India."

I get a picture of Lady Eleanor behind the throne, anxious to run the whole show as soon as possible, and Harold Hardy hanging back a ways off stage, just waiting on his wife's first opportunity.

I can't help snorting.

Hughene looks to share in the fun. Already a wee smile plays on her lips.

I wouldn't be too wee on those lips.

"Yes children," Mrs Hardy winds up in a chant, "before His Imperial Majesty we are all English children, made one together before one flag" — she gestures backward — "one throne" — the empty space looks down on her — "one Empire" — her arm holds out again the possibility of chocolate bars.

At last Hughene's lips have tasted the bittersweet in the Daughters' treat. I couldn't agree more. She can have a taste of Ukrainian that will make her forget English, Scotch, you name it.

Feet scuffle. Everyone's standing. Hughene and I scrape up from our desks, looking to see who's noticed.

Singing:

> . . . *our gracious King*
> *Long live our noble King*
> *God save our King.*
> *Send him victorious*
> *Happy and glorious . . .*

I think of Eddy's greatest glory and steal a glance at Hughene. She's not harping the majesty of dull George either.

One button pops, pulling him out, and then I have him shielded toward her, revealing his true majesty. Then he rolls back his ruff, getting more majestic than I intended. Hughene looks faintly concerned. His head is royal red and if anyone sees me I'm dead. Hughene's face is Scotch sour. I try to shove him back in my pants. She can't take a joke. He hurts, rammed down. We're not English, he and I. Fuck the Scotch.

A finger lifts like an eagle's claw under my clavicle.

"Dumb boy," Mr Waters says.

I go down on my knees to escape the gouging knuckle.

Stan Waters wouldn't do anything worse, he wouldn't. He knows how to take a joke. The time he called Ray Macomber up to his desk after a spelling test . . . "What did you get?" he said in a real pleased voice. "98," Ray says in tones too big for his broadcloth. Mr Waters' voice drops way down low: "You usually get a hundred." Then before anybody expects it, he picks the Webster's off his desk and crowns Ray with it. We try to hold our gasp of laughter just to hear Mr Waters' next words: "Dumb boy. Next time get a hundred." . . . He couldn't do worse to me, he wouldn't.

The knuckle doesn't let up on my collar bone. I don't know whether to cry or to yell.

"Sit," he says, releasing me suddenly. The look on his face is pure disgust.

I feel as sticky inside as that ice-creamed floor. I don't dare look at Hughene. But I don't care about the other faces turned to stare at me.

"Thank you," Mr Waters says in a public voice, moving up the aisle. "Thank you ladies for everything you had to tell us."

I don't suppose any of the IODE noticed.

"Oh dear," says Mr Waters. "I'm afraid the ice cream has wasted away."

He stops beside a lake of the stuff, then steps carefully around behind the desk. He's making a show of opening the duffle bag.

"Ladies," he says, "I'm afraid our luck has run out."

The Daughters carry on like chickens with their eggs snatched away. Mr Waters says only the usual polite things as he shoos them out the door.

The class is moaning and groaning. Hughene won't look at me now.

"I'm not entirely sure," Mr Waters says finally, once the door is closed, "that everyone is this room knows more than before what the King means to Canadians. Nick, could you tell us what he stands for?"

I stare as steadily back, liking Mr Waters still, but helpless to answer.

"Okay," he says easily, "can any of you dumb ones help our bright boy out?"

But I know the help we need isn't in this room, nor in the poolroom either. For the first time now I've got a sense of what's coming.

Above five o'clock Delbert Hampden steps with the mayor into the poolroom. Delbert has something to do with the Legion.

"Nick," he says to my Dad sitting in the barber's chair, "we'd like to talk to you."

The games running on both tables stop. Merle Guttormson

who never plays, but sags against the wall all the time, sidles near us. If he had a tail and a grin, we wouldn't have to call him "Monkey"; he'd just be it.

"Talk all you like," Dad says without paying Delbert too much attention. "I wouldn't mind some intelligent conversation for once."

Delbert pauses like a chess player who's never seen this opening before.

The mayor chews thoughtfully on his cud. I look for handcuffs, or at least a padlock, bulging in his pocket. But he's along as usual for the ride.

"Have you been told," Delbert asks as if it were still a Kingside opening, "what your boy did in school today?"

The eyes of empire are upon me.

Dad sits with his hands folded calmly over his Buddha belly.

"I assume," Delbert's lips tense for the three-move checkmate, "it doesn't matter to you?"

"I'd guess," Dad shrugs, "it would matter only to the girl he showed it to."

There is some sniggering from the boys with pool cues planted on the floor.

"That's not the point," Delbert looks away to the men about the room. "It's when he showed it that's wrong."

Boizha, I should have never brought this onto my Dad. He mustn't be pushed into talking politics to cover my ass. Or else he'll give away his idea that Canada should be a republic.

"We both got carried away," I say quickly. "You know how it is."

A few of the boys look at me. Delbert and Dad pay no mind at all. He's going to say, Screw the money we pay for a king. Use it to pay off our provincial debt. We'd still have the money left over for one president to run the country.

Delbert's the one who breaks the deadlock. "A man doesn't show his prick during the anthem of his King. I think your boy needs a real talking to on that score."

Dad sits up straight. There's a hush in the room. Don't say it, don't say it!

"I don't see why. The former king give up his throne that way, didn't he?"

Even Merle Guttormson lets out a monkey grin.

Delbert is clearly sizing up Dad's bulk.

"That's unpatriotic," he says, the moment his jaw flexes in decision.

"You got no disagreement there, Mr Hampden."

"No. I mean you're unpatriotic. To speak that way against the country that gave you a home."

His fists are clenched tight with his thumbs pressed right against his thighs. The men with pool cues look like the remnant of those noble six hundred.

But my Dad is unconcerned. He's still in control of himself and his moves!

"I didn't say nothing against this country, Mr Hampden. I only noticed something to you about the former king."

Delbert's face is pinched with this effort to remain reasonable.

"You know King Edward didn't show himself off that way. It was your son that did, Nick. So I don't suppose we can hope to make a citizen of him either, eh? Not if that's the kind of talk he hears at home?"

"I am a citizen," Dad says simply. "This *is* my home. I talk the way I want here."

But Delbert is desperate now. He'll risk anything.

"Well, if you were born here, Nick, can you tell me why you still haven't learned to speak the King's English? A man who's at home should know the language, shouldn't he?"

"*A bas anglais,*" Dad says as level as you please.

"What's that?" Delbert says with forced ease.

I don't know whether to breathe.

"I was wondering," Dad faces him unafraid, "why you never learned to speak no French, Mr Hampden."

Dad worked for the French farmers once at Duck Lake. He speaks it even yet.

"I guess," Delbert's lantern-jaw is starting to heat up, pretty soon it will glow, "you foreigners all stick together, eh? You speak any language except English without an accent, you want to fight for any common cause but the freedoms which our British institutions give you."

"I didn't know," Dad slumps back, his winning move in view, "you Legion boys did business away from your beer tables."

Delbert has nothing left to say. His desperate gambit is lost, his purpose exposed for the paltry thing it is.

Then the mask slips, unhiding all that meanness.

"We don't know much about you, do we, Nick. For all we know you could be a Stalin lover. The way you foreigners won't come out in public, it's little wonder your women go crazy."

My guts twist, but my brain tells me we've already gained the victory.

Dad studies the man for what he truly is. Everyone has seen him exposed.

Then, before I can stop him, Dad stands planted on his footrest, his trouser buttons stripping away. His prick, when he shakes it in Delbert's direction, seems shamefully brown and old.

"There," he says so awfully deliberate and slow, "is that enough public for you, Mr Hampden?"

And walks stiffly by the poolplayers, by me too without so much as a glance, toward the stairs in back.

I watch him go in silence.

Faces lean over the rail, not daring to break the silence.

Then a bull-shouldered man says, "Where did you come from?"

The ferry slips by in the current, straining on the cable sagged across the river. A monkey-backed man takes up cable on the hub of his great wheel.

"St. Louie," Fine-day finally mumbles.

"How come you're on the river?"

I stare at them there, men and horses and black cars floating so easy when here we sit so cramped and muscle-weary.

"Have you got any guns?" the big bull man bellows suddenly.

Many-birds, through sun-puffed lips, mutters, "I wish I did."

"That's him," an official voice says.

"Let's get him," jabbers another.

But this time we got to stay clear of them.

"Many-birds!" I shout as the ferry guys untie their boat beside them. "For shit's sake help to turn us out!"

Many-birds paddles instead like a madman toward them. Jack seems to come to his senses, though. With the three of us digging against our own shipmate, the canoe finally swings out. Then we bite the current.

"Shit," I hear a voice behind us. "Whoever yelled, Let's get 'em? We should of coaxed 'em in, you dizzy bastard."

We pull away now with even Many-birds paddling by a kind of reflex. Water pitches over the bow, pooling on the floor again.

"Slow down fershitsake," says Many-birds as we make the bend in the river. "I want out fer awhile."

I check behind and catch the old man doing the same. But a rowboat is no match for a canoe. They've turned back to the ferry.

Now that the paddlesplash is stopped, I hear our heavy breathing.

"Let's go in," Jack says quietly. "We'll keep a watch on them."

To stand up is such relief. Even in water by the shore. We drag the canoe up, feeling the pleasant crack of knees and backs. Many-birds wastes no time in adding water to the river.

"You keep a watch on the canoe," Jack orders him. He is striding away behind a clump of bushes.

Fine-day is climbing up the hillside. I've got to get up where I can see too. The old man doesn't stop me from tagging along.

We both climb stiffly, glad to be out of the glare of water. But the earth is hot, smelling of sage and buffalo beans and crumbling clay.

Finally we see plains roll, woodedly, where the valley cuts through so deeply. The boys at the ferry down there are just standing on shore. They couldn't catch a cold unless you sneezed on them.

Then I see Many-birds in the tail of our canoe. He's edging along the bank, stealing back toward the ferry.

The boys don't know they're about to catch a cold.

I unbutton and begin to pee on a wild-looking plant.

The old man hasn't noticed yet. He's fiddling to start his waterworks flowing. Then I'm surprised, stealing a glance, at how alike they are . . . so brown and old . . .

Our quiet ends with Jack dancing in the sand, his back to the water.

" — he's gone — "

I try to reason with him. But he isn't with me any more. He sits in the twilight on the stoop, just sits.

"Dad," Phyllis says from the inner porch door, "supper's ready."

We sit.

"It won't go nowhere," I say. "We won't lose by it."

Dad's voice is vacant as the majority of lives in this town. "I already lost by it. I lost control of my mind."

His throat is thick with something strange I've never heard. I don't dare to look him in the face any more.

When I leave at last to see to the poolroom, I take the sidewalk around the side of the building.

The boys look up when I come in. No one jokes a thing.

As each billiard match ends, I figure out the time and money. But no one needs me to decide on a rule or anything. I ring up silver for a pack of smokes, some snuff, business as usual. But mostly the night is pretty quiet.

Phyllis brings me eggs scrambled on toast. I'm not hungry.

"How is he?" I say in a voice the boys won't hear.

She only looks at me. "Like you would expect."

He's still sitting back there when I close at ten o'clock.

"Why don't you come in, Dad? You'll catch your death of cold out here."

He sits in darkness like a forsaken idol.

"Dad, I wasn't thinking. You know I wouldn't deliberately give them an opening on you."

The light from the kitchen window falls in line with the porch beyond us. It's this silence, not the dark, that I can't bear any more. So I'm not sure if the voice is his, or my imagining, when it comes.

"Don't blame yourself. Don't blame yourself ever. Blame me; I'm the same as her."

I try hopelessly to reason with him. He doesn't answer again. Not once.

Then I don't know how long we sit there without talking. I don't even know if he stays out all night. I go to bed at last, like he tells me.

When I wake with the sun on Marsella and me and Eugene in bed, the curtain isn't pulled around his bed. Just then I hear the sound of a hammer, the ring of his last, muffled by leather. He's working, at least. His steady rhythm is broken by a spell of coughing.

I think of Mother's tuberculosis, the way they moved her to the San. Then as quickly I put it out of my mind. Dad is no way like Mother.

Only someone has to come next day to school to tell us, "He's got pneumonia. Doc Graves wants you to come home to pack his things for the hospital. They're putting him on the train to Melfort."

Bud Cutler from the Hotel and Delbert Hampden from the Legion already have the train fare collected. Half the town comes out to see my Dad carried on the car.

I wish it was me lying on that litter. The engine snorts steam, the platform shakes, and then that shuttle arm pounds the train along the track. I watch the porch of the passenger coach as long as I see it swaying between the rails.

I'm surprised, when we get home, to see the mayor hasn't padlocked the poolroom door. But by suppertime, Mikey Betrofsky has skidded a granary into town. He sets it down between the Hotel and Hardware. Before another day is out, he is all set up in barbering. Delbert Hampden, they say, helped him to buy Pete Wasylyshen's old chair in Nisooskan. That farmer Betrofsky. He couldn't even cut hay.

"Hey," old Fine-day has stood up suddenly. "He's got 'im."

I look downriver where our canoe wobbles toward us. Wild horses couldn't have dragged me back to that viper pit. But here he returns. With Many-birds!

Many-birds must have a gun in his back. I don't know how else Jack would bring him along. Or why. *Boizha*, a lot of help he still is.

> Jack Cann can do no wrong
> But Jack does nothing right.

When those palookas cleaned out the last of the Coke and Wynola, leaving just their ⊬⊤⊤ on the poolroom wall, Jack tells me, "The Lord keeps his own accounts."

"Yeah? Well the wholesaler keeps accounts too, you know. We're out of business unless we make those grasshoppers pay up."

Jack be nimble, Jack be quick . . . But Jack hid out with our old broomstick.

So at least the church people were lucky enough to be rid of him for awhile. Hadn't they just overlooked mentioning how he was too goody-two-shoed to be seen in a poolroom?

And if I hadn't whipped him out in the schoolroom, do you think anyone might have looked on my father's shame like he did?

Jack

Truly he taught us to love one another I remember the way our daddy read to us after evening meal from the great, hide-covered Book. There was never enough to eat on that table, but his voice was love and his word became our meat and drink. His eyes would not hide from us their pain, but his mouth never faltered, either, in the word of the Lord. With my own eyes I saw those lips made Word *love your enemies bless them that curse you do good to them that hate you and pray for them which despitefully use you and persecute you that ye may be the children of your father which is in heaven* So have I worked in my weak way to make his Word flesh again.

Today I have helped him who hates me; I have rescued Many-birds from the grip of prison. I have done far more than to pray for him who despitefully used me *for did he not make a whore of her who restored me to that still small voice? Oh, she was a whore, all right; I saw her with my own eyes* Many-birds looks around at me from the front of the canoe. I must have groaned *for I know I'd prefer even to lose this outward light than to look again on such a sight for the Lord was not in the woman and when I wrapped my face in my mantle and went out and stood alone the voice was no more with me* I still prayed the boy and the old man to come with me, but Nick would wait where we were, thinking, God knows why, those men had meant to persecute him. But I knew, yea verily, who the true persecutor was. So I retraced that shore myself to the ferry landing and there, sure enough, our boat was beached.

Many-birds, it appeared, was locked in their equipment shed. For an instant I was tempted to let him stay there *for I was very jealous for the Lord God of hosts since he had wasted her excess of Love oh the Word made too much flesh* until I heard the Word speaking to me, only I grew afraid, hearing tongues I could not fathom *then I wondered could the Word equivocate? or might the devil somehow use God's voice to deceive you?* until at last I made out a bystander, though not that foreign tongue itself, doing the speaking.

Then I doubted, through an ensuing silence, what I should do, till I remembered to pray *bless the Lord o my soul in all his judgments and remember to keep his commandments so I ought to bless this man whom I should not judge, yea, not though he has done evil against me*

"Aimé," an authoritative voice was slowly working itself up, "how many times you need reminding this here ferry don't answer to nothing but English?"

Again the bystander spoke, but this time with an accent. "I t'ought mebbe we might lock up also this one."

I could see him feigning not to keep watch on me, even after I stood alone in the other men's gaze.

"Don't see why," the commanding man presented his bulk to the whole lot of bystanders. "Ain't only one man escaped, hasn't he? And we've got the one is Indian. Even admitted his name is Many Guns."

"Many-birds," I said involuntarily, still with a mind to truth more than to any love of my enemy. I wasn't aware, even now, how far the mind must lag behind acts of the spirit.

"But for 'elping 'im to get away? The Mounties will wan' to talk to 'im, for sure."

"Well — "

I didn't have time to consider my peril; I was faced with a fool's way of sparing the persecutor — hallowed means, nonetheless, of making the Word incarnate.

"The fellow you've got locked up, whom do you say he is?"

So the ferry man, I guess it is, moves to block off my retreat. Tall men like him, who are bigger than most, have to be fooled quite a lot.

"That convict," he lowers over me, "is escaped from the P.A. pen. Yesterday the Mounties came and made me responsible for this here crossing."

"You've nonetheless got the wrong man," I say quietly. "I'm Dr Cann with some TB patients from Nipawin. Now you've some of you laid hands on this unfortunate fellow, have you not? I surely hope you haven't put them to your mouths — not even once."

The men on board the ferry slip their hands into their pockets. Or go to wiping them, at least, on their overalls.

"What can we do if we have, Doc?" a trembly-thin man asks. He appears himself to be consumptive.

"Wash your hands and face immediately with strong soap and water. TB, you know, is caused by TB germs. Is there any strong soap up in your house?" I address the ferrymaster briskly. It is best, with his type, to take charge without any suggestion of falling back.

"What's a doctor doing," he falls back on bullying, "out paddling sick men in a canoe? It's a mighty long haul from Nipawin to Saskatoon."

"Sunshine and fresh air, my good man. It's part of the cure before they get there."

"Never seen a single canoeload of patients come by before. Why not, when this is the only river goes to Saskatoon?"

The poor fool is too grossly held by flesh to this world. I only look at him, letting him know by my silence that he cannot apprehend the Word.

"Well, why did the bugger tell us plain his name was Many Guns?" he can merely bluster. I see a slow-witted man can have no defense, save his bulk, against the ways of God. So I shouldn't mind his size.

"Many-birds," I say, "is a very sick man. Many-birds is an Indian and knows how to paddle a canoe. I just hope to God by this means we can save him. Now if there's anything I can do to prevent you from getting his disease, I mean to try. The first thing you've got to do is cleanse yourselves as thoroughly as possible."

Into the sudden scatter on the gangplank my inquisitor is forced to say, "There's soap in the kitchen sink. Aimé, you bring the padlock key on the table, eh?"

When we are left alone he says, "I didn't touch him, Doc. I had to stay with the ferry. But I got this swelling on my knee. Would you mind taking a gander at it?"

I have seen similar knees before, with as much water and nearly as much hair on them. Time was when I would have lain hands on the affected part and simply relieved the man of his misery. Now I am pained for us both. I can only offer him advice which he takes in all humility. My heart goes out to him in his suffering, weighed on by so much flesh.

Afterwards he says in conversation, "I got nothing against Indians, Doc. I didn't mean no harm to your patient. Those

Northern Indians are different from the ones down here. I was to Cumberland House once and those are fine people you got up there. They got gumption enough to make a living for theirselves. But the ones down here are spoiled by their mixing with us whites. You can't count on them for nothing. And the worst ones are mixed in the blood, if you know what I mean. Them bastards ain't just lazy, they're plain crazy. Especially when they got a drop of French in 'em.''

He says more of the like *and I recall a whore without naming names but Crystal wasn't a whore when I married her. The Lord was in her, even if my daddy didn't think so, for he was afraid that Love could not be present so long as she'd not been saved. So who made the whore of her: my daddy, for doubting? or I, for believing? or the Lord for Loving her unto salvation? His Word, departing with her, has never told me. He has continued all this time silent* and has even paddled since we left the ferry, though we two still steer at cross purposes. I imagine Many-birds is grateful for his release, considering all the charges we could have brought against him *so wasn't there even a hint of rape in the whoredom of my love? How else, Lord, would I have been so fooled?*

I am looking at the wrinkles in Many-birds' bull neck when I recall *how God has sometimes required us to be His fools consider Hosea whom He called to fadge together with a whore so was I not called unto whoredom to make example of His Love?* what fools I made of the poor ferrymen — for what other purpose than to prove we are all the children of our father in heaven? *but shall the devil be restored unto the family of our heavenly father?* Now who are we, His children, to say whom Love shall love, or Love not love? *Lord forgive me for my unloving heart if I have not heard your Word aright I just could never comprehend Your speaking with the devil's voice*

Many-birds

The goddam world's against Indians. I only tried to sell them something like white guys always do, but they kicked me and punched me down. You'd think I was giving it away to their women or something. Those white guys just got no fucking use for Indians.

Even the guards in P.A. beat me up every time the jailbirds did. None of 'em ever give a shit for me. Well, I found someone now who does, and I'm free to go see her if I want. And then word gets out some fucking Indian has broke out of jail, so any Indian comes along will do to serve his sentence.

I served my own already, thanks a lot, though why I should I never knew. That white guy never cared enough about his car to keep an eye on it. He never drove it out at night anyway. Day after day passing me on the road to town. Never stopping once to ask if I'd like a lift. I didn't see why he could drive through our land when I got to walk. They never locked him up for stealing the land in the first place.

Anything I ever done, some white guy showed me how to do it. So why shouldn't I be just like them? Only do it first, before they done it to me? But then some chickenshit bohunk scalper got me when I wasn't even looking. Stole away my manhood so now I can't so much as beat Rubber Neck to a piece of ass.

Fuck. I'm done. The old ones were right. A scalped man belongs to the dead. If he's so unlucky to be left living, then he might as well finish the job, fershitsake. No living woman will want him.

Agnes . . . she was the only woman who ever wanted me. She likes Indians. She said so herself, that she was part Indian. Agnes, who filled that window with light. And our bed with great heat. Agnes who for once give me a chance to be a man. I got to show her I can still do a man's job.

What if I never find her? Or she turns me down? That story of the guy at Medicine Hat who only lost his war bonnet, he never got to fuck the chief's daughter like she hoped. They say he was put under by the whole Blackfoot nation the minute his cap blew away. So what chance can a bald-headed fucker have?

But I still think those white guys are only half of my goddam troubles. There's got to be something bigger up there that's dead against Indians. Thunder Bird, are you scalped now too, that you don't have the Power to look out for us?

Fine-day

. . . . skin on fire . . . white man too, his shirt stained a darker blue through the back. So could the boy catch it worse than us? What if it should happen the same way again?

Nothing you can do, my fears whisper . . . your fault for pushing in here again . . . always fighting the flow of things. No wonder the Sun is turned so fierce. Won't you ever learn, old man, from your old mistakes?

. . . . my father told me to stay home, that I wasn't old enough to go with him to the halfbreed troubles. But I still listened from my sleeping robe as he sang his Power Songs out by the Warriors' fire. Just then Coyote yelled. It scared me. My father stopped singing and I heard him in the silence give his pipe to Pointed-thigh. The leader was taking a long time. He must have been smoking it now.

Then Pointed-thigh said, "Stay home. Coyote says not to get mixed up in their troubles."

I was so relieved I fell right to sleep. But when I woke up, my father wasn't under his robe. I found him down beside the River, loading his canoe.

"Let me go with you," I pleaded. "If all the Warriors are cowards. . . ."

But he just said, "Listen to Coyote like they do. Until the day your Helpers tell you different."

Only I went sneaking after him in my dreams . . . followed where I wasn't supposed to. And on the fourth morning I heard He-who-carries-a-cross say, "Look! The Sun has come up clear. That's good. My god says we will win. If it had come up cloudy, we would have lost. . . ."

But he didn't know my dream was sending the Sun to hide at noon. So I alone saw when the redcoats started running . . . breaking their lines . . . to drive right over us. I tried to cry out but they were yelling worse than Coyote. Then our men finally heard them.

My father outran everyone. I wasn't far behind, dreaming us out of there. I could hear some Warriors sobbing behind me, my own voice, perhaps . . . too loud, anyway, for my father to hear the shouting of Buffalo Hunter behind us.

The rest heard and stopped. I looked over my shoulder. Only

four mean-looking Soto were still running. Buffalo Hunter
pointed his rifle at my father nearing the River. I called out to him
. . . plunging down the bank to his canoe . . . he never heard me.

Then I seemed to be looking both ways at once . . . one Soto
fell down . . . the Rifle spoke. Three Soto leaped on my father's
back . . . falling . . . he appeared to float there in the midst of
blooming prairie lilies, three handles sticking up from his back. I
watched as our birch bark swam safely to the other shore. Then
those three "braves" disappeared into the bush.

When I woke up, the Sun was bright. But I couldn't help
seeing how it shone through the tipi wall, turning everything the
colour of falling leaves.

About mid-morning the women started to play the Testicle
Game. One carried Two Little Bags on her stick, and the others
were trying to knock them off. All the men stood around laughing.
I couldn't laugh. I was keeping my eye on the Sun.

Clouds came up. I asked the Sun to stay out. But the girl with
the shining hair didn't hear me . . . seeing how my dreams had
made it happen this way. Still I was trying to believe that nothing
bad could come of dreams. . . .

People yelled. My mother had dropped poor Bags off her
stick. Now another woman ran off with him and my mother didn't
chase her. She came and stood beside me . . . watching. . . .

I watched all that afternoon for my father's canoe . . . it wasn't
coming. I no longer saw but only felt River run by. . . .

Toward evening some Warriors came on horses . . . a band
who had some Warriors . . . desperate for food. I went up to them
there among our Warriors. What did I care . . . when our manly
ones hadn't dared to paint their faces red and black?

"Have you seen my father?" I asked one who was wolfing a
whole fillet of fish. His eyes were watching too . . . but he only
shrugged.

Pointed-thigh glanced at me.

"His father is Double Runner," he said to them.

Painted faces turned to me . . . still I felt no fear.

"He had the Sun on his canoe. With markings like this."

Their leader looked kindly at me. "Not too many got away."
Then they started talking about other things.

Pointed-thigh got up. He went to Badger-call's tipi. Soon the
women were out working . . . lodges coming down. . . .

I ran to my mother. "We can't go. We've got to wait here for Father."

But her eyes were bright with fear. "Redcoats will come and kill us too." She went on loading our travois.

So I had to catch the dogs . . . then load my own canoe. Pointed-thigh came down beside the River.

"We're not going on the water. We're crossing over to Great River."

"But how will my father know?"

Pointed-thigh grew as quietly insistent now as River. His silence seemed as final as my dream.

"You know he'll be looking for us here on Elk River."

"Coyote warned him not to go. He's got us into trouble. The redcoats will be coming . . . have to break camp."

But I had expected as much from such a Warrior. . . .

Later I found myself trying to explain it to my mother . . . how it was only a bad dream. . . .

"Don't you know he's gone?" she said when she looked at my eyes.

"He's going to come back."

"No . . . he's gone to the Sand Hills. He can never come back."

Then I saw again those handles sticking out of the water . . . and the sun died in my heart.

"You mean he's gone to the Green Grass World?"

I wasn't going to let myself cry, I wasn't . . . I had to be a man now . . . but I couldn't face those shadows under my mother's eyes.

"Don't waste your life like him, my son."

"What do you mean?"

"Don't listen to their boastful tales."

"You mean you believe . . ."

"No . . . yes, listen. He wouldn't have gone to fight if they hadn't promised him that Green Grass World. Don't you see? There's nothing but death waiting there in the Sand Hills . . . dead shadows . . . who eat nothing to be full . . . say nothing to be heard . . . see nothing to be seen. Don't you understand? Oh my son . . ."

Then she was weeping . . . I felt too cold to cry now . . . still so cold . . . the shivers run down the length of my spine. . . .

I look ahead at stone-troubled waters . . . three figures there in front of me clothed in light. Now my head is feeling strange . . . snowing inside . . . I know my eyes trick me. Ghost Dancers flit across the River . . . I blink. Now I see nothing ahead . . . trees beside us . . . an island. Then I feel the Current push like a hand against us. As we put into quiet water, the River changes and turns to stone . . . clean-swept . . . shining like the Wolf Road. Now the light begins to grow. Fire. It spins, knee-high, at me . . . licking at the floor. I shiver. And yet I am no longer afraid. . . .

Suddenly I am alone . . . none sits in front of me . . . thinking how the fire has come for me alone. Then as swiftly as it came it goes away . . . ay me! it isn't satisfied to punish me alone. For now the other canoe carrying that boy darts out from the bank . . . without any boy or even Many-birds in it? But can it be . . . my father paddling? Even now, in the knee-deep water, three Soto chase him . . . as knife blades gleam. My father slumps . . . slides under . . . where prairie lilies bloom. Hands reach for the curve of his vessel, swimming barely out of reach. And they will get in, and we will be the next to die, my paddlers who have re-appeared like shadows before me.

Something tells me to look again . . . shadows gone . . . but in the other canoe a man rides alone . . . where I thought I saw three. And could I ever forget the dip of that shoulder, that smooth sweep of paddle?

"Father! How is it you are still alive?"

I seem to cry again . . . still he doesn't hear me. He is paddling away upstream. Of course. Boat-with-many-guns would be down here beside the ferry landing.

I stop to debate whether I dare go after him . . . but after so long how could I be denied the truth of things? I get out on shore, leaving four men behind (one slumped) and am surprised at how swiftly I race over the rocky bench. Got to beat him around that bend . . . where his canoe is already drawn up?

Suddenly I see him disappearing high into the cutbank. I look for some footpath up there . . . nowhere. So how am I stepping into this fissure up here in the wall? I've lost my bearings . . . but as soon as I pass through, I see the stone gates are real enough . . . hearing them grind shut, their rocky echo taking so long to die away. . . .

Once more I glimpse that burning whirlwind . . . only a terrible wind rises against me, threatening to drop me into nothing. I cling with my feet to the rock, edging ever downwards to the light. As I come closer, it seems to grow darker. Still I can see in such blackness . . . if it does hurt my eyes like the Sun. Maybe I'm blind and staring right into it.

But as I listen to this wind, I recognize nothing from the blessed world of the Sun. There is nothing here in my mother's unseen world . . . no truth of things among un-seeing shadows. . . .

"I hear you," I am suddenly thinking in words like fire.

Every hair stands at the back of my neck. I strain to see anything which might not be nothing.

"Father, is that you?"

Nothing answers . . . something is here before me. Instantly, *behind* my eyes, I seem to see my father as he looked in that morning mist. But I know for sure I am not looking. My eyes are closed with dread.

Now something passes once more behind my eyes . . . no longer any picture . . . more like tongues of fire.

But when I hear myself say, "Lost Double Runner?" my heart just about quits. "Found him, you mean. Father, I was so scared that I'd lost you forever."

. . . . nothing now. No more fiery answers . . . now I seem to be in dread of nothing more than Something.

"Father? Let me come into your dream. Please don't leave me to my own dream any more."

I don't know where the feeling comes from that I won't be let to stay here.

"Father? I won't be alone any more. Let me stay here, Father . . . or I'll end up hurting someone else."

Then at once I know the dream is ending.

"Father," my terror gets the best of me, "what have I done to deserve this?" For just now I have glimpsed the arrow darting like fire into my back. I fall, and even as I fall, I feel great wings bearing me up.

Soaring Hawk! But now so dreadful. . . .

My fear knows no bounds. I can't look up, can't even open my eyes . . . light upon eyelids beginning to redden . . . as my inward eye watches our updraft ceasing . . . settling now so gently. Finally the dreadful clutch loosens and I am let down on the earth again, gulping great odours of the grassy earth, now hearing with real ears the voices like distant water flowing over rocks. All of it holds me so enchanted. For once I could feel at peace with this world.

Singing is turned to speech, speech into my son's voice. My son's voice? So he is like me after all!

"See," I hear him saying, "I knew he was okay. I told you he'd come to."

. . . . my son come back in spite of me. I open my eyes. Oh . . .
it's that white boy . . . not my son. I close my eyes in disappointment.

Why couldn't I have stayed in that world? . . . and yet I can't
help hearing the music of this world. Suddenly my eyes are
opened: I am to father this boy.

"Son," I try to say. But the word sticks like sand in my throat. I
can only look in his eyes . . . brown like mine . . . out of a face so
much like burnt milk. . . .

. . . . hold yourself back, you dreaming old fool. You don't
want to set another boy on fire.

Nick

It is the Thinker — gawking around for any old place to flop —
who notices him. Not Jack, plowing the water like a wooden
Indian. Or me. For sure, not me.

He has to be all right. He has to. Though why I couldn't see
what had to happen —

Fine-day's not the sort of guy you'd see if there was anything
at all to look at.

I hope he'll be okay. No one knows how long he's been out.

It's too marshy here to lay him down. His black head is hot.
It's so stinking hot in this muck. The air just sings and stings with
mosquitoes.

We try to lug him up the cliffs.

Boizha! For being so scrawny, he's a heavy bugger. I'm nearly
busting a gut. But the path is no help. So steep. Must be a hundred
feet up.

Dirt crumbles underfoot, rolls. We nearly drop him. For once
Jack holds on behind.

Shade. Just over the ridge. Drop him here. Set him, I mean.

Too lung-busted to move. Calves like flat tires rolled on the
rims.

Those closed eyelids flicker. Then the whites begin to roll.

I wipe the sweat out of my eyes.

The old man looks me in the face. Dazed.

"Sun," it sounds like he says. Awful garbled.

"That's what I told 'em. I said you were only a little heat-happy."

But my relief is pouring off my face.

He doesn't seem to notice, at least.

I'm looking for water when a house appears out of the trees. A hut, really. I come around to the front. A man is sitting on a bench against the grey board wall. His chin is resting on his breast. A black cat curls, asleep, against his belly.

I hesitate to wake them.

But the old Indian is dangerously dry.

"Excuse me, mister — "

The hat comes up.

It is Dad. His teeth are snaggled and yellowed; his eye-rims red. He doesn't recognize me.

"Do you have — " I fight this absolute craziness, "any water, mister?"

His horned hand strokes the fur of the waking cat. Its eyes come to life with liquid fire.

The man talks some kind of crazy language. Tongue of the lost forest spirits.

I run.

I come upon a church in another clearing. It is open. Light stains the floor. Blue and yellow glass in the windows.

The altar is bare, pews sitting empty. I peer through the grate of the confession box. A blue-yellow light sits inside. But the curtain is trailing from one corner. There is no one here to hear me.

I sit down on the cushioned seat. The whole place smells musty and cold.

I can't bear the silence.

Next door the rectory is empty. Doors nailed shut, as if no one was returning. A spatter of holes appears next to the upper window. Bullets sing across the silence. Then smack against the squared log wall.

I light out across the hollow, making for the height of land above the river.

Markers against the sky. Cemetery.

But I can't avoid it.

I walk through carefully. Too many people here for such a tiny hamlet. Too many names on that cement obelisk. Joseph Oullette, 90 something. *Ans.* Old and young alike heaped in a horribly glutted grave.

Silence whispers.

Something awful has happened here.

I can't help myself. I run from the place of the dead.

Oi boizha! There's Jack Cann coming along, lard bucket slopping water.

"What the — Jack, what happened here?" I try not to shout.

"Where?" Jack speaks plain good English.

I'm back in the land of the living. That other shit was crazy.

The old man is standing with his arms spread out. Crazy as a bedbug, he'll jump off the cliff.

The thing like speech gurgles in Jack's throat.

I jab my elbow in his ribs. Water sloshes, spills.

I race over the remaining ground in silence.

The old man doesn't budge as I grapple him backwards. He keeps his feet, staring fixedly above the river. Out in space there a hawk, I guess it is, wheels. So he isn't bat-crazy after all.

"Many-birds," I snap at that useless hobo lying off in the bushes. "Can't you watch a sick old man for even a few minutes?"

But the Thinker hears nothing, dreaming maybe of his feel of pussy last night.

"Let him sleep," the old man says, so reasonable now, I'm ashamed.

Still that silence looms back there; threatens to overtake us.

"Would you mind gettin' me some berries to eat?" The old man points me back the way of the graveyard. "I'm really hungry, my son."

"I'm not your son," I fight to stay reasonable.

After a time he says distractedly, "You'll have t' find it out fer yerself."

Dad is the only one who ever makes sense. The rest of the world is crazy.

Fine-day

Alone . . . Hawk wheels, no fear of harm to other hawks, no need of help from any of his kind . . . he soars off into all loneliness before the Sun, topping those shining heights, then touching the edge of light itself. . . .

I feel my blood beat up. How long since light last thrilled at my tip? . . . mind just bubbling to embrace? . . . fearing only that I won't be able now to hold it in . . . waste it all burbling out. . . .

. . . . but only Hawk comes bursting from the sky . . . bone stinging to earth . . . down there the instant blowup of feathers . . . so this time, were I to feel such a clutch, would I even flinch at the lasting peace?

Then I seem to have taken hold myself . . . sighting up the River . . . straddling riffles where the bush curls back on skin as red as wheat . . . so spumy wet for me . . . there where Soaring Hawk swoops, skimming waters so yielding to touch . . . he pounds up to the living light. . . .

. . . . wet? . . . my hand is all wet . . . and bone so sore though it's done being bone . . . won't ever learn . . . no matter what I touch . . . cannot bring a living thing with me out of the dream. . . .

I look around quickly. No one, at least, has caught me. I almost wish one had. Though maybe it's too late for me . . . since I feel doomed to die, as I dream, alone. . . .

MONDAY

Jack

A sickle edge of moon, white as cloud, sticks into the field of grain *a thing which I greatly feared is come upon me* I had not found it out before now *I was not in safety neither had I rest yet trouble came* hobnobbing with the sun the whole day long it was up there harbingering that tryst while the sun's light hid it *knowest thou a thing hidden from the foundations of the world declare if thou hast understanding* but I would never dare to look into it nor could I say why *His Word let out the fallen one was free to come among the sons of heaven* it should come as such a shock.

The moon drops down from sight. The old man was adamant about going on. He said the setting sun couldn't hurt him any more. He preferred travelling by night to paddling tomorrow beneath the blaze of noon *have pity upon me have pity upon me o ye my friends* so we took him at his word *how long o Lord must the just suffer and the innocent perish wilt thou hide thyself forever* but our enemy grumbled from the moment I delivered him *Lord hide not thyself overmuch from us for where are thy former lovingkindnesses which thou swarest in thy truth*

Once had He sworn by His holiness that He would not lie unto me *I who was eyes to the blind and feet was I to the lame* He said, Son, my peace I give unto you that you may sow it unto a final harvest. And even on my deathbed I knew it was true; I felt His Love reach down and touch me. He said, Son, I want you to forget this sclerosis, for I am going to make of you My light of the world to a dark generation *for my covenant will I not break nor alter the thing that is gone out of my lips* Now my mama and my daddy and my brothers and sisters who'd come home to the bedside, they all said they heard nothing then. They thought I was unconscious. But I remember saying, "Lord, even if you let me live, I'll never be able to preach. For I am the least of your servants, a stutterer and a stammerer, Lord."

"Even so," His Word spake unto my soul, "you are to shine among men" *and your seed shall be as the sun before me. It shall be established for ever as the moon and as a faithful witness in heaven. Selah*

I came to, looking into the shining eyes of my daddy.

"The Lord gave me His promise," I murmured. "I'm going to heal my generation."

"Shhh," my daddy soothed. "Not now." Then I saw his eyes were shining with tears. He seemed to be whispering, "Forgive, Lord, this doubting Thomas. Hide beneath the multitude of your tender mercies your servant's sin."

Mama just cried and cried.

But true to His Word a night came when I arose from my bed and walked. I actually walked! My legs were as awkward as a pair of stilts — and about as far removed from me, it seemed — but I tottered out of that sickroom door into another life.

Mama was sitting where life had pretty much kept her: in the front room of our partitioned granary.

"Praise God," she breathed at first sight of me. "Praise His Holy name!"

Then it was as if she were my substitute, newly paralyzed but glad of it, as she sat rooted and rejoicing in her old rocker.

My daddy leaped to his feet and took me by both arms. I think, were we not true Christians, we'd have done a dance right there.

"Glory, glory to God in the highest!" we were all yelling, even Joseph, the last of my brothers remaining at home.

Then our daddy wiped his eyes and said, "This my son was dead and is alive again, he was lost, and is found. Joseph, run to Uncle Henry's and have him take you round to the whole clan. We are going to celebrate tonight. Joseph, go and tell them we are to give thanks unto the Lord!"

That evening our yard was jammed with wagons and with teams of horses hitched throughout the grove. I was too played out to walk any more, but I was sitting, at least, in the tiny sitting room. So was everyone else who was not standing. Now I could meet them face to face; no one had to look down on me prone any more in my bed.

As soon as everyone was there, my daddy led the meeting of praise for God's goodness. There was no one who failed to give thanks for the restoration of my body. When the last voice had prayed, my daddy talked to God again, thanking Him for the prophecy he was given at my birth. Then he said "Amen" and started to talk to us.

"Most of you always thought Vernon was going to be the preacher, didn't you? But the Lord made known to me at Jack's birth how His hand was on this stuttering, stammering child. I want you to hear how it was my unbelief that nearly took my son's life. But I do believe now that he is the one who must change the world for God."

"Why Wilfred," Uncle Ellsworth burst out, "have you lost your m-m-m-mind? It would take that boy an eight hour day just to preach a five minute sermon."

For seventeen years I had heard the like from these people but suddenly I wasn't thinking of myself any more. I was only jealous for my father's good name.

"You c-c-c-c-" I started to say, and then recalled a time before I was stricken when Vernon and I had skipped school to work for some threshers. We had done it to buy ourselves trousers, instead of bib overalls, to wear in public. Yet when these same relatives had crowded into our kitchen that night to admire just common dressed-up country boys, they had started to take on over Vernon's new fashions, not mine. His trousers wore a stripe, and nobody bothered after that with my plain grey flannels. I went back in the bedroom and opened the red shirt Vernon had bought. It was with the extra cash the straw boss had paid him because he liked him; Vernon was saving the shirt for Ruthie McCunn to see first. I put it on anyway and went and stood in the doorway.

Vernon didn't see yet, so to the rest I might as well have been invisible. I drew myself up to my full, slender height.

"I got new cl-cl-cl-cl-cl-" I tried to say "too."

The room erupted in such hooting and catcalling as no child should have to suffer.

"Well, would you look at the cluckhen trying to crow?" Uncle Henry Arbogast said.

"Ain't he the funniest thing you ever saw?" said three or four more.

So on this night of my rejoicing, I was to be an occasion for mirth anyways, as if the Lord would do deliverance just by halves. But I had a habit, I guess, of making things worse any time I opened my mouth, for here I couldn't even stop myself from shaming His Name.

"You c-c-c-c-can't," my tongue came unstuck as if from frozen metal. It was while I stopped to suck the damaged part that I realized Uncle Ellsworth could say whatever he liked — however much he wanted to be responsible for, through all eternity. "Well, you can then. B-but glory to God in the highest, and on earth peace, good will toward men. For I have the peace that passeth understanding, Uncle Ellsworth, and you may have it too if you only heed with that irrepressible will of yours His ineffable Word. For you are quite right: as a preacher I am neither inevitable nor ineluctable, and only you are free to hear that Word where it is truly spoken: in the still, small voice of your still small heart."

Uncle Ellsworth looked at me as if he had just seen a ghost. All the relatives, in fact, seemed more astonished at my talking somehow than at my walking clean out of graveclothes.

"What's the matter?" I said. "Don't you think the Lord is able to teach a fool wisdom?"

Only their gaping faces proved I was no longer deemed the family fool.

It was still a long time after, when the Lord had delivered me well into His ministry, that I could look on my Uncle Ellsworth as a fool of God. I had returned to the town of Nipawin, to the people who had sent me out under a bigtop tent — under the benediction of God. And who should I see there on opening night but my old-time mocker? Uncle Ellsworth was standing, too late for a seat, as near to the front as he could get without getting right up on the platform. His weakly handsome face was set, not in derision but in defiance, to make a real fool of me. I took note of it and the next instant I forgot him, so caught up was I with the Lord's anointing.

I looked out over four vast aisles of human faces, each with its precious burden of uniqueness and particularity, and began to speak. A hush fell on the multitude, and then a deeper change — one that never failed each night to move me — as if the myriad atoms of personality were now resolving into a greater oneness of the Spirit. I forgot everything but our at-one-ment as we were borne together toward the mount of God.

I don't know how long it was before I became aware of a man beneath me, bawling like a calf. At first I wasn't even certain it was a man. Then I caught sight of Uncle Ellsworth with something awful in his face. I didn't even know I could foretell what was about to happen. But in the instant I felt ashamed for him, that God should have to humble him this way, that he should even be come unto his brother down in Egypt. My heart which had been averted from him, now turned with a rush to accommodate his abasement. I reached down in love and put my hands on both his shoulders.

The look my Uncle Ellsworth next gave me, obstructed in mid-bleat, in my turn astonished me. I had a sudden feeling of freedom, of a liberty I could hardly imagine, to be the holy fool of God. I was amazed to consider we were all of us at our ease to do whatever God pleased. I imagine I even let out a laugh which echoed up in heaven. For the next we holy fools knew, people were swarming all over us to be touched and healed in our embrace. I toppled, my sermon now forgotten, off the platform into a rising tide of believers.

I might have been a different sort of fool, however, at my first healing meeting. Isn't it strange how one can do exactly the same things with such a world of difference in one's heart? For I leaped my first time too into the midst of the congregation. I was still a youth of twenty-one and beholden as youth so often is for the good opinion of my elders. I couldn't begin to fathom a Wisdom which would laugh at my calamity or mock me in my fear. I believed the true servant of the Lord to be above the world's foolishness, and I was only afraid I might impair, by my low frailty, the dignity of the Most High. So I struggled under the awful burden of good opinion, while in my heart I felt excluded from the permissive will of Heaven.

Now these of my flock were good people, even dignified people, but how could they be expected to understand what still bewildered me: a way to shine before men without assuming the character of a fool? Yet every time I got up to preach to them what they wanted to hear, I was under condemnation from the Lord who said, Son, I am going to make of you My light of the world to a dark generation.

I wasn't doing what the Lord of Hosts had commanded me. I would read the Gospels and the Book of Acts and see God's people healing the sick and casting out devils, and then I would look at my ministry and see nothing at all confirmed with signs following. So one Sunday when I felt especially oppressed by the power of the Lord, I surprised myself, I suppose, as much as any of them. I stopped short in the middle of my sentence, beginning to stammer. I felt my voice, so fierce was the stutter, to be turning inside out. Then I felt the faces rushing towards me, or no, I thought, it is I who am hurtling towards them. In truth I was. I had leaped from the platform. For a moment I glimpsed my shame run out of itself, dashing away down the aisle and out the door. Then I hit the floor and it was as if the Lord had simply pushed me out of myself so my foolishness was left behind.

"Is there anyone here who is suffering, who needs by God's grace to be healed?" I cried. Even I did not recognize my voice, but I could hear God's voice ringing now in my ears, Son, rise up from this bed of sickness, for I am going to make of you My light of the world to a dark generation.

The people startled up, amazed at the wave of power which swept over them. They sat dumbfounded, doubting what they heard, even denying what they had felt. The only person not taken aback enough to meet me halfway was an old lady with a withered hand. I knew she spoke German mostly, so she might not have even understood. But I reached out to her, feeling the tingling power of God in my right hand, and I prayed only these words, "Lord, drive this demon out."

The following day the saints of Kewgardens S.D. 1666 cast me out, though the old woman had been gloriously healed. The elders of my congregation, after a meeting that went on all Sunday long and half the night, concluded the Age of Miracles was now past. I wasn't to use their church any more for a mockery. Next, the school trustees, who served doubly as elders of the church, forbade the use of that country school.

I was left to doubt, more than anything, myself and my presumption. So I went home, a fool once more, to my father's house.

"I still believe the Lord meant what He said to you," my daddy sought to resurrect the heart in me. "I believe you have just set out with signs following."

But I felt perhaps the majority were right: the way of a fool was right in his own eyes. Somehow the old woman was only a healthy misunderstanding.

Only the Lord wasn't through with me yet: one sign was still to follow. A man with a sty in each eye came to the parsonage in back of the church in Arborfield.

"No," I said. "I don't have that feeling I had before."

For without such a wildness, I thought, how could I ever convince him to convince himself? Only a fool could believe in his own foolishness. But the man had heard enough about that meeting in Kewgardens School.

"Touch me. Just touch me anyways like you did that lady," he pleaded. "And we'll see."

Maybe his fatuity needed merely to make use of me. At any rate, the moment I lay hands on him I found myself staring into the deepest, clearest eyes I have ever seen. Those phlegm-and-milk cataracts were dropped away.

"I can see," the man said. "Blessed Jesus, I can see!"

I too saw, for the first time, beyond my folly. For if I felt nothing, then nothing was dependent on me. It was entirely between the man and his Maker.

"I have a friend — " the healed man appealed to my newfound subtlety. "I know others who would come if — "

It was as if his unfinished thought were a force driving me out of myself. I could feel my heart tipping, like a snowball, over the crest of a steep hill.

"I can't do it," I said, trying to prevent the precipitous rush. "My daddy just got moved into a town church. I don't want to see my Mama driven back to the country again."

"But," my daddy said after the man had interceded with him, "hasn't the Lord called you out to be His witness in these last days? What could my ministry accomplish, Jack, so long as I knew you were not inside that perfect will for your life?"

I thought of all those peaceful Sunday mornings when I had lain, relapsed, on the chesterfield in the front room and felt the hymnsing swell through the wall. Then I would hear my daddy's voice speaking serenely and saintly on the other side, and I couldn't keep back the tears from my eyes. He had suffered too long in the ignorance and indifference of those country schoolhouses.

"Where will you be," I said, "when they drive you out into the wilderness?"

"With your Mama, Jack, and with my Lord."

But after I had crossed, some nights later, that terrifying threshold of the not-me into mystery, I wondered how I could ever go on this way, passing from the humble sitting room into the presence of the suffering alive. But I would step, again to my wonder, through the door between the chair and chesterfield, and the Lord would be waiting on me in His temple even as the sick waited on Him. They all believed He looked tenderly, through me, upon their affliction and they bowed their heads and worshipped. I worshipped too, though fearful of the moment of stepping out of myself. For what might the Fool yet do before he was transfigured? Yet nightly the Lord wrought His miracles in me.

When of a sudden the people of Nipawin invited me to preach, I surprised myself by welcoming any change which might require less change in me. For Jack Cann the stammering man was quite unknown in the big town of a thousand; but to the country people around Arborfield, Jack Cann had managed his greatest miracle by merely stepping through a wall.

The Lord works in mysterious ways His wonders to perform. When, at the end of a month of meetings in Nipawin, He had provided a tent and a trail of meetings running clear across Saskatchewan, I couldn't remember who Jack Cann had been to doubt Him. The way seemed to part before me and the waters stood up on either hand like glass. I could see clear to the other side, and I felt the haunting strangeness of those heaps poised overhead. So I walked, dryshod, in the faultless liberty of Love.

It was all of eight years before I would emerge, one winter night, in a meeting in Essex County, Ontario. I recall only that a young woman stood before me, a grim, hollow-cheeked face resembling the photograph negative of a black woman, save only for the eyes which stared back at me so blackly haunted. I felt an icy chill pass down my spine.

"What is your sorrow, sister?" I asked hesitantly.

She shook her head. Then, as if the words were ripped from her belly, she said, "I won't ever have my own children."

This negativity seemed to surround her like a cloud; it fell like cold drizzle on my soul.

Before I could speak any word of faith or hope, she cried

fiercely, "Why not? Why not! When any cow can have a calf. . . !"

I actually trembled to think of laying hands on her. But the Lord had taught me about doubt; to prevent it from spreading, I prayed in a loud voice, "Lord, drive this demon out!"

The life poured from my hands into her. It passed as a flash of lightning to some distant cloud. I could feel myself drain empty of light; then she seemed to be stored with a deeper darkness than before. Just as the frigid waters broke about my head, I caught my last glimpse of the farther shore. And then I escaped with nothing more than my life.

"You know best, Lord," I prayed in the dark days that followed. "You have ever required the trial of your saints."

But when the people still flocked after me, beseeching the miracles He had done for others, I could not bear the thought of some who could yet be spared their living misery.

"It doesn't matter about me, Lord," I prayed again. "I can live with my own misery. But I don't want your Word to be broken, Lord" *remember Abraham and Isaac and Israel to whom thou swarest by thine own self, and saidst unto them, I will multiply your seed as the stars of heaven and all this land that I have spoken of will I give unto your seed, and they shall inherit it forever*

Did He not keep His covenant with me when He restored me, in the person of my Crystal, unto Love? Then why do I seem to recall yet waxing wroth against the Lord? Unless it was his own wrath that I was filled with. Or that I grew desperate in such another winter of our discontent, when we were sorely tried. For I seemed ever to forget, and then recall, and even to forget again what hitherto He required of His hallowed fools.

I know one afternoon I had gone across the fields to Brother Cardiff's place to ask of him some potatoes. Porridge was all our fare those days — gruelling oatmeal porridge. So while I was there, Brother Cardiff took me aside to reprove me of a certain matter. We went out to the sunporch, though it was cloudy outside and unheated in that misnamed leanto. As we stepped through the wall, Brother Cardiff said to me, "Brother Cann, are you sure you're doing the right thing by the Pentecostal Holiness people down in Nisooskan? Are you sure you ought to be stirring our times in with the sacred *Revelations* the way you do? I know I've heard you only the once this week, but aren't you a little afraid you might be exchanging the Word of our Lord for the ravings of men?"

Now it seemed to me just the sort of thing I had heard from country people before. I had been preaching in town those nights from *Revelation* Chapter 12 on the wonders revealed to us in our time: 'And there was war in heaven: Michael and his angels fought against the dragon; and the dragon fought and his angels, and prevailed not; neither was their place found any more in heaven.'

It happened that Spain was on everybody's mind: Spain and the heroic defense of Madrid. Not too long before this, a man from Montana had come to our district at the invitation of the anti-Fascist League; he was a member of the International Brigade, but he was mostly an anti-Fascist. And he told of the trials and the tribulations of that country, until I began to see in my mind's eye a vision of the seals opened from heaven, and a people afflicted with the sting of scorpions' tails, and they desired death, but death relieved them not.

While I sat in that meeting, I thought of many things: of wars and rumours of wars, and of war in heaven where the great dragon was cast out, that old serpent called the Devil and Satan, which deceiveth the whole world. And he lay in wait upon the earth for the wonder which had already appeared in heaven: a woman clothed with the sun, and the moon under her feet, and upon her head a crown of twelve stars. And the dragon stood before the woman which was ready to be delivered, to devour her child as soon as it was born.

Suddenly I understood everything in life which had perplexed my life. The powers of destruction were here among us. We were living in the end times and didn't see it. Now I looked deep into the womb of time and saw where our sorrow had its issue. The dragon was waiting to make an end of the child. *But had He not said my seed should be as the sun and the moon before Him?* So were we not caught up, in spite of ourselves, in those great issues which were to be a light unto the world?

So I said to Brother Cardiff, "What do you mean?"

"What do — Well," he said, "for one thing, has it occurred to you that you are making a laughingstock of Scripture?"

"What do you mean?" I said.

"I mean that the Battle of Armageddon will not occur in Spain, nor even in your own heart. Just who do you think you are, Brother Cann? A second Son of Man?"

I felt that giddy sense again, so long forgotten, of being free to play God's fool.

"Whom do ye say that I am?"

The Word stopped Brother Cardiff in his tracks.

"Wha — " he said. "Brother Cann, you're not — "

So I repeated the Word of the fool. Now a change crept over Brother Cardiff's face. I could tell from his eyes what he was going to say, before he even knew he would say it.

"Brother Cann, I'll keep no company with blasphemers in my house."

"Get back, Satan!" the fool mocked at him. But I reached in Love to save the rest of him. "O ye of little faith, wherefore didst thou doubt?"

He removed his hand, an impatient gesture. He was refusing to play the part most pleasing unto the Lord.

I dropped to my knees on the icy floor.

"Teach him, Lord," I prayed. "Show him what you revealed to me and Uncle Ellsworth. Make him to know the truth of his humourless pride."

"Don't be an utter fool," I heard the voice speaking angrily above me. But I prayed more earnestly that he should see the truth of things he denied.

"For God's sake, stop your nonsense, Jack!"

Then I began to pray with all my soul for him.

Suddenly he tried to pick me up bodily. Now the wrath of God, which had been shut up like fire in my bones, overcame me and I called down that fire upon his rebellious head.

"Smite him, Lord!" I cried in His holy wrath. "Smite him who would prevent this freedom of Thy fool."

Brother Cardiff cast me out on my face in the snow. When my sack came flying after, I looked through the door at his face set in such self-righteousness. Then I turned my back on a man who sought only the face of respectability.

Later the Cardiffs came, with horse and sleigh, over the snowy field where I walked.

"Get in, Brother Cann," said the eldest boy, Joshua, who was driving.

I merely heaved the bag off my shoulder into the box.

"Get in, Brother Cann," said the man himself from a chair in the sleigh bed.

"Many thanks," I grinned in expectation.

"We were worried," Brother Cardiff said without looking at me, "about your wife alone in that shack." It was all he said.

Crystal, when I came in, was sitting by the stove. She smiled at Brother Cardiff while he set down the still-steaming pail of milk. Then they drove out of the yard, the sleigh bells now leaving us farther and farther behind.

And shall I be prevented, for my single sin of wrath, from passing over Jordan? Must I be set apart to be destroyed here in this wilderness?

For a moment I see clear to the bottom of the river *where strands of human hair are swayed* within my paddle's reach *I glimpse the stone-cold faces as we pass over, and then the watery tresses close round them again* I start back from a sudden school of fishes which swarm up like doubting thoughts.

We are alone in darkness. Now the stream runs shallow above a bed of rocks. Still we glide on in silence, with only a click of wood or the thump of stones for company. Now and then a man's voice grunts with exertion *and then I know I can't last, for destruction from God was ever a terror to me and by reason of his highness I could not endure* though I don't know why it should frighten me so much since *both the moon and the sun went down* it was merely a jest taken in earnest *hast thou considered my servant Job that there is none like him in the earth* now I can't for the life of me think what it was *still he holdeth fast his integrity although thou movedst me against him* yet I feel strangely moved to pray, yes I must pray quickly for the old man here who was nearly killed by the sun, and Nick, whose mother went crazy and whose father was taken in the hour he expected not *for the Lord turned the captivity of Job when he prayed for his friends* for even him our enemy, Lord, may you teach him that his folly is but freedom to do whatever You please

Fine-day

I reach nervously ahead . . . bear down and out through a long backstroke . . . reach again to torment the water. I must not jostle the boy's paddle . . . so lift my blade to the left side . . . safely up and over. The last time he wheeled and gave me such a glare. I don't think it was just the raindrops. He really does hate me . . . so it's best to be back here . . . better for everyone when I'm alone. . . .

Still something urgent cuts under me . . . not letting me alone . . . something as swift as the River, like my dream of Soaring Hawk . . . more like those awful hands bearing me up, the ones carving and carving. But how do I now tell the boy that I need him? . . . mistaking him once already for my second son . . . when he's got such troubles of his own? Why must I always go around like that, believing my dreams are true? It's only brought trouble to everyone. . . .

Then I think how a dream like that should help the boy who's lost his father. What he really needs is hope, if even for a moment . . . even if he should wake up like me and find nothing else changed. . . .

It's this feeling of hope that won't let me alone . . . that would maybe let me live in the dream if I learned not to insist on it. But how to share it with the boy without more urging? . . . and then I see it as clear as the Sun. Draw it on the side of this vessel like my father did his Sun Spirit. Make it so . . . a picture of Soaring Hawk gliding over the River, our boat on water with us two inside . . . untouched by water . . . just a dream . . . but were he to see it just once for himself . . . not my fault then if he happened to see his "father". Well, no crime at least to hope. . . .

I get so excited, I almost believe I see Soaring Hawk up there, sweeping along Wolf Road this same way as us . . . up the long River of Light out of seeming darkness. I look to see if the boy sees . . . whether I am dreaming . . . something . . . looms over his shoulder . . . Soaring Hawk again? . . . skimming above the water. Oh. A ferry. I had not seen it before. A man stands upon the railing . . . then plunges so loudly into River.

"Man overboard!"

Voices cry . . . confused . . . no sign of the drowning man. He's swallowed up . . . where the current simpers, swirls. . . .

The boy cries out . . . something about his mother. I don't understand . . . the white man twists around, his face twisting now with such a terrible pleading.

Only Many-birds acts like the real Many-birds.

"He's drownded, fershitsake. Place will be crawling with cops!"

And now I see a real dream alright . . . where we drift beneath the shadow of a cable. HANGMAN'S NOOSE.

The River murmurs how I'm good for nothing.

I might as well be hanged.

Jack

Curse God and die, she said. But he would not

Porter

The Lord giveth and the Lord taketh away. Blessed be the name of the Lord.

I won't stand to hear, in these desperate times, how the Lord has fixed His canon against self-slaughter. There's just too many souls stricken with a drouth that none can help. So the Lord goes out and looks over His barren land and He's got no choice but to call in some of His mortgages. And the destitute man looks at all the waste he cannot change and he turns his back, in sadness and relief, on the farm he's made his living at. Now it may not be that way exactly, but I know the Lord will understand and *forgive* poor Harry, no matter what some may say. And I will take his body home, when they drag it up, and grieve for my dearest friend.

"Have some more sandwiches," I hold out my lunch bucket to the boy who's lost his father. Life goes on, at least for those of us holding onto mortgages. "Now don't stand on ceremony. You know how long salmon will last in heat like this."

The boy looks nigh to being famished. Still he looks scared to be a trifle in my debt — I, who have so little to give.

"Go ahead, son. Please. I — I just don't feel like eating none myself."

The boy sticks a hand the colour of burnt milk into the pail. Lord have mercy on the children. And on every soul in this world that has been undernourished.

The boy doesn't need to say thank you. He squats back in the grass, away from the running board, where his scalded-looking ankles stick bare above the tops of his canvas shoes.

I wish there was something I could do to help. Maybe when this terrible business is over, I could catch up with them, at least to get that boy home again so's they could hold a funeral.

"Hey mister," the young Indian fella breaks in on my thoughts, "you savin' the rest of that fishy s--- or somethin'?"

The old fella, whose whole countenance says he has accepted his mortality, looks at me out of eyes that are sweetly concerned. I look at that gentle head, at his hair bunching like sweetgrass, and for a moment we understand one another in a way that passes thought.

I recollect myself and pass the pail.

"You're welcome to all you can eat," my eyes include the young fella too.

But I am possessed again by this uncanny understanding of I know not what. Of a secret sympathy between myself and the wild young fella and that stranger fella out there in darkness and poor Harry, now dead. And the minute I think that, I get a tingling sensation along my spine, like someone is hovering above me, Harry's spirit perhaps, and I know I'm not afraid to die, I've come to terms with that, so why am I so frightened? Then I realize it must be a moral shock of sorts, that my convictions are somehow shaken, like they were when I run into that wild-eyed fella along the shore.

I was walking along the bank, hoping and not hoping to see Harry's body washed up, when I saw a shadow lean out from beneath a tree. My heart leaped with an impossible hope that it could be Harry. But as I ducked under the shadow of those leaves, the shadow stood up and whispered, "I only am escaped to tell thee." I took one look at those white eyeballs and then I hightailed it. I was aware, as I ran, that I myself was escaping some outrage, but what it was I wouldn't even care to know.

I believe Martha might understand. She already knew more than she wanted to last night, after Harry had come over to stay and sleep. I saw the line of her chin whiten as she turned down the lamp and then I could see her eyes still fixed on me through darkness.

"Wes, you're *not* going to take him, are you?"

But I couldn't accept it any better yet than Harry.

"Might as well help him off the farm as on it, I reckon."

"You've helped him enough, I should think. More than enough for your Christian duty."

"Well, you don't think I'm going for myself, do you? That the likes of me been so long in the furrow would ever skip my traces now? *Do* you?"

"Shush up your nonsense, Wesley Porter, before you make me think it's what you really think."

"But if you thought my helping Harry was taking aught from you, Martha — "

"I never said a thing of the kind. We ought to be our brother's keeper; no woman could uphold you more on that. As if you needed to be told — "

"I wouldn't have you do my chores, if that's what you mean. Not while I'm off gallivanting, as you see it. I'll go ask Ernie Koob if he won't do my milking, at least, and slop the hogs."

"You're really going to take him, then, spite of anything I say?"

"I don't see — Oh. Well, I never meant to say you should stay home. Of course you should come along to Battleford and speak to her too. We'll make a regular day of it."

"A day of it? Is that all you see? A day of it, when so many days lie ahead?"

Which isn't all I could see, to speak the truth. But what mere man could have foreseen the river?

"I see there's a chance here, Martha, for you to help Flossie to her purpose like you hoped. Though why any woman would want, or even *not* want, to marry ere a man is beyond me."

"It's beyond you too, I suppose, to go chasing after that poor woman, expecting to make improvements on Omniscience. Well, if you bring her back here when the Lord has seen fit to send her away — Well, I just hope Harry Bartook will drive you where you have to go."

Isn't that the way it is with a woman? You sleep beside one of 'em for thirty years until your kids are grown and gone, and then you discover one day you've still got to get to know her.

The smell of night air fills my lungs before I realize I have heaved such a sigh. Martha will be alone now in bed. I accept it; I just wish there was some easy way to tell her.

Lord forgive me if I have done aught to hasten Harry's end. And forgive me, too, if I have intruded upon your Omniscience. I know I've maybe kept Harry farming longer than he wanted or You even expected. But I've not meant to meddle. It just hurt me to hear folks say of my friend that he couldn't stand success, that the moment he got a dollar he quit working to enjoy it. You know how he tried, Lord, in his own way to look after the farm. Why, remember that time he rang out the Fire Department to souse a brushfire, and then sent the town a bill for the fence they'd flattened? Now if that's an outrage — and I might admit his way of dealing with folks could be wrong — at least his gall gave me the courage ere to be right. So restore in me my shaken convictions, Lord, and I'll not ask who these strangers are. Let me remember Harry as he was, and I'll do my best to accept his passing on. For You have recalled him, Lord; so I believe You must have needed him. Then blessed be the name of the Lord.

Many-birds

Thunder Bird is wearing me. Fershitsake, that's what's wrong. How the hell could I forget that stuff? If I saw him that time, I got to act like him. Like the holy men would do in those stories my old man used to tell. You had to wear the sign of the thing you meant to keep under your thumb.

Fucking rights. Old Bald Head Moon, wherever you went, you don't worry me now. I'm not going to end up like your prairie chicken enemy at Medicine Hat. Agnes will outshine your piddling little light.

"Old man, I like the way you moan. Ow-woooo! Come on. Swallow that fishy shit an' let's howl away Old Moon."

He stares at me like a lump a shit.

"You want the rest of these buffalo chips?" I say to the kid. They burn in my mouth. Buffalo Maker may have ate seneca root, but Fuzzy Nuts ate up his makings. So let them all eat shit, if they want.

When Fuzzy Nuts seems scared to trust me, I give him a friendly grin. Now he won't know what to expect.

I think even I'm surprised when he takes it. I give a shit.

"Old man," I say. "Why don't you jump in the river too? It's maybe as wide here as your old woman's cunt. Why don't you finish yourself off so we can hear that old bitch sing?"

I get up and look over the raft. They are all watching what I'm gonna do next. Good.

"Hey, old man, why don't you take the plunge? Go look for yourself like you were before. Maybe you got lost there inside her. You could make her piss you out again."

All is quiet like a pack of beavers chewing. It feels good to have them scared of me as that. Feel the worry drain clean outa my mind. Stupid to worry. Never have got outa the pen alive if I worried. Keep your mind a blank. Every day drain it dry.

Then I feel something else about to drain. Icy tea the lunch man poured us.

In one snaky motion I am unbuttoned and out. The old man looks like a frog eyed by my snake. I swing it once for his sake.

"Water to water," I say, "dust to dust."

It's what the priest said over Billy Left-hand after he got outa the hole. Throat cut the same day. In the dining hall.

At the last minute I think to stick out my cup. My friends all sit, blinking like owls.

"What's wrong with you birds? None of you ever laugh?"

I put the cup to my lips, swallow fast. Hot.

"Very sweet," I say, rubbing my belly fast. "Good for you. Want some? What about you, whitemen? Try some Ind-yun tea pee? I seen lots of you tipi creepers before. No? Too bad. It's very sweet."

Lightning. Strike like lightning. So they'll never know where it hits next. Then I see my penis still hanging outa my pants.

"Go ahead, old man, you can jump in safely. My rope here will save you if she won't let you out."

The lunch man is sitting like he's scared to get up. That fat fucker. But he's watching all the same. I give him a grin.

"Don't look so worried, loverlips. She's not going to make you kill yourself. She'll go clear home with you."

At once I know a way to beat that fucker, Bald Head Moon. Outshine him myself.

The cool air licks at my crack. Between my legs I see the old man grin at last.

"Hey, old man, I think you should kill yourself. That would be the funniest thing. Here, it's easy. So easy a guy like you could do it. Let me show you."

I flip over the rail, headfirst. I hear them all gasp just before I start to fall.

Upsidedown I grin at a starry sky. Old Bone, I think, your light is put out. You won't dare to show your face again.

Then I land, like a cat, in mud to my knees.

Jack

At first I was relieved when, of his own free will, Many-birds sought to confide in me *if I have found grace in thy sight, shew me now thy way, that I may know thee, that I may find grace in thy sight* for I presumed that God was acting upon some need to restore folly to the bosom of Congruity. Gladly I let myself be led by the way, confident *'twas grace that taught my heart to fear and grace my fears relieved* that God must want, could even choose, to work by indirection so that His greater direction would be revealed.

"Bless me, father," Many-birds was urging as soon as we were passed from hearing, "for I've sinned real bad."

Still I must confess I found this somewhat disconcerting. For had not St. Paul forbade us to mediate between men and God? If, however, God wanted a witness to see the Devil made His Fool, why I must be His man!

I could nonetheless be hardly taken aback by what I heard. Many-birds was proving to be a minor devil indeed, one whose folly you would not *not* imagine. Then again, I wondered, might not his lack of originality leave him even more free to follow God's subtle motions? I resolved to let my heart remain as open as his own to Divine suggestion. Yet I couldn't say why, if the beggarly life of the man was to be hidden deeper in Wisdom, my heart should now be left so terrifyingly open. I was in a state of un-natural excitement; otherwise Many-birds' trifles would not be so unnerving.

"I was nine years old," he said, "and just come home one day from school. My mother was standing at the clothesline, pinning up the wash.

"I said, 'I'm going with V — Freddy to play at Many Guns house.'"

It seems his mother was a truly gentle woman, conscious of her duty to her children.

"'You haven't brought in the wood for supper.'

"'I'm going with Freddy.'

"'You bring in the wood, then.'

"'Why doesn't Freddy have to?'

"'He has other chores to do.'

"'Like what?'

"'You look to your own life, son.'

"'Freddy doesn't have to do nothing after school.'

"'He's up long before you in the morning, to split the day's wood and to light the fire for breakfast.'

"'I'm going with him to Many Guns. He's going right now.'

"'First bring in the wood, then.'

"'No.'

"'Then you don't go today. I'm sorry.'"

Many-birds was silent for a time — a silence asking no reply. I hastened to doubt the worth of what might yet be wrought in him. Only God's deepest Fools could prove His deepest mysteries.

"I didn't quite hit her, you understand. I only struck the clothesbasket out of her hand.

"Then I saw what had happened to all her wet things in the dirt. Their whiteness was smeared with mud. I don't know why the sight of them made me so mad. I wanted to wipe my feet all over them.

"'Many-birds!' my mother cried out in such a pain of love.

"I looked at her weak woman's mouth. I wanted to hit her, to put that silly expression on the other side of her face. I raised my arm. It wouldn't move. Was I so weak I couldn't rub out that reddened stupidity? Then I think I must have seen red myself. I remember starting to shriek. But I don't remember passing out."

He paused, as if now awaiting some response. Suddenly I didn't know what to say. I supposed if this were a truly humble and a contrite heart, it would not try to magnify so much its littleness. I didn't doubt that this story of dirty linen was a worthy product of a shallow mind; but the mind-annihilating fury of a nine-year-old, was this not the more desperate melodrama of some empty Self refusing to accept its own nothingness? Surely if this were but a case of the creature come, in spite of nothingness, to know and so to be itself, it could not be to me so deeply disturbing a spectacle.

But who has not found out, when you wrestle with the Devil, that he proves to be ever a slippery fellow? I assumed there must be something further here, and that my heart must not be averted from him, for it did seem motioned of God that we should now accommodate him. So I looked to Many-birds to walk with him still the second mile. Surrender, man, the very vanity of your confession; stop playing the hero of your own villainy!

But this time he would not look at me. I was horrified to see him posture now with his own back turned *thou canst not see my face for no man shall see me and live* hoping thereby, I suppose, to magnify in my agitated breast his own poverty of spirit. But already I feared that such must prove too much for me.

"There was this man who loaned me his car. I had needed one for a long time. The man had a new Model A, and he agreed to let me use it.

"I had it for a year. I made good use of it. Then one day I drove it into his yard. He met me by the woodpile, before I had a chance to get out.

"'I know times are hard,' he said, 'and nobody has much of anything. But I can't afford any more to let you drive around on my good name. Do you realize I can't even take my team to town without being dunned for your gasoline? Is it true, what they say, that you drive away from the pumps with just a backflung promise that *he*'ll provide?'

"I looked sadly at the man. 'Is that what you think? You think I meant you?'

"'Who else did you think was paying your bills this past year? Do you suppose you could have got away once if I'd not been obliged to honour your accounts? Come on, get out of my car. If I can't afford to run it myself, I'm not going to run it any more for you.'

"I got out of the car," Many-birds spoke still with his whole being averted, spoke quite matter of factly, "and grabbed up the axe from the chopping block. I would teach him to doubt my destiny."

Though now I must misdoubt myself, whatever I intended by listening to the man. For I believe I have barely escaped with my life. Oh, I ran. I daren't wait to see revealed the end of *things too wonderful for me which I knew not* a man whose farcical beginnings had grown so terrible to me.

Stranger yet to tell, ever since I've gotten free of him, I've had the strangest sensation that he is right behind me. The feeling grows so certain, sometimes, I feel the flesh creep on the back of my neck. But as soon as I whirl on him, he's gone — or jumped behind me again. I swear I've gotten so jumpy now, I could almost whirl out of myself.

Fine-day

Jack

There comes a whisper of leaves from beneath the aspen, a still, small —

Silence. Only silence speaks.

Listen, then, to nothing. Only do not go within the shadow of that tree.

i committed murder, father
i killed my little brother
i felt his heart come to life on the point of my knife
he was only a baby, father
and just the thought of his dying went through me like a knife
if i loved him so much, father, why would i think of it the minute my folks drove out of the yard
i tried to stay away from his room, father, as long as i could
i shut myself up in the kitchen
then i noticed i had the butcher knife out of the cupboard
i remember standing over his crib, watching him breathe
it hurt me just to draw a breath
why wouldn't i hurt my own self like that
i suppose i was thinking, if this is worst, no worse can come to me
but father, this is worse
i don't have a brother
i never had a brother
still i need my brother to stand for me

No, answer him nothing. He seeks only to make you in his image.

Yet if I ignore him, nevermore of silence.

And should you answer, nevermore of solace.

Then how have I come, without even willing it, into the heart of this shadow? Do the stars no longer shine?

No, there is nothing, nothing here at all save that voice whispering of death: a voice which, disembodied, might never die itself.

O wretched man that I am! who shall deliver me from the body of this death?

Nick

I thought I was going to be all right again. I felt fine on board the ferry, even with the old guy eyeballing me so mournful. Then he ups and gives in to Thinker, to his crazy idea that we go on in the dark.

So I yelled, "I'm not your son! What right did you ever have to say that, anyway?"

Because I couldn't tell them how I was scared to step into their box.

I still can barely see, when I lean out past Uncle Fred, *Baba* lying in her box. Her nose is like wax. She isn't sleeping. She isn't like us any more.

The priest steps out from behind the curtain. He stands beneath a silvery picture on the forehead-wall. He belongs to it — the Mother Crooked-Cross Church who holds a Baby Church in her lap. While the priest looks on, the singing stops.

Uncle Fred and Mother and my aunties step out, and the singing starts again. The priest shows them the coloured book. Uncle Fred kisses it. Mother kisses it. My aunties kiss the book. Mother is crying. Then they take our hands to go by the box. I startle as I edge around the lid. The thing in the box isn't *Baba*. Iris and Marsella edge away too. Then Marsella begins to cry. I see her face in the side of the box. Same as ours: crying, but alive.

Mother stoops to kiss the thing in the box. Her straight hair falls onto its face like chicken feathers fluffing in the dirt. Mother looks up. Her eyes tell me she won't let *Baba* go.

She grabs me to kiss it too. No. I don't want to. It's only somebody's dress filled out with sticks. The face of Marsella's doll left out in the rain. I want to kiss the book the grownups did.

Mother pushes me up. I can't hold myself up in mid-air. My head bobs. And touches the thing.

The cold jerks clear along my spine. I yell.

Auntie Sophie takes me away in her arms. She is warm-smelling as *paroha*. She is crying hot tears.

Mother cries. And screams.

Uncle Fred has to carry Mother out the door. His eyes look like eggs in his walnut-hard skin. But his nose isn't stiff. The nostrils widen and blow.

Baba wasn't in the box. Nobody was.

I'm nobody's son.

Jack

The dead of night brings forth an infant son *and swaddles it with darkness. Now there appears a great wonder in heaven, a slender young woman clothed with the sun and the moon under her feet*

And she being with child cries, travailing in birth and paining to be delivered

But there appears a new wonder in heaven, a great red dragon standing before the woman which is to be delivered, for to devour her child as soon as it is born though something tells me it is not the thing which has unmanned me. What is it then, that makes me now so fearful of my very shadow?

I John heard a loud voice warning, Woe to the inhabiters of the earth and of the sea! for the devil is come down unto you, having great wrath, because he knoweth that he hath but a short time

I know my father's voice was first, if not the last, to warn me *for what father would in truth devour his children* He said, "Jack, I fear the devil lays in wait to ruin your ministry. Shouldn't you tremble, son, when you say she isn't saved?"

Still I was barely returned home with good tidings and a promise from Crystal's house. So I said, "No, I don't, Dad. I know that she must be glorified according to His will."

"I don't know, Jack. I can't help feeling worried that there's something wrong over there. Didn't you say the elder brother — what's his name? the cowboy one — didn't you say he might be something of a black sheep too? Doesn't it strike you there's a pretty deep failing in a Mennonite family that raises only sinners? I believe it happens to them sometimes when they depart from their German ways. Jack, I don't know.... You know I wouldn't mean to gainsay the girl herself . . . that it's only your being called of the Lord which I'm concerned about."

But I was afraid I couldn't explain to him about the wonderful freedom I enjoyed. I didn't think my love could ever survive his judgment on the wedded sort of fool.

"Daddy," I said, "this is of God, believe me. He has spoken to me like He did before."

Only He had neglected to add how He could make a fool of me even in marriage.

So when the relatives came and sided with my daddy, I denied them. This very shadow cast by the light of my life, I argued, was in themselves, not in the sun. It had to be so. The Word of the Lord was against them.

Nonetheless I returned deeply disturbed to Gethsemane the day after New Year's. I was on the verge, I knew, of doubting.

"Crystal," I whispered among the sleighload of laughing young people, "what would happen to us if you weren't saved? Do you think we could be wed when all the Scriptures warn against it?"

For answer she buried her face in the cold of my coat. And clung to me through that whole awful waste back to the school.

But two weeks later God was to grant me the privilege of leading her into His presence. What greater right could be given a husband than to father his soulmate in the body of the Lord? Crystal stood before me the moment our class was out. A young man was troubling me about my methods of Personal Evangelism. I answered him quickly, as sweetly as I could. Then Crystal was alone, save for her girlfriend lingering discreetly by the door.

"Would you —. I want — " she managed breathlessly. And then it was said for all eternity " — to be saved."

"Yes, my love," I answered exultantly, not forgetting to add "in Christ" for the edification of the friend. But I gazed upon Crystal lovingly, openly. For just an instant her eyes met and twined with mine. Then she coloured like the summer rose.

So it came to pass that we were trothed to become, that June, one body in the Lord. Nonetheless I was feeling again that unalleviated burden of a needy humanity outside our cloistered walls. I grew restless now in the yoke of do-nothing instruction. Lord, I said inwardly, I do believe Your promise, and I await its confirmation with signs following.

Then one March morning I stood in the pulpit of a country church. It was our Christian duty, from the Institute, to go out on such ministering visitations. I don't recall my text that day, or even a word of my sermon. But as I was speaking, I began to sense the terrifying presence of demons in that room. Out there towards the back. Yes, lurking in the corner. There, in the eyes of that strapping teen-age boy. I think I have always hesitated before demons. But that day I stopped whatever I was saying. I walked across the platform to where I could get a clear view of him. The thing looked at me from out of those hooded eyes. I could feel the hate spit at me like fat fried in hell.

"Demon," I cried in a loud voice, "I command thee in the name of Jesus Christ of Nazareth to come out of that boy!"

First the congregation sat bolt upright, hearing a new quality in my voice. Even the Sunday dozers came to with a start. The second thing was that the boy let out a wild cry as his hands tore the clothes off his back. Then his body began to twist and he knocked a scatter of hymnbooks off the benchback. A confusion of many tongues fell from his lips. Then a woman sitting near him broke out into shrieking hysterics. It wasn't a lovely sight. But I held the eye of those unclean spirits and suddenly I felt the power of God surge out in waves to the back of that church. The people were instantly stilled, and only that boy's body writhed and moaned on a sea of calm silence. By this time I was to the corner where he sat. I stretched forth my hand upon his head and the power of God stiffened my arm like a bolt of lightning.

"Malefic and Mithrai-as, your names are given unto me! Come out of this boy and depart forever into perdition."

With a horrible curse, then with a cry like some dying animal, the babble of voices ripped out of that young body. The boy, when the demons came out, slid like cooked macaroni down onto the floor.

I stooped and, with the praise of God on my lips, raised him up. The boy leaped, half-naked and dumbfounded, like the Lord's own Fool to his feet. But his face was alight with the joy of his Lord. At first the crowd was struck dumb. Then, as I was turning to walk up the aisle, they thrilled into the strains of the doxology.

This, I thought at that moment, is what I have always wanted. I have wanted to see people delivered. I have wanted to save souls and feel the people's reverence before God. Most of all I have wanted to join people, and have them join me, in this transfiguration of plain fools.

It was, of course, the end of my career at Gethsemane. I informed Peter Giesbrecht that afternoon, and he agreed it would be foolish for me to stay on. So I and the Lord were to take the road again into the wilderness!

Crystal cried for joy when I told her. And for sorrow when I said I must be leaving soon. She asked if we could not be married at once, and she would come with me. But it seemed prudent to stay apart just yet. I ought in private to cohabit first with Folly, without whom no miracles were born.

"We'll write," I said. "The Lord in our absence will strengthen our love."

Praise God He did. Never, in all my years, have I waited so longingly for that which my soul did yearn toward. At last, on the day of our wedding, I stood at the altar and suffered the power of God in me like a stinging fire. I even feared, when I leaned to put the ring on her finger, that the jolt would lay her in paroxysms upon the floor. But it didn't. Nor, that night, did Crystal seem to know at first which were the wise and which the foolish virgins. But finally she that was ready went in with the bridegroom and the door was shut. And the freedom of His Fools was past belief.

So, in those hot summer afternoons which followed, my unvirgin wife and I took our joy of the Lord in one another. Together we experienced that transfiguring power of His Highest Folly. O this, I thought, this must be what I have always wanted! This may be forever my redemption out of solitary frenzy, for now this is mine to have and to hold!

God confirmed at once my hope with the gift of a tent through some of His servants. Now every afternoon and evening I faced hundreds under the banner of that bigtop, and the sick were raised and gave to God the glory. And every night and morning my wife and I were met again beneath Love's banner, and God gave to us the glory.

Then were we given a sign that the last promise made to us at Christmas was about to be fulfilled. So all through the heat of that autumn, Crystal and I grew together in the Lord, she in her way, and I in mine. Now surely this was a time of wonder-working power!

Yet, the Christmas following, Crystal lost her baby. We were home to her parents' house in White Fox. The boy child, perfectly formed at six months, was stillborn in her parents' bedroom. He never drew a breath.

We buried our pretty baby twelve miles away in the Mennonite Brethren burial ground. And for a time we were numb. What, my heart cried out to God, do You mean by your promises, to answer them in this way? But I could only blunt my rebellion by turning numb again. I feared for Crystal, however, when after a time her numbness threatened to put her in that adjoining plot of earth.

Then I saw my doubt had almost corrupted her. I had to help her now, the best I could, to overcome the devil. So we believed again. God was good; the devil was bad. But I think at such a time as that a woman's very blood must tell her to sorrow. So I brought her home to my mounting hope of another child. Still our promised babe was not forthcoming. Labour as we might, we could not make another. The power was passed; we seemed to be plain fools again.

Lord, what is man, that thou art mindful of him? and the son of man, that thou visitest him?

I was preaching in the Vixen country schoolhouse, two miles from the Hildebrandt farm. The place glowed for me in more than the light of a 9 p.m. sun. For I could see the wraith of my childhood sweetheart moving year by year, row by row, from the little desks at the left to the large ones at the right. I could see her with careful eyes set upon some columns of figures, labouring neatly to tally them. Her clever drawings decorated all the walls. Then my heart was driven wild to see her sit before me as a child. But was this the child promised me? Even as I spoke, I wondered.

The Lord had worked His wonders, too, this week in our little room. Forty-four souls had made profession or renewal of their faith. The healing lines stretched, beyond the blackboards on one side and past the windows on the other, out to the poor and needy souls waiting in the summer twilight. These came with consumption in their chest, but the Lord gave them lungs to lunge through the crowd, hollering hallelujahs! They came with crippled limbs and the Lord threw down their wooden crutches. People yelled and screamed God's praise at every miracle, and nearly shouted the walls of the building down. My, but it was wonderful to be at the centre of God's holy storm again, with His power leaping from my hand like lightning a-purpose!

It was a far cry from the drouth that had stricken our house and the land surrounding. God raining down on such thirsty hearts and souls — why, it was a beauty too great, almost, to be borne! I thought of Crystal back in her parents' house, and all of them there in formal mourning for the old woman buried just a week before. They needed now to be here, the whole family. How their hearts might be revived in this outpouring of God's spirit! It was only too bad the grandmother hadn't lived to see it with her old eyes. For she had had an eye for beauty, she had indeed. That lovely woman had made this desert to bloom like a rose. And had she been able to find her faith restored —

I recall my astonishment, the week before our wedding, on coming into the garden in the Hildebrandt's front yard. Crystal was waiting to see my face as we strolled, arm in arm, behind the privy hedge. I could but draw in my breath at this paradise in bloom. The blossoms were ranked in profusion of pinks, reds, yellows, purples, blues, and whites, all in circles within squares within circles. And they bowed to the sun in saintly harmony, even in highest order.

"What —" but I shook my head speechless.

"Isn't it beautiful?" Crystal said, heedless of this challenge to her own petal-hued charm.

"But who —"

"Grandma. She does it every year herself. She won't let a one of us in here with a hoe."

"But surely she's aware of the drouth laying waste this land?"

Crystal put her head against my shoulder.

"She carries the water herself, Jack. On a yoke of pails from the well. Father says she did it that way in Russia, too. She never let the garden die through the worst of the awful famine."

Of a sudden I felt a deep kinship with this old woman whose language I couldn't speak.

"But it almost broke her heart to leave her garden when they fled. If she'd just been able to get carrot seed or beets, I suppose, they wouldn't have had to."

Then she stopped in surprise, tightening her hold on my arm.

"I'm glad they came here instead."

"Praise God," I said. "We were in His mind all those many years ago."

"Yes," she breathed with the scent of musk roses. "Even forty years ago."

"Even as your Grandma, Crystal, brought her garden with her in her mind."

Her eyes lighted on me in sudden recognition.

"So all things do work together for good?"

"Did you ever doubt that, my love?"

Much later, I know, she did. In the midst of our desolation, it was hard for us to remember. So it was too, I suppose, in the midst of an old woman's desolation. But Crystal's Grandma gave way to despair and death. She forgot, when the well went dry, that God had some other good to give her. She watered those flowers to the last trickle of water from the ground. Then she just sat in her chair in the garden and withered with the blossoms on the stalks. Mrs Hildebrandt found her asleep one afternoon in her rocking chair within her desiccated garden. But Grandma Hildebrandt wasn't sleeping now.

If she had just been able to hold on till this week, to see again His showers of blessing! If she had only placed her faith above, and not in wells below. But her death was a lesson to all of us. I hoped Crystal's parents would recognize that when they finally came to service. Jake, I knew, had already glimmerings of a higher theology. And who could say? Other eyes might be opened.

But the next evening when I caught Mrs Hildebrandt's eyes amidst my audience, I felt as if I would be unmanned by doubt. The next aisle over sat her daughter, as demurely downcast as ever. Now beneath the black hat and veil of mourning, Crystal's mother looked pained beyond expression. It was clear she believed I was getting around the will of God, not working through it, and what was clearer, she believed she must also suffer me. But I couldn't bear that look of dogged patience which settled over her. I longed to say outright what had claimed the life of one of them, what might even take others. Yet whatever I spoke, my words seemed to beat back in my face. It was as if she were saying to me, You are a fool if you presume to speak for God.

Quite naturally I experienced a feeling of frustration such as I had never known in front of a crowd of people. There were feet shuffling and throats clearing, and over all hung the conviction that nothing could ever happen here. God would not work miracles in Vixen regardless of what He'd shown a bare night ago!

It was the devil making a fool of me, not my Saviour, and I had to put a stop to it! Lord, I prayed, there is no greater damper on

Your power than doubt or unbelief. Touch that poor woman in her sorrow, that she may learn how You do hate suffering.

And then I preached like the Fool of old, yea, like a man possessed. But nothing, nothing happened. The storm had moved off, leaving me quite dry outside it. My well had run out.

O, I have had failures before. Many times. But in single instances, not throughout a whole night of wonder-working power. The power would be there, no matter if it slowed; it would come back in trickles, if not in waves. So there would always be something occurring to rouse people's belief, to beget more belief. Only this night we begat nothing. Then my eyes were opened.

"Crystal," I said after the humiliating end of the evening, "do you want that baby? Do you really want it?"

She didn't look at me, only nodded dumbly with her hands folded upon her lap. Her mother, after the closing prayer, had looked at me as if she sorrowed for the Fool, not mere fools.

"Then we're going to have to get away from here. Go down on the plains where people are really at wits' end, where the wells are all gone dry. God's calling me to where it's worst, Crystal. Where people are fed up with suffering."

Her luminous eyes lighted on me momentarily.

"You sense it too," I said. "Your mother wants us to suffer as your people always have. You see what that did for your poor Grandma. Pain begets pain, and misery is the mother of misery."

Crystal's eyes brimmed crystal tears.

"If I'd had — " and then she lay down on the bed and turned toward the wall.

"What is it, darling?"

She had never cried outwardly. So I dreaded any thought of some unreached sorrow. I reached to knead the muscles in her neck and shoulders, like she often did to mine after an exhausting bout of healing.

"Don't go grieving again for that lost baby," I said. "That's a year and a half ago. You'll have another one. The Lord will provide."

Her voice against the wall sounded utterly hollow.

"Mother said — if I'd only — had the proper food — "

Then she gasped as if her breath used speaking had been too much for her. I was left to feel as if a stone, or maybe the stone-cold bodies of two family members, lay between us. So I was to blame, was that it? I had killed my babies — me with my belief in wonders, not in wells. This is what the evening had been about. My wife was returning from me to cleave unto her fathers.

Now I lay there, bereft and broken. None but my Lord could comfort me; but who knew when He would choose to do so? So I lay in that house, an alien, listening to the breathing which now would be forever strange to me . . . then I must have slept because I dreamed I was returned to my father's house in Arborfield. The clan of Canns and Arbogasts were gathered and I led the way out through the darkness to the great spruce tree on the east side of the house. Alone I mounted its branches like a ladder, not minding my needled face and arms, nor even my hands torn on the coarse and scaly bark. The balmy scent of resin climbed in my brain until that moment, oddly wonderful, when I emerged into another world, standing on the tip of the tree. The stars stooped close and swollen about me and, as I stared, their holiness blazed clear into my head. I began to jump for joy and, as I leaped, the heavenly hosts swarmed all about me. I was, beyond expression, exalted. Lights seemed to tingle and burst at the back of my throat. Then, in the midst of my dizziness, I heard the throats of my family, even those who had called me leastest, opening in hosannas to the Lord of Hosts. And there was rejoicing on earth as there was in Heaven!

Yet in all of this, my heart remained humble, knowing each in his turn must be caught up someday in the twinkling of an eye. But o! to live daily in the wealth of that blessing! When I sank gently to the earth again, the tree held still its loving arms about me.

It was a mid-morning such as this before I recalled the dream of Joseph. Surely the sun and moon and eleven stars were to bow down before him too. But rankled with jealousy, Joseph's brothers sold him into Egypt. So the Lord made fools of them when He brought them unto Pharaoh's court. I considered how I was here in Egypt already, newly given such a promise. So at some point it must be needful to depart, a forerunner, out of one's father's land! Instantly I forgave Crystal everything.

We had nonetheless to suffer the heat of an Egyptian summer before my daddy and mother came down onto the plains to see us. We had the bigtop tent pitched in the hamlet of Eyebrow and the crowds were gathered inside, secure out of the surrounding des-titution, to wait upon the Lord. Times were hard. There was little for the people or their minister to live on. But Crystal had rallied before God and her husband. She took interest again in life in its inward part — our material blessings being too few to count or even to count upon. She had taken up the pencil that she had not used since we were wed, and she exercised her clever talents to the full. Out onto her paper poured images of her childhood: the farmhouse set in its bush, the leanto horse-barn, her brother Thom's splendid palomino, and finally, some wonderful portraits of her family, all carefully shaded and rounded, till they smiled off the page at you, true as life. Only her mother's eyes, I felt, were not quite right. But then eyes must be the hardest to draw expression into; there is no animating soul behind the paper.

I set out to convince Crystal that her work was good enough to be displayed. Good enough even to be put to work for the Lord; why not do some sacred drawings? Scenes, perhaps, from the life of the Man from Galilee. There were so many splendid pictures to draw from: the blind man whose eyes were anointed with clay and Jesus' spittle; the amazement of the scribes and pharisees at that man let down through their roof — he who was not only cured of the palsy but whose sins were forgiven him; or the consternation of the disciples at sight of Lazarus come forth in winding sheets: it was all there to be witnessed by believing eyes.

So Crystal went to work, reluctantly, to cast her spell over all these scenes, putting them on the platform in a wondrous new light. The people who witnessed the miracles of her hand were more than ever opened to the miracles of God from mine.

We were gratified, too, and grateful to God at this time for the side of salted pork my parents brought us. It stopped the hunger of our bellies without quenching any hunger of our souls. The first night our company was with us, Crystal sat in her place upon the stage and worked at her easel while the local choir sang. She was as radiant now as she had ever been in the midst of the congregation; but she was busy at last in the service of the Lord.

As I looked to the top of the big tent, it seemed as if a shaft of light shone clear from Glory to illuminate my wife's mortal presence. It was an awe-inspiring wonder to me; God was preparing something for us, I knew it. And in that moment, I think I had never felt less of fear or doubt or personal inadequacy in my life. My faith was enough to move mountains. So I couldn't help myself, I had to stop the choir right there to ask if they knew the hymn, "Shine on us, shine on me, Let the Lighthouse shine on me." Boy, did they ever! They sang until the congregation saw the light and helped raise the roof, voices swelling in one mighty volume. I felt all our souls mounting upward, near to being raptured.

All the while we sang, Crystal had been working on a lovely picture of Zacchaeus, the little man who climbed a tree to see our Saviour. The crowd, when they saw it, were already as high up there as Zacchaeus was. And they too could rejoice in what they saw with their own eyes. For just a moment I couldn't help but wish they would recall the end of that story, how the convert divided half his riches with the poor. Then as I began to preach, it didn't matter, I knew all the riches of God were mine. For His anointing came suddenly upon me and I began to tingle from the soles of my feet up through the crown of my head. I forgot the presence of my father and mother, I forgot myself entirely, and the spirit of God was loosed upon my tongue in living fire. The sea of faces became a blur before me and my voice rose and rose until I could no longer hold it, it blew as a puff of wind into my hearers. "People," I heard that breath whip away from me, "people, something is about to happen! God is here! He is about to reveal Himself to man!"

Suddenly the crowd was all up on its feet, and a mother with a child was passed as if from hand to hand onto the stage.

"Madam," I said to her trusting face, "what ails this son of yours?"

In a needy voice she answered, "He has been dumb from birth." Then, maybe fearing the laughter of the crowd, she added, "He's never been able to speak a word."

She need not have feared with me to play the fool. I looked at the boy. He eyed me soberly. I turned my back on the crowd. Touching his lips, I said in a loud voice, "Be thou made whole!"

The little boy slipped and almost fell, so great was the force that struck him through my fingers. I felt as if my hand would be jolted off. Then, miraculously, his lips were opened and in a crystal voice he said, "Behold the angel of the Lord!"

"What's that?" I said loud enough for everyone to hear.

Then in a voice that transcended all brute dumbness, he cried, "Behold the angel of the Lord with a sword in His right hand!"

I held my hand aloft, my back still turned, for the crowd to look upon. There was a sudden scream in the crowd and a gasp as of a mighty wind.

"I can see, I can see, I can see!"

I whirled round to see a man, blind from birth, leaping in the aisles. Then he raced up the sawdust path between two tent poles and out the door, safe as any man with 20-20 vision.

Pandemonium reigned. For five minutes I could not make my voice heard above the tumult of the people. Then they were streaming from everywhere to get into line to be touched.

I worked that night until I was ready to drop.

Back in the empty farmhouse that had been furnished by willing people, my father waited up for me.

"Jack," he said, "I want you to put your hand upon my head."

"Daddy," I said, "I am your son. You should be giving me the blessing."

"No, Jack. God has blessed you beyond conception. I would like just a little of what you've got, if it is only His will. What you have is more precious than rubies or diamonds."

"Daddy," I reminded him, "it is as precious as the crystal windows of Heaven through which God looks down at us."

"That is so. That is truly so. Forgive me, Jack, for ever having said a word against her."

And so I put my hand in God's anointment on him. The jolt stiffened my arm and drove him to his knees. The power has lingered that way upon me for hours after I have preached.

"Forgive me, my son," my daddy said, clutching my knees in his arms.

"Daddy," I cried, "there was nothing ever to forgive."

"Stay as humble as you are, Jack. Don't let anything change that. And I pray that God might work His will through you in these frightening end times."

Thus I myself was called out of my wilderness at last. I was redeemed out of my terrible aloneness into the human fellowship of family. Crystal and I were no longer driven forth.

In the days that followed, my Mama remarked often, "Jack, you have been amiss in not bringing my daughter home to me. Jack, you know we have missed both of you."

Crystal would only look shyly to the scrubbed board floor.

"I know, Mama, I know. We'll have to make it up to you."

As soon as we were alone Crystal would hold my arm in hers and say, *"Ich liebe dich."*

"I know, my dear, I know. As I love you in English."

But I could not bring myself to go to White Fox again and

suffer her mother's disapproval. The thought of those pained eyes was nearly enough to unman me, let alone to still the power of God in me.

"Another time," I would say. "There isn't money for both to go. Why don't you go alone? Someone, I'm sure, would feed me. And I suppose the ones who see their faith imaged in your drawings could spare you, too, for a time."

"Do you want me to stay?" she asked, not looking.

"Not if you feel you should go. I'd like you to stay, dearest. But we need, sometimes, to have something just for ourselves. Now if the Lord would only give us that baby, maybe I'd go with you. You know how your mother feels about that. . . ."

Crystal looked at me with a hint of the old, mysterious smile.

"Would you — "

"Would I what?"

She only smiled.

But to try was to believe again. And our rapture, every bit of it, was restored to us. And I did cleave unto my wife until I thought there would be no more of me. But o! to be so lost as that! to be such fools!

Yet when the tide came and went, we were still hopeful. We prayed together, lay together, prayed together. I put my hand upon her womanhood and felt the wave of God pour into her. I spake into her very womb to open it. And still the Lord withheld His promise. Autumn passed into winter and our joy leaked out. But we struggled together in the widespread whiteness of a desperate winter. Still all lay dormant as the snow. At last Crystal turned her face from me, though not from me herself.

Just when I felt anew the sap of spring rise up in me, just when my heart was quickened again in the rush of the new season, Crystal awoke one night as from a dream. She was wild with lamentation. She cried so fiercely that I couldn't quiet her. She kept saying "No, no, no" in a voice as hoarse as the returning ravens, and she pushed as if to remove some presence off of her.

"What is it?" I said, feeling some of her terror. I confess I myself was nearly frantic. "Now what is it, sweetheart?"

In the end I had to slap her to her senses. She let out a terrible cry and slumped into a dead faint.

When she came to, she clung to me in desperation.

"What is it?" I said. "It was only a dream, Crystal, dearest. It was only some nightmare troubling you."

But I felt the shudder go through her, felt her mouth moan deeply upon my neck.

It was daylight before she ever told the dream to me. Told? I had to descend myself into darkness, yea into a maze, in search of it! Blackness everywhere. Almost visible. The darkness of everlasting night. Far off, voices. In a void, yet vivid, somehow, and slow as the beat of blood. Swelling. Now chanting in a solemn chorus. The fall and rise expectant. Sway and lilt, sway and lilt enchanting. The hum breaks suddenly into song. Not yet nearing. Yet ever so near. A song without words, without meaning. Only high and low tones, coupling and uncoupling. Still somehow significant. Then out of the reddened darkness a hand. Touch of fire along one shoulder. Naked flesh revolted. Another hand burns. Then something in one scaly motion covers her. Savagely. Her vulva searing at the mouth.

"No no no!" her mouth spouts lava in the light.

"Crystal!" I cry. "Satan! Call on Christ to save you!"

The thought of the devil in her flesh leaves me impotent. My right hand hangs unfeelingly at my side.

"Crystal! Call—"

But she collapses, weeping, in my arms. Beneath her breast the heart flutters like a bird against a pane of glass. I hold her in horror before I realize such dreams may not survive the light.

Then it is given me what to do.

"Crystal, the devil has — has oppressed you. Do you—" but I find it hard even to think of it. I manage, finally, to say, "Do you still feel his presence in you?"

A shudder runs through her. I feel that bird about to break the glass. I look upon her face with its eyes tight shut. Her mouth is twisted out of mystery.

"Crystal?" I say in my urgency.

She shakes her head violently, just once.

"Crystal, for the love of God! There is time to rid yourself of this oppression. Don't you recall the wonderful saying of Peter, that 'God anointed Jesus of Nazareth with the Holy Ghost and with power who went about doing good, healing all who were oppressed of the devil for God was with him'? Don't you hear that promise, Crystal? Who is with us? God. God is here as much as Satan."

Inasmuch as her mouth has ceased from its wretchedness, I take heart.

"Darling," I cry, "the devil is mounting his last assault on me. We are doing God's work too well. There is war in heaven, and the dragon who has devoured our child is about to be cast down."

Her eyelids flicker and my Crystal's glance lights on me, then hopelessly away.

"It was only a dream," she says despondently.

"Only a — "

But she doesn't want to hear any more. She covers her long, lithe limbs in an old nightgown and leaves the room. I can hear her in the kitchen, preparing our pitiful breakfast.

I am checked; I don't know what to do with what is given. A dream is given. A devil-sent dream, meant to fool us. But what if our whole lives were a dream, like Jacob's, of angels descending and ascending? Did he not wake to find his head pillowed on a rock? And did he not find, years after, that dreams may have this extra truth — that an angel could actually meet him, and wrestle, and even cripple him? Now of whom was that: God, or Satan? And how would the fool ever know whose servant he really is? *By their works ye shall know them*

At last I go into the other bedroom to work on my sermon.

That night after service I can only say I know whose servant I am. For I have felt the whole evening long God's wonder-working power in my right hand. I rejoice in His continuing power to heal us of all oppression of the devil. If this be a dream, well then, I can only say, does it hurt or heal? The outpouring of the Holy Ghost must be its own witness.

But when we retire for the night, Crystal tells me simply, without looking, "I'd prefer not to."

I understand this shock she has suffered. I don't press it further, though the time is certainly auspicious.

Our sleep is uneventful. My heart rises on the morn to praise its Maker for His care and goodness. This glorious light of morn is no nightmare, surely.

Crystal is nonetheless not recovered. There is a shadow fallen across her which dims her accustomed lustre. That night, as I preach, I glance at her. I am frightened by the sense that her glory has departed. She sits there so absently. . . .

. . . . until we do glory again in the land of the midnight sun. We have recently met Brother Cardiff of Lacjardin. He has brought us homeward into the lake country showered with Mercy, and has given us the house on his other quarter section. It is only an old settler's shack, but at least there is somewhat to eat. Brother Cardiff ministers to our needs as the raven to Elijah: it is Heaven-sent fare. Crystal seems to take heart again in the sun of God's plenty. My own heart opens as a flower to those beams.

"Do you think," I say one Monday, returning from services in the hopefully-named town of Pleasantdale, "that God meant it as a sign to bring us unto Lacjardin?"

Crystal, bathing in the glow from the window, turns to me at last with her secret smile.

And now the nights are too short to trouble us. We labour nightly in God's vineyard, first in public, then in private. We plant God's seed with the promise that as ye sow, ye shall also reap. And in the towns around, from Nisooskan out east to Naicam, the fields are white unto harvest. Only in our bedroom is the harvest un-yielding as a field of snow. . . .

. . . . the snow comes too early this year. October 8. For days the world fades away in the veil of the blizzard. When the sun does struggle out, it is wan and white with frost. Now the light of a wintry afternoon stripes the far board wall and the sun itself parti-tions us, crystal walls of light between. I admit our failure, but I will not accept defeat.

"If we must," I say at last, "let us surrender ourselves in public, even reveal ourselves before the congregation. Maybe we are hiding our light under a bushel at home. Let's ask God to heal you right out in the open, as He does the rest."

Crystal only looks at me, her tall neck bowed with private grief, and I know it is no use. But oh it grieves me to see her suffer so, this apathy deepening on her like the winter snow. I can only praise God that she has not sought, willingly, to wear this mantle of suffering. Yet methinks, almost, it would be better if she had; there would at least be that gladness for her in it. Why Lord, I plead silently, why these others and not us. . . ?

I am awakened in the midst of night to her crying, "No! No, no!" and I come up from the depths as lost as a drowning man. I reach to shake her, but now her voice rises one full octave in her terror. She shrieks at last, hysterically.

I fumble for the lamp on the dresser, turn up the wick, strike the wooden match. The light flutters and then rises like a prayer.

I approach the bed where my lost wife is bedeviled. I feel in my soul there is nothing I can do for her. I may only wake her in a series of moments. But then she will sleep again. These nights are neverending.

The moment I approach the bed, lamp in hand, and touch her shoulder, she cries as if in greater pain.

"Crystal!" I plead unto the gates of heaven.

She flings round in her distress of winding sheets. Her eyes go first to the light and then to my face. And then I remark her glow of recognition. I am struck dumb when she cries in renewed terror, "No no no." She shrinks against the wall, lies helpless in foolish horror. I stare at her, amazed. Then the light winks once, catches, and winks out. We have forgot to refill it with coal oil.

"Crystal," I say into the frozen darkness. "It is I, your husband."

"Yes," she says, muffled by a despair of bedclothes.

I cling to this acknowledgment as to a piece of floating wreckage.

"You've got to get free of the devil, Crystal. Or we are done for. I'm going to pray as I have never prayed for your deliverance. But you've got to believe. Do you believe, Crystal, that God will save you?"

"Yes," she speaks hollowly as from a crypt in the wall. Then some other will, not her own, assumes her being. "No. I don't know."

The thought of doubt at such a moment unmans me. Has she betrayed me already, succumbing in a secret moment to Satan? All at once the wrath of God, our God, a jealous God, pours out of me.

"Which is it to be, woman? Him or me? Declare yourself this instant for God or Satan. Now choose whom you will serve!"

My once-true wife says nothing, nothing at all. She is passive to this her utmost destiny. How could she care so little, so terribly little, about such momentous things?

Fortunately God gives to mind one event, one characteristic image, from her family life.

"Crystal, you mustn't give up! Don't lose hope like your Grandma did. Be not conformed to this world, only place your trust in higher things. Crystal?"

The darkness seems to have taken her. She is given over to demons. But my pity is awakened for both of us. She can't help herself any more than I. God alone must succour us. I must pray. Pray alone.

Even as I mount the steps of darkness with my last entreaty, as my voice carries now in rhythmical petition, my mind departs in wonder at our Lord's delinquency. How could He let His chosen servants sink unsuccoured into this slough of despond? By what right should He choose when He chooses, and ignore when He ignores? Has He not promised, Beloved, I wish above all things that thou mayest prosper? And did He not say, I am come that they might have life and that they might have it more abundantly? Then by what right should He give to those that have, but to those that give, He taketh away? Why would He fool us so utterly?

At the thought of *His* folly I grow maddened. At last I prepare to storm, with my prayer, the gates of Heaven. Lord, I cry in one final effort to catch the bottom rung of Jacob's ladder, Lord, you come down to us and learn what it is to suffer the torments of the devil!

The words are no sooner spoken than I am caught up in a seeming whirlwind and am transported beyond sight or thought or hearing. For a long time I know nothing. There is nothing. Then I see at last I am alone in an empty house and an awful thing awaits me . . . awaits so near outside my senses. . . .

I awake to daylight and a vacant house. In my passage into every room, a drear chill takes hold of me. Crystal is gone. Her few dresses are not hung in our closet; her dresser drawers are bare.

Suddenly I stand convicted of the thought that I must never see her again. . . .

I am not fooled. The next evening they come to tell me she has run off with her lover. I have to stand and listen how she came to him, where it was on the banks of the river by Nipawin. They imply, with devilish cruelty, that she was so relieved to find him, she waded to her waist to embrace him. Then he caught her and swept her off her feet. And they never saw her more. The lovers were united in their secret place. Only her body —

No! She went with him. She went the only way a woman could. But they twist the truth like lies. They are of their father the dragon, and the lusts of their father they will do. He was a murderer from the beginning, and abode not in the truth, because there is no truth in him. When he speaketh a lie, he speaketh of his own: for —

— the river whispers, she is dead, she is dead, she is dead. Now its secret thought runs even to a frozen ocean. O my foreboding soul! My lovely Crystal cold?

I loved her. Why would she leave me? She was so good and gentle. Even the way she sat here sustained me. Smiling her secret joy in all things as unto the Lord. No wonder He claimed her for Himself. She met her lover, radiant with this imminent translation, and Death took her in His arms —

Since when has Death been styled the Lord of Heaven? Is God, our God, that dragon Death, who devours women and little children? Then how have I hated Him! All my livelong days I have dreaded Him. I will not go to meet my Maker. I want no part in Him forever.

Yet Crystal loved Him. She preferred Him to me. How could she?

Because she started sleeping with Him. At first in my bed; then in the cold, cold ground.

Whose fault? Whose but her own? I gave her of me all she could have. I brought her gloriously to life.

And because I would not go to Him, He came to her. Because I would give Him no part in life, He granted her my portion, even unto Death.

Then who was that dragon?

The father of lies. He was a murderer from the beginning. And in Him is no life at all.

But she lives with Him. Not me.

Who then is the father of lies?

I. I am that murderer. I killed her. O, and our unborn children! My self-slaughtered by myself.

It is too much to be borne. Ever, ever to be born.

In me gnaws the worm that shall never die.

Would that I could die. But Death would not surrender her.

Then who would ask to be made an eternal soul? O —

Immortality: the gift of grace through Jesus Christ our Lord. Jesus wept. For men. Thank God Jesus wept.

Not for God. No one weeps for God.

The river weeps. Like Jesus, the river weeps for me. It knows, like Jesus. The river is the way, the truth, and the life.

Suddenly its truth startles clear to the bone. Almost it overwhelms me. I drink it in, suck deep, but it bubbles out my nose.

And yet . . . how is truth so black? I always believed it to be Light. No, the strangeness is, how have we ever seen at all in this dark?

There, almost, I see the awful thing. Its veil floats by. Lifts. I see —

No, I must not look on that. That way nothing lies. O, I must have lies.

Eyes, return! And rise, bare bones, to trick dry fear in flesh. Stand up, skeleton, and sing. And o, ye osseous ears, now hear the Word of the Lord!

God is the father of lies
Even He who said He was and is and is to come
Then must God die
He saved others; Himself He cannot save
God is Good
Good is Dead
So why should Truth be known?

TUESDAY

Nick

Let me alone. I want to sleep. Just sleep.

But he won't.

"Come on," he says in a funny, fluting voice. "Try some of this stir."

A tin plate is stuck in my hand. Carrot tops. A lump of something in gravy.

"It's not so bad as it looks. It'll help heat your insides."

I never saw him before. So why does he think he knows me? A guy younger than me; no fuzz on his cheeks; like some bad dream insisting I remember.

I don't want to dream. Just sleep.

"Come on. I know it ain't much for someone nearly drownded. But we got to put life in you somehow."

For the life of me, I've got to get out of this dream.

"Wake up," says a voice.

I open my eyes on light spitting out sparks. A low bonfire. Other fires. I don't know why bonfires make me think of a poolroom.

Here comes a face I know I can ask.

"Don't I know you from somewhere?"

He looks away; spoons something out of the gallon tin on the fire.

"Here," he hands the plate to me. "You spilled the last batch. Be careful of this; there's not much left."

I have a hunch.

"You've run away from somewhere, haven't you?"

"Don't let him bullshit you," blusters a voice that I somehow recall.

The young guy looks away in confusion.

But the voice belongs to a stranger. He's arguing over there by the next fire. My hunch fades away: was mistaken anyway.

I'm not mistaken that there's some kind of bond between this young guy and me. His eyes tell me he feels it too.

Yonder a mosquito voice whines. Then the familiar accent takes up again.

"Mister, you ain't got no reasons whatever to back you up. The trouble with this country was never bohunks. You're just looking for someone besides yourself to blame."

I'm not sure why I feel so suddenly at home.

"You're damn right I'm a Chuk, mister. Damn tooting right. And my mother was a Ski. But I was born here, mister. Where were you born?"

No answer. There never was to that one.

"I thought so. Hell, my father busted land here, mister. Made it grow wheat instead of buffalo grass. You can't tell me it was bohunks caused the ruin of that land."

"Well," the mosquito pitches up to full whine, "you tell me why bohunks get all the relief when British citizens like me are left to starve? I say there's something wrong with the world, the way MacKenzie King is running it."

"And I say the reason you're a bum, my friend, is because you're a bum — not because my father took a thing from you. But the reason I'm a bum is because the mortgage company took my father's homestead. Land that was ours, mister, before you laid eyes on this country. But the company took back my new equipment and then they took my land. By God, there oughta be a law."

"There is," another voice booms away across the fire. "To help the companies. Big business, it's drinking our blood. And politicians are all the belly of the blood-sucker. Just read down any Board of Directors."

"Then maybe, my friend," the bohunk says, "that little twerp MacKenzie King is to blame like you say. Only me and you are bums for different reasons."

The fires have died down. The boys are back to ordinary grumbling again. I don't know why I'm so worried that the bohunk should have given the Mosquito an advantage.

The young guy's face comes back to worry me some more.

"Your friends are going to be all right."

I don't have any friends.

I see some old Indian coot lying by the fire. Two Indians. And a tall, weird guy, looking like death. Those are no friends of mine.

"Who are you? Why do I know you, anyway?"

The kid seems to know how much he haunts me. For an instant, he looks haunted himself. He swallows, hardly a bob of Adam's apple.

"Since you think you know so much about me" — he falters — "maybe you know where my father is? Have you maybe seen him somewheres?"

I catch at some fleeting thing. Gone.

"I look lots like him, people say. Taller. I mean, he is. Missing a thumb and forefinger on his right hand. Lost them in a boxcar coupling. So the railway let him go. You'd know him if you ever saw him. The way he could stroll a catwalk. No? Hell, I keep forgetting you ain't been riding the rods."

But my expression must fire up his hopes again.

"You saw him, then. Was he all right? Where was he? Oh, if I could just see him once. Just talk to him. We never blamed him none, you know. He was our father. We never looked on him as another mouth to feed. I'd like him to know he's still my old man, no matter what he told Mom."

Then I know. Know it for a fact.

"Your father's dead," I say matter-of-factly.

He blinks at me like an owl waking from a dream. His eyes appear to go a little crazy.

"You don't know nothing," he says.

He gets up, begins to shuffle off.

"Where you going?"

"I got to make a train."

I listen, but hear nothing in the distance. With almost a sense of relief I watch him go. Still I wish he would've told me how I know what I know.

I could sleep now if it wasn't for the damn bickering. Home Sweet Home.

Where was that?

Nowhere. Anywhere. We're knights of the road. Look at these guys. Every one carries his closet on his back. Two, sometimes three coats. And trouser legs stuffed like *kielbasa*. We're all going everywhere and nowhere.

From back in the dark a terrible moan gets my hackles up. There's nothing there. There can't be, that's all. But the groaning goes on.

Then I know I've got to see for myself.

I go up the steps, push through the darkness.

And look.

Aaaa, just as I thought. There's nothing here but that guy whose father died. He's the one doing the moaning. So how do I know it was his father that died? For once I doubt myself. Then feel a ray of pity for the kid.

"I came to tell you I wasn't sure of what I said. I'm sorry. I don't know who it was. Somebody's father died."

He gets off his elbows at the sound of my voice. I give a little lift, as he struggles up, under his arms. My hand closes over a — tit.

"Wha — " I say out loud in my astonishment. Then change it to "What's a nice girl like you doing here?"

"Shh. Don't say nothing. I don't want nobody to know. If the bulls catch me again, they'll send me for sure to the Women's Jail in Battleford."

Again I miss some fleeting thing. We are both quiet for a time. Thinking. She makes no move at all. Then I realize I have my hand still on her breast.

Fershitsake. She's easy.

At least she wouldn't squawk if I pulled out my cock.

But something in my memory of her eyes alarms me.

I search her face in the dark with my fingers, trying vaguely to remember. Doubtfully I reach her on the lips. She kisses me back, her lips parted. Suddenly her tongue is in my mouth, licking the backs of my teeth.

Boizha, I can't be a-scaired of any piece that wants it.

We sink side by side onto the grass, fumbling under one coat, then another spread out on the ground. Then I'm trying to get my buckle loosed. My pants slide down clinging-wet. Finally I feel a lick of air on my red-raw skin.

She lies there limp and moaning. For a split second I'm scared, no matter what I tell myself. Her eyes were too crazy, her face was too sharp, her hair so chopped and ugly. . . . Aaaa, I'm only worried about getting a dose, no worse than sniffles. So fuck it.

I lay heavily, after. Too coldly heavy. She senses. Then starts to cry.

The bridge rumbles as the train trundles on.

"Get off!" she says.

She is pulling up her trousers when the first dark figures run by. I crouch with my ass against the willows, watching a swarm of men mount the bank and fan over the tracks.

"Goodbye," she says and is fled into the darkness.

"Wait," I call. "I don't — "

There is only a growing roar upon the trestle, the hollow rumble of steel over the pit. Now into the empty midst the engine pants. I see it spouting sparks in the dark. The bankhead trembles. Then the engine comes to earth again. The shaking dwindles, is absorbed along the land. Men run along the cinder track, are swung up in the silence. As soon the nameless faces whirl toward the distance.

I still don't know her name.

My name is Nick. I'm Old Nick now.

Boizha, I'm as bad as he ever was. If not worse.

Many-birds

They gabble like a flock of his geese. Ones that couldn't fly off in all the cinders an' shit. Goddam honking hoboes.

honk honk honk

Twenty pair of eyes swing round on me. Eyes like slitted buttons, blinking. The *gobble gobble* is stopped. Turkeys with their wattles hanging.

"What's wrong with you guys?" I say when I see they take this sort of talk serious. "Why'n't you get some women out here, instead of all this fucking powwow all the time? Ain't you heard what a good time could be had by all?"

Twenty pair of eyes blink. Twenty peckers hang. Let them all go hang. I won't myself for much longer.

Then one of them fuckers peeps and finds a egg under him. *cluck cluck cluck* the racket starts again.

Those jailbirds used to kid me how kings kept no-nuts in every palace. They said they would be kings too, just by cutting my nuts off. But a real king wouldn't put up with shit like that. He'd light out for the woman he loves. Well here I am. So what's wrong with me?

It's Goose Neck's fault. That bugger is crazier than a bohunk barber, fershitsake. No wonder she left her closet empty too.

Agnes? Are you waiting for me where the lights shine behind that bank? Can you feel me getting close to you? Agnes, I give up my crown for you, the woman I love.

I got to goddam find her. Before her husband does. Get away from all these no-nuts before my nuts get shrunk like pounding berries.

Sure as fuck I didn't ask to sit around this joint. I could see them buggers hopping, way across water, like hoo-er crabs jumping out of the fire. Then Goose Neck was crying how she fucked off on him. Next thing I know, we're tipped over our heads.

Fershitsake, I remember thinking, isn't it just my luck to wade this goddam river to find her, and then go drown in her fucking backhouse? It made me so mad I grabbed at Goose Neck to be sure he drowned with me. But when Fuzzy Nuts pulled me off his back, it was Fine-day. Goose Neck was already hanging to the boat's belly. The first to climb on again.

And I'm a cocksucker's uncle. Why didn't I see before how his girlfriend outlook was the same as mine? My *nikocak*! Fellow husband who will lead me safe the rest of the way. My fucking troubles are over.

"Hey," I lay a hand on his bony shoulder, "get yourself looking like a buck, at least. We're gonna leave this dump."

I see us paddling down a river strung with lights. Then I remember that canoe guy, what he said about tipping out in front of his woman. Well, I think, the one I go about with won't get another chance.

"We're taking the bridge. I paddled my ass enough."

I got a friend in my pants, though, who's nearly ready for another chance.

Jack

He whirls and runs out. And I get out with him just in time but ribbons of light like steel rails run away from us, or are they going blink blink there below? Then I stumble and his arm crooks round my neck; I tremble to see the void up under us, all around us *but thou art with me, thy rod and thy staff they comfort me* Then it is finished. We clatter down some wooden steps and come to earth again. I'm so relieved I could laugh.

"Well," I say, "thanks for the help. You're making a regular career out of helping people, aren't you? Did your woman thank you, too, when she left you for that other man?"

Many-birds' lip curls off that jut of jaw.

He is almost child-like to manage.

"So are we going to stand here, for God's sake? Or are we going to save her from the fate worse than death?"

Then my poor fool doesn't know what to think.

"I'll tell you what, my friend. The first thing we need is a car." Now, of course, he is totally in tow. "Sure, I've managed to borrow cars from folks — before they ever knew they were so generous. So what do you say we scout along this street beside the river? It looks ritzy enough, don't it?"

His eyes follow mine along a heavily treed crescent where the streetlights gleam like diamonds in the grass.

Suddenly he is slapping clumsily at my back. "Well fershit-sake. An' here I thought you knew only one goddamn way to honk."

"That's just fine, friend. But let's leave the laying on of hands to me, eh? What do you say?"

He grins. And is not scared off by my returning grin.

"Okay, I swear to you that we'll find that woman, and I'll bring her bawling into glory."

Briefly he looks confused. But we are little more now than two shadows flitting toward a darkened house. *In my father's house are many mansions* So why does he go charging in front? Who does he think he is, trying to lead?

Then the hedge gives way upon a glistening expanse of lawn.

Lord, if it be thou, bid me come unto thee on the water
He stretches forth his hand

But the tall, double doors of the garage will not open. They are bolted from inside.

"Pray that ye enter not into temptation."

Many-birds looks foolishly at me as I disappear around the corner.

I peer in at a window. My face is striped by the latticework. I try to raise the sash. It is locked.

Still not a sound to be heard in the whole neighbourhood. Only secret wealth whispers behind the lace next door.

We have heard the joyful sound, Jesus saves, Jesus saves!

The tidings are now spread all around on the garage floor. I try not to cut myself on the shards sticking out of the sash. Then I'm on my feet, feeling my way along the flank of a sleek automobile.

When the bolt flies, I swing the door to. There is a bone-jarring bump; Many-birds' yelp is caught in his throat.

Why sleep ye? Rise and pray

"Wake up," I say with my hand on the double door. "Or you'll get it on the other cheek."

He is humbled the moment we see what awaits us in the stable.

"Do you know what that is?" I feel my blood race.

"A Hudson," he growls with savage pleasure, rubbing his nose.

"A *Hudson?* This is a 1935 or '36 Cadillac, my friend. The kind we doctors drive. Too bad you don't know anything about medicine."

I bend to look in at the driver's window. Suddenly I can't avoid any more the dark face of my familiar. He is grinning in the polished glass like a Cheshire cat. I could hoot, he looks so pleadingly hopeful.

I'm just one tiny latch away from being back in the driver's seat.

"Find me some wire."

He comes back like a retriever, haywire in hand.

Immediately I lay hands on the car. I feel a thrill in my fingertips. Then the noose is edged inside the glass, I cinch up and the latch clicks, and I open the door, sliding in one motion beneath the wheel. The seat is crushed velvet, exquisitely soft.

"Hey," Many-birds barks, "I'm drivin' it, fershitsake. It's my woman I got to look good fer."

How long, ye simple ones, will ye love simplicity?

"Sure thing," I say easily. "But first you're going to earn that right. Push us down the drive, eh? We can't start it here."

The narrow rubber tires roll soundlessly on the concrete floor, then slow . . . as Many-birds stops to pant.

"You got the bugger in gear or somethin'?"

Be not deceived; God is not mocked

He shrinks down again from the sight of my eyes; I watch behind to steer.

The car stops directly in the shadow of the house. I hear a foot on gravel and then Many-birds yanks open the passenger door.

"Your turn t' push me," he hisses, sliding across.

Now I must hump in righteous rage the bumper of my car down a rich man's lane. Many-birds swings out onto the street, running one reckless tire over the lawn and curb. I'm pleased when Wisdom counsels to get me behind him and propel him yet a hundred yards.

"Okay," I say, forcing a grin at his window, "you get to crank."

He gets out reluctantly.

"Okay, but I'm drivin'," he says balefully.

"Sure. I pushed most; now it's your turn to bust a gut."

I slip behind the wheel and switch the lever to on. But I wait until he's bent over, hunting the crank. Then I hit the foot starter. The mighty engine whirs into life.

Many-birds almost scrabbles onto the hood. Through the window I give him a genuine grin. Now as he races around to my side, I let out the clutch and roll in solemn splendour.

"Fershitsake!" he yelps like a coyote pup. He is running alongside, his canine countenance straining to be human.

"Get in the other side," I say through the glass.

He shakes his head.

Because I have called, and ye refused, I also will laugh at your calamity; I will mock when your fear cometh

"So howl," I say, stepping on the accelerator. "Wake up your dog-god to help you."

My intention is just to keep on going. *But Balaam said unto the ass, Because thou hast mocked me, I would there were a sword in mine hand, for now would I kill thee*

I debate whether to swerve and run him down.

"Fershitsake," he gasps over my shoulder, "you fuckin' promised —"

"All right," I take pity on him, I don't know why, "you can get in, then."

The trees and hedges and houselights are starting to run in my passenger window. Now I see in the rear-view that he is running for all he is worth.

"How d' hell can I?" he cries from afar.

"On the other side." I wave him over.

When he crosses behind, I slow to a walk. He swings in from the running board, panting, though his eyes spark with a magneto pulse.

Just this once I send up the kite that will draw off his electricity.

"How often you go running on wild goose chases, friend?"

"I ain't till *you* tramped on it."

Then he grins at me, forgetting to scowl.

He that troubleth his own house shall inherit the wind: but the fool shall be a servant to the wise

I grin back, putting teeth into the jest.

"So you finally came forward, did you Brother Many-birds? You chose at last to humble yourself before God and man? Well then, I'll be as good as my word. You are now free to see that woman of yours — to see her for what she truly is. Where did you say she's at, friend?"

"She's stayin' wid her sister," he mumbles in a greatly changed voice. From the corner of my eye, I catch him looking at the floor.

"What's her sister's name?"

"Elsie, Elsie Ernst."

"And where might Elsie Elsie live?"

He shrugs hopelessly. But now he attends, I see, on my every word.

"Brother Many-birds, let not your heart be troubled. I am the way. You follow me and your faith shall be rewarded you."

At that moment the river on our left gives way upon a bridge. I stop at the red light, then turn right to follow the park. I pray that I am right.

Almost at once I see the sign I am looking for. 'Drink Coca-cola.'

Brethren, are you washed in the blood of that sign?

We pull up to the curb before a grocery store. The sign rainbowing over the window reads, 'Yin Confectionery.'

Well, I think, so long as the telephone book isn't in Chinese. Else the Virgin will have to wait tonight for the ram to feed among the lilies.

I look at that brute of a man turned into a quivering lamb.

"Buck up," I say brightly. "I'll have her address for you in two shakes of a ram's tail."

Then I saunter up the steps of the grocery, knowing he could as soon drive off without me now as without himself.

A little bell tinkles as I push through the doorway. This balding, bespectacled old Chink stands behind the glassed-in counter. His hands are folded neatly above his grey-smocked waist. I notice they are mottled — to match the dots like India ink upon his forehead. I try to think what the pattern of the dots reminds me of.

"Evenin', little grandfather," I say easily.

The man looks at me with the blandest indifference.

"Got a telephone book handy, old fellow?"

He only looks at me uncomprehendingly.

The wisdom of the Orient, I see, is hardly what it's cracked up to be.

"Looky, looky, telephone booky?" I hold an imagined receiver to my ear, cranking an imagined handle.

He shambles away toward the back. While he is gone I find his Eastern philosophy to be of no avail. I fill my pockets from the counter with Sweet Marie bars and Dutch Masters cigars. The old boy comes trotting back, watching all the while. *For if thou shalt not watch, I will come on thee as a thief* But the fool is content to clutch a ragged book to his breast as if it were the scriptures.

O say is her name written there? Is it written in the Lamb's book of life?

My dupe arrives somewhat breathless. He shoves the book at me upsidedown over the counter.

"Thanks," I say. "But I don't read Chink."

I turn it over and thumb to E. Early to bed, early to rise, I'll have her first, a religious surprise. Ernst, C.D. Ernst, Elsie. "Now there's my baby, I don't mean maybe, there's my baby nowww-ow." 821 Ave. C. North.

"Where's Avenue C?" I ask old Merry Andrew. "And don't bother to say it's between B and D, not unless you're passing from Birth to Death."

He looks at me like a Dumb Beast. I take his pencil from his smock, he unresisting. Good for you, old fellow, you're getting wise. Finally I let go of his collar.

When I've circled the address, I give it right up under his nose.

He points to his right, over a bin of rice.

"How far? Next door? Or halfway to China?"

Somehow "China" looses his English tongue. He sets off on a sing-song recitation as if he were one of the Wise Men in the Sunday School Concert.

"Twenty-fift stleet, twenty-fouh stleet, twenty-thlee," he gulps for air, "now closs on twenty-thlee beneath low subway, go up hill on Avenue A, next twenty-nint stleet. You find Avenue C on oth-ah side somehow."

"It's that somehow," I say, "that wollies me."

"Say," I remark once more the mark on his forehead, "don't I know you from somewhere?"

The dots are slanted and squiggly, like sideways sixes. *Here is wisdom. Let him that hath understanding count the number of the beast. It is Six hundred threescore and six*

"No? I suppose not. Well, man, it's been my pleasure neither buying nor selling with you," I say, barely able to hold back a shout of laughter that racks my throat. "Good night, old chap."

I sweep out the door on a wave of triumph. I have managed to do business without taking the mark; I have deceived even the beast.

"Have a see-gar," I say, swinging up into my wonder-making machine. Many-birds remains hunched in his seat like a gargoyle. *Having eyes, see ye not? and having ears, hear ye not? and do ye not remember?*

I shrug and press the cigar lighter, then settle back amidst this luxury of pin-striped cushions.

Slowly I draw the unwrapped stogie under my nose. Its pungent aroma sends up a wonderful darkness in my brain.

"I'm gonna see Elsie who lives on a hi-ill," I sing half under my breath, "if she won't do it, her sister wi-ill."

The gargoyle glares at me. My lighter pops out. I hold it, hot as the devil's hoof, right at the ready.

"You shut yer fuckin' mouth like dat."

"Sure thing, Joseph. Just like your Lady did. Chew on a new cigar, why don't you?"

He glares, then takes the extended offering. I light my stogie, watching him the while. Smoke rises through my nose, making me feel lighter.

"Here," I punch the lighter in. "She'll be ready in a minute."

"You mean — ?"

"Oh, her," I say innocently. "I thought she was always ready."

And I ease out in the street, admiring the while our padded instrument panel.

"You fucker, you ain't said what you found out."

"I've found out things too wonderful for you, my friend, which you're better not to know."

"Fershitsake, you better tell me — " he stabs the air with his unwrapped cigar.

"Whatever you say, friend. But don't say I didn't warn you. She's staying on Avenue C, which might not stand for Christmas, then again it may."

"Stop d' car."

I oblige at the green light.

He is already butt-shifting himself over to where I sit.

"Get lost you cunt."

"My friend," I say so gently, cuttingly, "Avenue C is not two shacks built together on an Indian Reserve. It stretches clear across the city. Now how would you ever find it if I get lost?"

Soon there is a line of cars honking behind us.

Many-birds stares murderously at me. I don't remember anything about them killing the angel who brought the good news.

Then he looks slightly less dangerous.

"That's better," I say. "This will mean a whole lot more to you if you have some faith. Give me room, now. We wouldn't want to be picked up with a stolen flivver, would we? At least not for overcrowding the lousy steering compartment."

Soon we leave those hornblowers to eat our dust.

We have to dodge a street car clang clang clanging onto "twenty-thlee stleet." But we stay out of its tracks up the pavement of Avenue A. The lights of the city begin to fall away on our right. For a moment I am held spellbound by this sea of light. I yearn to lie contented on its gentle breast. Then, of course, I do recall myself. "I come not to send peace, but a sword." Only go slowly, then; don't force him to turn your own sword upon you.

I slow for a blinking yellow light, and read the sign for twenty-ninth street. We turn up a boulevard middled with trees. The light barely filters through to us. Finally we enter no-man's-land itself.

"This should be your house," I say, looking at a row of three-storey, rundown dowagers. Then, before I know it's out, "What kind of house are they supposed to be running, anyway?"

Many-birds is mumbling again. I try to look question marks at him, try not to get him waving that sword again.

"How d' you know dis is it, fuckhead?"

So he must have some doubts himself about the sort of house that would keep her.

"Well, what are you waiting for, Solomon? A loan?"

"Don't go away on me," he says almost pleadingly.

Now he advances his pitiful banner up the walk.

Stay with me flagons, comfort me. For I am sick of love

A light snaps on inside.

The voice of my beloved! behold, he cometh leaping upon the mountains, skipping upon the hills

A face appears behind the glass in the veranda. Then Many-birds is talking.

O my dove, thou art in the clefts of the rock, in the secret places of the stairs, let me see thy countenance

The door doesn't open; her face is turned back within the house.

Many-birds makes one move to kick down the door *but in three days he must raise it up again* Then he whirls and paces down the walk. I observe him through closely slitted eyes, sparing him the shame, but apparently he doesn't see me *being in an agony, for his sweat is as great drops of blood falling down to the ground*

Then the door clicks and Many-birds steps softly inside. I maintain this posture of sleep, my head back and my eyes closed. For the first time I realize how desperately weary I am.

"You shouldn' be sleepin'," he rebukes me in a sad voice.

"Hmmph," I say, coming to. Unexpectedly I give him a genuine yawn. "Where to now?"

"Anywhere," he gives his usual lunge of voice. But this time it falls strangely flat. "Go fuckin' anywhere. Dis here's d' wrong address."

Then, as if to make up for the sound of his voice, he glowers at me.

I will rise now and go about the city in the streets, and in the broad ways I will seek her whom my soul loveth

The car slopes on its descent of a new face of the hill.

He that sitteth in the heavens shall laugh: the Lord shall have them in derision

I'm not going to be able to hold it much longer; it tickles in my throat like bicarbonate of soda.

"Stop d' car," Many-birds says abruptly.

A squeal of brakes masks the peal of my laughter. But I can't stop. I press in desperation the pedal to the floor. The car begins to skid. I'm howling silently now. Then we plane out, bouncing over some railway tracks, and come to rest. I brace against the wrath to come; a door slams; Many-birds is out and running back toward the tracks. Then I lose sight of him wading through weeds in a vacant lot toward that tent.

My beloved is gone down into his garden, to the beds of spices, to feed in the gardens, and to gather lilies

I gasp like a girl. Then I am not so bursting with it any more. I wipe my eyes.

The tent has disappeared *the veil rent from top to bottom but I must not look at that* and then Many-birds reappears, stalking in and out of the light, a blanket draped over his arm *my God my God why hast thou*

He climbs in, closing gently the door, and mutters, "Drive."

I feel my mind race away in front of us.

"What did you do?"

"Guy was sleepin'," Many-birds grunts. "He never woke up."

"Say again?" But I hear in that rising pitch of voice how my mastery is lost.

"He ain't yet," he mocks at once, "or you'd be runnin' like shit from d' cow, eh?"

"But how — "

"His tipi was held down by bricks is all. Fershitsake, are you waitin' fer d' sun t' get him up?"

I put the car in gear and let her rip.

He only clipped the robe of the Lord's anointed. He never stretched forth his hand against him

"Say," I try to get the upper hand again, "I know well thou surely shalt be king."

"Shit," Many-birds' face blurs with acid regret. "Dat king can go fuck himself fer all I care. Let's get some beer."

I must show surprise, for he holds up a fistful of money along with a watch.

"Fershitsake," I say. We laugh, each for his own reason, but I am driving as quickly as I dare.

Many-birds turns to see out the rear window.

"It's dere, behind us."

Then I am lost, till I see green lights printed in the mirror.

"Barry Hotel," I finally reverse it aloud.

Now we seem to have just abandoned the car somewhere on a street above the river. Since I am so disoriented for the moment, I don't object to Many-birds taking the lead. I know only that we have turned our backs on *a pillar of cloud from* that smokestack towering over the river. My reason assures me it is now for the best.

We turn a corner and a man lurches out of a doorway before us. He stumbles and goes down at my feet.

Lord, does thou wash my feet?

If I wash thee not, thou hast no part with me

I step over the man as if he had leprosy.

We stop before the side door of the hotel.

"You go buy it," Many-birds puts some money in my hand. "Twenty-four is good fer now."

He is looking away across the street already, interpreting the darkness.

"I don't know what to do. I never bought beer before. Here, why don't you?"

"Fershitsake," he ignores my momentary panic. "You ain't goin' t' get me locked up so easy as dat."

Still I eye the door in reckless desperation.

"Fuck," Many-birds says. "I'll be happy t' drive, if dat's what's eatin' you. I'm a good drunk driver."

As I step over the threshold, I hear him say, "I'll be across d' street. You better fuckin' come back — "

His voice is lost amidst the clamour of the room. I step into the cavernous brilliance where the hubbub itself swells me down the aisle. I sense the blur of faces jeering as I pass, but then I look and there is only a fat, florid man shouting across the table to a squeaky-voiced fellow. That tall man with the big ears beckons me; but the waiter goes to him instead. I glance down at the sawdust aisle and at once am skewered by roasting eyes. I rush forward, only to hear the voices stand and sing, "Let the healing waters flow." And then I am safe and secure down in front of the altar. The brown-vested minister holds his hands out to me, I reach him back with something, he goes and comes with healing waters, handing me the whole case of them.

"You've forgot your change," he calls, but I am embarked again through pandemonium, the crowd now praising and hollering hallelujah for another convert brought before the throne. I pass out the door, reluctant to be lost from such good fellowship. Better, my heart tells me, to be lost with company like this than to be shut up alone in glory.

I look in vain for Many-birds who has disappeared. Though didn't he say he'd be across the street? Perhaps he's found fellowship in that vacant lot.

I cross over the street into a swarm of sprawled bodies. A cheer is raised from a nearby company *for he commanded them to sit down by companies in the green grass. And they sat down in ranks, by hundreds and by fifties* Many-birds sits crosslegged in their midst.

"Where's my change?" he says as I transfer with both hands to him the case. Then he seems to forget it, cracking the cardboard box.

"Who's got a church key?" another man asks, holding up two dark bottles.

"I do," an Indian man grins toothlessly.

"Praise Jesus," says a plump woman with frizzy hair. She might be Indian too, unless all our faces have turned Indian here in this darkness. She smiles pleasantly as she passes the lidless bottles around the circle.

Many-birds raises his glass in salutation.

This cup is the new testament in my blood which is shed for you

"Man, this is coffee," a middle-aged man says.

"Haven't I seen you somewhere before?" the plump woman says to me.

I swallow the bitter liquid, feeling yeast swell up in my nose. I blow to clear my sinuses, hawking wetly in the dust.

"No offense," she says invitingly.

But even after she is turned to talk with Many-birds, I wonder at her words.

I drink to keep up with the company. The beer sits heavily in my belly. I feel it fanning out, and rising lightly, after a time.

The toothless man guffaws at something a bony-cheeked man says. The woman looks at me again as if she is still curious.

"Di'n't I see you once in some meetin'? Ain't you a preacher?"

There is a catch in the chatter of the company. I feel all their eyes upon me.

"No," I say firmly. "You mistake me for someone else."

The hush is released, the voices run on again amicably.

"We need a fire," the bony-cheeked man says as more bottles are opened. Some of the company walk off, tilting heads and bottles back. I drain another beer in two long swallows. But it isn't helping. I've got to get control of myself.

"What time is it?" Many-birds asks the moon.

"Damn near closin'," a voice sings out of the air above me.

"Goose Neck," Many-birds hiccoughs, "be a good bird an' fly over fer another case a beer."

I walk as on a sagging tightrope across the street. My knees are so terribly heavy, compared to my head. Inside, the hubbub is as loud as ever. I go into the beer parlour. This time I am neither hailed nor hissed. The crowd talks every man to himself, every face flushed with new insight. I look not on them, feeling myself alien and apart.

When I return to the street, my way is lit by the infernal flame.

"What took you so long?" the woman says.

"Man, this is coffee," the middle-aged man says, swigging from both hands.

Many-birds says nothing, looking glittering-eyed into the fire.

I drink in desperation.

"Don't you never say I took yer last beer!" the bony-cheeked man hisses.

The middle-aged man holds his head low like a bull about to charge.

"Bullshit, he did it!" The long, bony finger is pointed at me.

"Did you take my coffee?" the middle-aged man glowers at me.

"Dere's more in d' case," the woman says, rocking the box in her lap. She cradles it against her breast like a baby.

"I seen you somewhere before," the middle-aged man eyes me narrowly. "Sure, down at Elbow. Cunt. Somewhere. You was makin' a Ass of yourself, wherever. In front of a whole lot of people."

"I was never," I say solemnly, "in Elbow in my life."

"'Course not. Elbows is bony. I know I seen you in Cunt, though."

"What ya mean?" the bony-cheeked man says dourly. "Who said my elbows was too bony? You wanna make somethin' of it, fella?"

He is looking threateningly at me.

"There's more beer here," the woman says again, tenderly.

We all look at her.

"Jesus," the bony-cheeked man gets up and crawls toward her. He noses up under the case and nips at her breast.

"Baby. Oh, Jesus, Baby," the woman says, holding his head with one free arm.

"Man, that's coffee," the middle-aged man says.

The hotel spews out a belly-full of men. They heave through the door, stream away beneath the lights. I hear the sea roaring in my ears.

"Do you know why," the middle-aged man is roaring in my ear, it isn't the sea at all, "I drink? Beer makes me famous. If I wasn't drunk, I'd be just another dummy. Nature, you know, is what I live by. Did you know that? It could be chicken today, feathers tomorrow. But nature is what I live by. Say," he says after a pause, "I know you. I seen you before around Nipawin, up there somewhere. You're that healin' fella, ain't you, that cured the deaf?"

"How often," I erupt on him, "do I have to tell you people I ain't the goddamn guy you think I am? Now fershitsake lay off me, will you, Jack?"

The assembled host look on, amused.

"Well," the middle-aged man says, "gotta be goin'. Got me a rodeo to go to. Did I tell you I got seven pairs of cowboy boots?"

He lifts his pant leg to show down-at-the-heel, broken-back oxfords. I take a sudden liking to the man.

"You sure bust 'em," I say. "The horses, I mean. It sure is great to see horses broken, eh?"

"Yeh," he says. But he is already moving off. "Gotta be goin' now."

He sits down at the far side of the circle and drains his bottle in one long swallow. Then I notice there isn't a circle any more. I sit alone and they watch, like an audience waiting for the curtain to rise.

'*Whence comest thou?*' the first player says behind me.

'From going to and fro in the earth,' I answer him.

'Well, you can't stay here,' he says.

He steps onto the lighted stage. Then the middle-aged man says, "I got me a rodeo to go to." This time he actually stumbles off into the dark.

"What's wrong, off'cer?" the frizzy-haired woman says pleasantly.

The policeman laughs rudely.

"Brothels and beer parlours in the open, eh lady? Well, we don't need any more of your type in town. Come on, gentlemen, let's move it along."

"You know, you're kinda cute," the woman says. She is up on her knees, her breasts swaying beneath her.

"Now I don't want any trouble with you," says the officer.

"It's no trouble," she says, grovelling beneath him. "I'd like you t' fuck me."

There are scattered titters from the surrounding audience.
The policeman takes a backward step.

"Come on," he says. "There's no more room in jail. I want
you people out of here, is all."

"Where?" says the Mother of Mercy. "Where can we go?"

"Anywhere. Just get in out of the streets."

"Cud we come home with you?"

"I got enough troubles without you. Come on now, get out of
here."

The woman lunges suddenly, catching his boottops.

"Come on," she says. "I want you t' fuck me."

The policeman is struggling to free himself. The people have
gathered from all across the lot.

"I've got my beat," he says. "I'm just trying to do my job."

"So'm I," she looks him full in the face, "tryin' t' do mine."

There are catcalls from the audience for the villain, and many
more cheers for the heroine.

"Come on," he says, struggling more vigorously backwards.

"Okay." She looses her hold and in the same instant he trips
and nearly falls over his boots.

"Oh," she says to his retreating figure, "please don't go. I
want you t' fuck me." She sits with her legs spread in the dirt.

He runs through a shower of laughter.

"Come on," she cries after him. "Fuck me. Fuck me!"

Her face is wet with laughter. For a moment her mockery
almost restores something. Then Many-birds gets to his feet.

"C'mon," he says. "We're goin' places."

So he brings you on a steep and winding trail to the river. And
somehow you wonder if you're not walking on the river. But your
legs won't stand the pitch and trough of running water. Then
you've found your car on solid ground, after all, and you get in
with the motor humming. Many-birds closes you up. He goes
round to the other door and starts the motor. Buildings and lights
start to flow past your eyes. You try to focus to stop the flow from
gushing. You hold it. You close your eyes —

— and when you open them Many-birds is saying, "Where d'
fuck are we? I must of turned wrong somewheres."

Directly in front of you stands the castle, its floodlit flanks and
turrets closing off the way, and how did you fail to see before that
orange is the colour of Despair?

Your farce has been to no avail.

Whomever you fooled was yourself.

Yet you want to cry out, "I got out of Doubting Castle. I made it out with the Devil, didn't I?"

Then you remember, while searching for the outlet, that it was God who made it out with the Devil. Now here the way is but a wall before you.

You weep bitterly.

Then, even before you turn to look up the short, deserted thoroughfare, you sense the rush of the awful thing coming.

Agnes

When he showed up at the front door, I couldn't believe my eyes.

"What have you come *here* for?"

"I wasn't finished my hoein'."

"My husband doesn't need you any more."

"Ah, you know what I'm talkin' about. Agnes. Agnes, look at me!"

The door to the kitchen was still closed. He couldn't have come in again without my hearing him. I looked back at that awful skull and crossbones on the step.

"I don't know what you're talking about. My sister doesn't need a gardener."

"Agnes, for f — "

"No. . . . Haven't you heard? The radio says the city doesn't need any more men. You better go home. You won't find work here."

"Agnes, have you forgotten the way we were together? Don't you remember how it felt like the wind was in our face? Fershit-sake, Agnes, you're the woman I love! Don't you put on this way with me."

I look over my shoulder for just an instant.

"I don't think you better let him catch you here. It's safer in that little hick town, I swear it is!"

"Agnes, fershitsake. You didn't go back to him, did you Agnes? Don't look away from me, woman! I been livin' four days now just for a glance from those lovely eyes."

The kitchen was still clear. Elsie and her boyfriend were staying considerate up in their room. I would of died if she seen me talking to a man looking so old as him.

"Goddam that nosy old Indian, but I would of been here sooner, Agnes. You didn't need to go runnin' back to him. Why would you want to dirty yourself again with a shitpile like him?"

"He'll be back any moment. He just stepped out. I swear I won't be held responsible for what he does to you."

"Agnes, I did this for you. I took the worst he could offer for love of you."

"No, no."

"Yes, Agnes, yes. Look what I give up for you."

"No, no."

"Once, Agnes, it was enough just to look at you through the window. But I can't take bein' away from you any more. Let me come in."

"No, no."

"Agnes, I come through hell to get here. We rowed a goddam boat — I could take you for a ride in it, if you didn't want your sister to find me here. Or that other bastard. No one would know but you and me. We got our own private loveseat on the river, Agnes. Just picture us there, floatin' beneath the stars with all them lights like dimes on shore. But you would shine brighter, Agnes, and whiter than the moon in the sky!"

I think I would like to get that white bathing suit if he does take me to Vancouver. I always looked so nice in white. I'll get the kind that shows off my figure real good. It'll keep him crazy for me as long as I want. Boy, just to have a man as crazy as the boys!

"Agnes, I got a Cadillac out there too, with a driver. We can ride anywhere you like. And I'll send him away. It'll be just like — no wait, I should tell you. You know what I been thinkin'? We're just like that onetime King and his woman. I been rushin' to come to you so now our long wait will be over."

"No, no."

"Yes, and we'll stand like them in that picture, our faces toward the sun, gazin' into a future so bright that ever'body wonders at us."

"No, no."

"Yes, and even though they won't let you be called her royal highness, you'll always be queen of me."

"No, no."

"Yes. Oh yes, Agnes, just like that time you gave yourself to
me — "

"No."

"Yes you did, my love. We did."

"No. I never. No — "

" — then how do you suppose your husband jumped me from
behind? How else would I of give up my crown for you?"

"No. No, you're not a thing like a king. Kings are tall and
handsome. Not bumpy as a toad. You're like the prince someone
kissed to turn into a toad."

"I'm — Goddam it, Agnes, you take that back!"

"Get away. You get away from here!"

"You — "

"Get away or I'll scream!"

"You fuckin' bitch!"

But he went away. I knew he would: it worked the other time.
And none too soon. The car drove off. The back door opened. And
there stood my prince with the beer.

Many-birds

She can't be gone. I can still talk her into it. Into more than she's
ready for.

I stop the car in front of her house. There is a wind singing in
my ears like from that other time. Maybe more like it's whipping
in off of our lake at home. Waves are running onto the beach and
back again. Foam piling up on the sand. The shore can take a
terrific pounding, like that.

I pound and pound on the fucking door. No one answers me.
She's laid between the sheets again. Goddam barber's stood up like
a little gopher for her.

I strain on my toes to see something — anything — through
them curtains on the door. She used to draw the curtains to hold
herself away a little. But last night her face was shining like the
Frozen Over Moon. I can't stop it now; I shiver with all the fire
gone out of me. My face stares back like some person that used to
be. Goddam my buggered head.

I am down the steps and about to go when I look up at those windows to the side. What the hell, I think. You come a long way to quit now. Why don't you crane up for a look? If she's gone, she's gone. But what if she left you some sign you didn't see?

I can't reach the window from the yard. Not even standing on all the flowers an' shit. But there's a pail hung on the side of the house. I turn it upsidedown on a flock of dandelions. It's a balancing act, fershitsake. Standing tiptoe on a pail drumhead, hanging down from a windowledge.

I peer inside. Christ! There's someone staring back at me! I drop like a shot-up mallard, kicking the pail in my fall. It clatters against the side of the porch. I hit on my back in a nest of stink flowers. I'm not hurt. How does even a plant get this whiteshit smell? I get up like a horse, front feet first. I'm ready to run. But I don't hear voices. There's nothing but horse-hoofs clopping one street over.

I turn around to be sure no one is coming down this street. My car sits there alone. Except for Goose Neck slumped inside. The sky above the trees is streaked with red.

I try to get up the courage to stretch out my neck again. Too bad the Goose Neck wasn't here to look for me. Be kind of my eyes, like that. Fershitsake. No fucking way I want his eyes to see what's here. That's Agnes's dress, the one she wore tonight, hitched over her thighs. Christ, I can see her panties spread out like a hanky across her cunt! There she is, big as life and twice as ugly, laid back on a couch with her legs apart. And she's fast asleep! Why, I could almost reach out and blow my goddam nose on her hanky. Or play drop the little fucker, like they taught us when we were kids.

But a white flag, don't it mean you're giving up? I stare at that white patch enough to burn a hole in it.

I rap on the glass but she doesn't stir. I rap again. I might as well be a woodpecker gone to work on the prairie. By Jesus, my spit runs at the sight of them spread joints! So why'd she never let on we'd been together? Not a thought of how we swam in sweat together. A toad, she called me.

She ain't budged a bit. A toad! The bitch. I wish I'd of given her warts. There, beneath the sign at the junction. Sign of my own, my own goddam mark.

The wind whistles in my ears like the wind of her rising voice. I got to yell or do something. I feel like I'll splash up on a beach somewhere soon. Thunder Bird, is that what you meant for me to do? To run up in waves over that sleeping, white sand? In wave after wave after hot hot wave?

I'm almost surprised when the window pushes up so easy. Then I get to thinking, maybe she didn't mean what she said after all. Maybe the bohunk was sniffing round behind. She could be throwing the dog off the scent like that. Maybe she left the window open in case I come back. Why else would she be sleeping alone in a fucking porch?

I get wind of my mare on the way up the wall. My plume rises near to steeplechasing me over. But I light soft on my feet as the morning's last moonbeam. There's a smell of something more than mare in the room. Old couches and stuffed chairs. Place smells like a train station. A cell, with the piss pail open.

Fershitsake, they left that piss pail here between the chairs! Case of beer bottles, fershitsake! So I have to go step in it. Fuck, it rattles.

Agnes ain't moved a muscle. She's had a few beers herself. I stand above her bare legs, listening to her breathe. Agnes, my love, did you get tired of waiting for me to come?

I go down on my knees, not touching her yet. I can wait a little longer. I'm happy just to gaze so close upon her secrets. Her belly rises and falls above the straps an' shit. Then I reach out to lick her with my tongue. But before I can do it, my foot is telling me, What's another foot doing back here in the dark! I spin round, my tongue damn near left behind like a frog's. Fershitsake! It's a man, by the trouser leg. Slumped back in a chair under the window. But he's out cold. Jesus, that give me a fright! Thunder Bird, you could look out for me more carefully with your eyes that glow in the dark. You could let me see better at times like this, couldn't you? Then suddenly my eyes are open to the whole fucking situation. She meant what she said to me. Or she wouldn't be so free with the view to him. Fucking cunt, anyway.

Thunder Bird, if these are your signs to me, what should I do now? I'd like to rip the fucker's cap from his bleeding skull. Maybe nail his balls to the floor. You say the word. Remember, we used to take scalps once a night outa Blackfoot tents.

For once I wish Thunder Bird would speak goddam English. His signs are so fucking hard to make out. I lean into the shadows to see what the fat fucker's face can tell me. No wonder it stinks in here. Look at him, how ugly he is! If it wasn't for that mess of hair. . . .

Shit, it ain't the bohunk! It's Albert Many-guns! He always said he was gonna cut my nuts off one day. But in the pen I wouldn't give him no fucking excuse.

Ah, fershitsake, he's sleeping at the bottom of a beer barrel! He don't know fuck-all. Look at that: I can drop his hand on his lap and he don't even move. And the hand is as heavy as a pump-handle. I lean once more over that bullbig face. His eyes are sewed tight. And his chest is jiggling up and down like my ass is gonna be.

I turn to kneel bravely before that holy place, showing him my ass. Thank you, Thunder Bird, for speaking so clear to me. Agnes, you may be finished with me. But you know I ain't quite finished yet with you.

I start pinching her knee, the inner flesh of her leg. No more of this sweety shit. She goes right on breathing like a bear in a log.

I look again at Many-guns. He's blowing farts in his sleep. The fucker can have my woman once I'm through with her.

I take off every stitch of clothing but my shoes. I shiver a little with cold or excitement, I don't know which. My sleeping beauty ain't sensed a thing. I pull on the front of them panties, peel the side over her lovely fat. And land my finger on the button. Then I begin to press real slow. After awhile the cunt moves a bit and I make little, exploring rushes. She is breathing harder than ever. I get my other hand up under her ass, still working with the first, and she raises herself just enough to slip the hanky down. I stop what I am doing and run the whole flag down the pole. Don't take care to fold it the way the Indian Agent done. Only to salute it once with my nose.

Agnes! How could you have left me so soon for another man?

She answers like the cow letting down her milk. I give one quick glance into the shadows. This is one pistol Albert Many-guns ain't going to shoot.

I kneel before the couch and show myself to Agnes. One last time for old Agnes. This last my Agnes. Agnes. Agnes!

She moans from her belly. I try to slow down, to back off, but the wind drives me on, drives me on, drives me onto the shore. Then I shower on the rocks, break in spray, splash in agnes agnes Agnes?

Her eyes are opened, kind of dreamy. Christ. I catch up my clothes with one hand from the floor, though still easing in, still easing out. . . . Suddenly I slip and dangle.

The moment she loses touch, her eyes swim to a point. I can see the risen sun in them, ducking that arrow point.

"So long, Agnes," I say, leaking across one of her stockings.

Her scream parts the air behind me. It feels like it parts the hairs on my ass.

Now why did I forget to unlock the door? Her scream comes again. More pissedoff than scared. My fingers are numb against the fucking button.

"What —" Many-guns snorts like a bull in a closet.

But I am skinning my bareass down the walk.

"Start her up," I yell to my stirring fellow husband. He looks up startled, seems at once to catch on. There is only the sound now of her screaming behind me. I hate his deadly silence. "Hurry!" I say almost to the running board. If he don't get us away soon, we'll get to be very dead geese. Both of us.

The motor sputters as I rip wide the door. Then it catches as I catch the floormats.

"Drive!" I yelp with my nose into the rubber.

The car leaps ahead before we hear a sound like pebbles hitting the side. The snap of a pistol follows after. And here I hang out behind with already one hole for a target. Thunder Bird, remember now, I never asked to be too holy!

"Shit," I plead, "can't you hurry it any?"

But my fellow husband ain't cussed me out once for getting us into this shit. He just looks down with those awful reddened eyes on me. Telling me he's been the one all along to blame.

Jack

I AM THAT I AM

Fine-day

The River has been urging my whole life against me. I won't fight her any more . . . lying heavy as stone underwater . . . my ears starting to ring. I could almost believe I heard . . . singing?

I open my eyes. No singing here. Just that boy again, kneeling above me. Nick, who is not my son . . . who is going to see his mother. Still his eyes look so concerned.

"Don't be af — " I try to say, then cough up black stuff, weeds and water, before my voice gushes out like well-water. "She'll be happy to see you." The words sound like a dream in my ears . . . if I really said them . . . then I'm deeply changed.

She will be happy to see you too, I hear him think.

"I said is there anything I can do for you?"

"No, I feel fine . . . now."

"I was . . . sort of hard on you before."

His eyes start to break with his words. I want to save him that pain. And yet to break . . . I don't know. It no longer seems so bad.

"Would you let me call you *geedo*, maybe? Grandfather?"

"Whatever you like. It doesn't matter."

Wait for her in that clearing near to the Sun, he thinks.

Something inside me has returned to life. I look around our camp where hopeless men sit . . . recalling the boy who used to stand behind me.

"There is one thing you could do, grandson."

"You name it."

"If you're going by that hill on the bend . . . could you maybe land me there?"

"Why not? The San's two bends farther on, they say. Can't miss it. *Boysha*, sit where you are. I'll put the boat in the water."

So I sit and watch him haul at our canoe. Now the River won't stop piping in my bones . . . in the old days we had whistles of bird-bone . . . so then I find I'm watching the water after all, trying deeply to remember.

Here near shore it eddies, skates, swirls, tiny snag lines starting up, darting off. Yet tighter inshore it has to backeddy, soapy bubbles building like dishwater. Only way out does it stand still as glass, still moving deeply, swept along.

Then I remember sweeping with it, cold, so cold, my last breath going, just as my head lightened . . . mouth clean as light . . . and my whole life seemed to burst.

Mrs Jameson

He approaches the desk just as the news comes over the radio.

"Yes?" I say, but when I see he is lost in the story, I listen too.

"Hope is fast fading that Miss Earhart and her navigator will now be found. The maze of radio signals which has continued to feed that hope has become ominously silent. Since 5 a.m. yesterday, searchers say, they have received no new report of these mysterious, unlocated signals. While the vastness of the ocean itself shrouds her fate, most participants in the hunt now fear that Miss Earhart's craft is sunk in shark-infested waters somewhere north of Howland Island. Closer to home, two people were drowned yesterday while swimming in the Saskatchewan River near Nipawin. Witnesses say — "

"May I help you, son?"

Even now he seems to take no notice of me. But as I notice him more closely, I see this boy could pass himself for a disaster victim. It isn't that his clothing looks slept in, or even that it's become his only refuge; no, he's managed, somehow, with his unbearable lonesomeness about the eyes, to put himself right into the Earhart story. Lord knows the calamities that have befallen his family to set him so adrift like this. But when you see them as we do every day of the week, you'd think you could at least develop some working immunity.

"Don't worry," I say. "They're doing everything they can. It's possible they'll save her yet."

I know how empty, how very bitter that cliché can be. But at least this time I'm confident I'm not having to rally a relative of the victim.

"Were you here to see someone, perhaps? Is it your mother or father?"

"Yes, ma'am," he says in a tone coloured by fear or guilt, I don't know which. I expect I'd feel a bit of both, looking the way he does. So of course it would have to be his mother.

"What's her name, son?"

Country people, you have to assume, forget how to talk when they come to the city. It takes us weeks here to draw back the curtain they pull around themselves. Now if it was my boys, they'd have already talked the doctor out of his stethoscope.

"Sobchuk, ma'am."

I recall the woman before he spells out their name. Transfer from the mental asylum. A spot on her lung. They're so awfully overcrowded up there in Battleford. Yes, it's that thin, frail woman with her hair looking like her husband chopped it. Little wonder, the way some people live, that we're constantly open for business. Now if we could only make our next port of call the tub room on the way down the hall— And yet his mother is neat about her person. Maybe when it comes to country husbands, there's not only no accounting for taste, there never was that taste implied by choice.

Still there's something, a flash of something, that I admire about that woman, in spite of all her melancholia. I might have chosen, too, to be sick if I were in her place. Rather than to be a beast of burden to one of those farmers. And if it weren't for the children. . . . I just thank God my Roger was a city man as long as he lived.

I re-file the admittance form.

"First I'll have to clear your visit with one of the doctors. Don't be afraid, son. Your mother is doing as well as you could hope. Would you mind waiting in the — uh, over in that area by the door?"

I can feel those forlorn eyes follow me down the corridor.

I wonder what his connection is with the Earhart story. Probably a backwoods superstition that if you save one woman, you save the other. But you have to wonder, living so close as we do here to life and death, what we could be hoping for in this search for two lost fliers. You'd think that common sense would hold your interest closer to home. After all, we have a few victories around here; we give some people some good years yet; we manage to cheat death a little while longer.

And when we do lose a patient, as we did yesterday in the middle of this corridor, do we lie down and quit? I'll tell the world we don't. While the body is still wheeling down to the morgue, someone else is scrubbing blood out of stone. That has to be the hook for us. Lung hemorrhages, no matter how irreversible they happen to be, are still involuntary; they are just something that *happens* to you. But the Earhart woman *chose* to fly off around the globe. God knows what for, but she volunteered to do it. I guess that's what we're all thinking about around here.

Nick

The shoes of the nurse echo like judgment.

And that sight, through every doorway, of women abed doesn't help much. They all look so feeble; even the young girls. They are racked by coughing and spitting. Sometimes their eyes turn listlessly. But the rest, with backs humped under a sheet, face in toward the wall.

Then I feel my dread bounce back from speckled marble walls.

mother you were right we never cared nothing for you mother have mercy   but stone is unpitying   mother stone is too cold to look at turn away please from the wall

yet what can you do when the corridor itself is stone when this whole living place is its own tomb stone

We pass a door with a deep, metal tub in the centre of the room.

if i could have a wash since cleanliness is next to   happy mother were you ever happy are you happy here at last

"Your mother's on the sundeck," says the sunny young nurse.

I look through the sick room to where she points. Beyond the white metal furniture, a glass door is partways open.

"It's all right. She's expecting you."

Mother cradles something in her arms. She croons. I stand uncertain on the threshold.

"Come in," she says in Ukrainian.

I hang back, fearfully. I am afraid of what she holds in her arms.

"Don't be afraid."

I understand her well enough. Just my tongue is tied by the Ukrainian language.

"It's only you when you were little. Come see, Nick."
At last I approach.
Mother draws the blanket back for me to see.
My face is stubbled with fur. Just like my Dad's.
Then I remember.

"Dad's dead," I say to Mother in English. Her face is wan and drawn. She doesn't seem to understand me.
"Dead," I begin to falter.
"Duh-duh-duh-duh — "
Her voice is quivering. So they do forget, once they fall, how to talk to people!
"Doh-doh — damn him!"
She is crying now, and moaning. She never cared about him any more than he did about her. She never cared for anyone but herself. Though she always accused us first to make us feel guilty.

Then my little self is wailing like a baby.
Mom tries to hush him. And can't.
"Goddamn him," I cry in my terrible concern.
And recall that bottomless anger at being left alone. Being so alone in blame of both of them.
My baby self hushes. Still he looks out at the world with such mournful eyes.
"*Diboizha*, little one," I barely breathe on him.
He will need that blessing. For the sake of all of us.

Mother's grip is fierce. But she weeps a river over me. And then I hear myself, too, mourning for him. I'm crying as awfully, now, as *that one* she said was always hidden beneath our bed.

Fine-day

Already the Sun has whitened in the morning sky. When she begins to lick the damp off my limbs, I stretch out, grass bristling under my buttocks, the buffalo grass tickling between my legs. Soon there's a hot smell of earth, badger dirt, getting mixed with the musk of wildroses. Here in the thicket of my crotch it is also getting hot . . . with the tingle of Sun eating at my root. So I just let go . . . give myself right up to her hot caresses. . . .

. . . . Sun has chewed the meat off my bones! My skeleton dances right in front of my eyes . . . such a click and clatter of old bone! I sit up. The dancing stops. I look around and see my shadow . . . looking at me full on the earth. Maybe Sun is telling me I am still of this world. But when I lie down again, old Skeleton kicks up his heels. Then the earth starts to shake: this whole hill moving here above a mighty whirl of waters: but I refuse to be shaken . . . until the trees in the cutknife start to walk. I sit up quickly . . . bones all flesh again.

Then I notice that the Bighouse across the River is on fire. Nine rows of windows all ablaze . . . flames reddening through every tower . . . but still no smoke. How can this be? If Sun herself is still in the east . . . it can't be Sun. Yet the light flames away over there . . . in another world. Then I think, maybe it is Sun's house . . . where she stays at night. But how would she live in our world without burning it up?

As soon as I think that, a door opens . . . someone stepping out. I seem to lose sight of him, among the trees and bushes, until he walks out on the water. Now he is crossing to my side, the light streaming away in front of him, and I glimpse again that brilliance out of such a blackness.

Maggie!

She comes up the bank, her hair shining as darkly as ever. She is slender too, just as she used to be . . . just radiant.

Well, old man, what took you so long

Maggie, what are you doing here

I live here

But I thought you were with

I was always here you can't get rid of me that easily

She smiles. I feel sunlight winking on my belly.

Maggie, you know I wouldn't

I know you wouldn't   that was the trouble   did you think I would wait forever

Maggie I am so   sorry   no that doesn't say it   I'm a sorry excuse for a man

No I told you before it couldn't be forever don't you remember

I never forgot anything you told me

She looks right through me. I feel a wind from her eyes blow chill between my bones . . . now I can't hide my nakedness.

Don't even try

Her eyes are warm again.

Maggie are you saying you would

She glances at my manhood where it rests . . . shyly . . . then looks back at me.

I hold her glance unswervingly. It tingles to those farthest parts of my flesh.

She turns aside, taking off her dress. I see first her swelling hips . . . that crisping of hair below her belly. I smile . . . to cover my fear. My fear of what? . . . that she won't really want it? Naturally she notices . . . and her eyes make me even more afraid. She can't want . . . me?

How do you expect me to if you look so forced like that

She stands there naked. But I can't stop grinning like a forced Weesakayjack, the time he had to change himself into a woman, and then I think how I must be making Maggie feel.

Thank you to think of me   now will you try to forget yourself

I told you it couldn't be forever so let yourself go

I breathe deeply . . . and let it go . . . always like that. Get used to letting it go.

Come here

She holds me close . . . I touch her lightly across her back, feeling each knuckle of her spine . . . feeling so near to her I would like to crawl inside her skin . . . if only to hold her mysterious life.

You do hold my life in these bones as I hold yours

And now her presence swarms through my open spaces. As soon as we are coupled we seem to rise and fly. . . .

Maggie am I dreaming again

She does not answer me. I look away to the four corners of this earth, to its farthest ends. How neverending it is! How the light builds unendingly too, till it bursts inside my head, flooding towards those ends of earth. . . .

Maggie shudders, crying out at the last.

Double Runner

. . . . I wake up weeping. It is only rain needling my face, my groin, with its tiny pins. I don't move, looking through a swirling curtain of rain over the River. The door in the Bighouse is closed up again. But has not the rain doused the fire over there? So maybe the Sun's house stands in our world after all.

Then I feel what a relief rain is to the root of me . . . touching around myself so gingerly. I'm burned pretty black, I guess . . . only I hope I still know the woman who may say it's not just some shadow. . . .

I let myself settle back in the soaking earth. And even my heart now wills my only Sun to go and come again.

Many-birds

Too goddam many guns. One of 'em's going to get me the minute I fall asleep. So drive.

But the first car that zooms the hill scares the shit outa me. I almost drive on the sidewalk.

"Hey lookout!" says Billy O'Jibway.

"It's hard to see. Fucking mud on the glass."

But I'm scared all to hell after running through gunfire. Swooping in like game to find our flock. Honkers settling over a marsh, big wings almost flapped forward. Bang bang bang and they veer off every which way. And then that lost, wild crying, getting out. Mary Bighead and Billy in back, you'd think they was the ones shot. They had just got in at the *Barry* and bang! it was like they brought it down on our heads.

"Fershitsake," I said running up over a curb, "hold your honkers 'till we're outa this hole, hey?"

Bullets rattled off of doors. A side window cracked like a spider web.

"What — " Billy said.

"You want me to stop and let you out?"

We flew around corners closer than two swallows. Nobody said to get out. Got to flock together to survive. One is so more open than four.

Now Billy says out of his no-teeth, "Hey Mawwy. Wemembeh that house? We got a woom theh with a bed an' a pail an' didn't come out foh thwee days."

I see Mary Bighead, like a goddam hunting dog, follow his pointed finger.

"Yeh, Billy," her scratchy voice softens up. "You never wasted that bed on no woman's beauty rest."

That's for sure, I think. That hairy head would be as restful as a wildrose bush. Though maybe you'd do for meaty enough.

"Hey driver," she says, "are you having trouble seeing or something?"

I look at her silly grin in the mirror. The sight of that face makes me stale again. Goddam used beer.

"Jesus! I could use some fresh air anyways," she says when I don't answer. "Can you find someplace sheltered, driver? Someplace I won't be shot at?"

When I don't turn, Billy says, "I can see you ain't seen Highway Mawwy do what she's famous foh."

Then there is quiet, finally, in the back seat. Nearly as quiet as my fellow husband sitting here, not a care in the world. He don't care how many times you shoot at him. He's used to it.

I look for some sign to lead us outa town.

"Can't see fuck-all," I say at last. "Can any of you make out a highway sign through this mud?"

"You'd see a sign, all right," says Mary Bighead, "if you'd only find me a safe place."

"Fershitsake," I say. Billy giggles like a goddam girl. But I turn off the big street into a nice shady little road. Jesus, put a bitch in a car, an' you'll stop every goddam block to let her piss.

"Hurry it up," I say as Billy helps hoist her outa the seat.

I look in the rear-view, checking for sneaky hunters. Then I see the dashclock is stopped. Little shit thing like that, why should it start me so bad?

The car front shakes. I wing up like I been shot. Ah, the bitch is only scratching her ass on the fender. Jesus, I got to get settled down. I can't go on listening like this for the snap of the next thunderbolt. Thunder Bird, I'm glad you showed your support for me awhile back in that rain. But now that it's cleared off, you got to help your Many-birds get clear of this place.

"Fershitsake," I yell through the window, "get off that hood!"

Billy has helped the cow on top. Here she's backing straight up to my window like she don't hear a thing. I'm about to honk my horn anyhow when she bunches her dress and drops them drawers. I get a glimpse of something dark and lovely. Next thing you know, my window's running wet with mud.

"Tuhn on yoh wipahs," Billy says.

I do. Quick as quick. The window comes clear just as them panties snuff out the sight of our last safe highway.

Billy helps her down like a queen from the throne.

"Get in the front," I say as they open the back door. "Sure, come on up here." I give her my best come-on smile, showing teeth.

"We'd have to ask yoh fwiend to move," Billy says.

He's too goddam cute. Bad for keeping teeth.

"Fellow husband," I say, "would you mind sitting in the back?"

We finally drive a block in damn near royal style. I feel lots better now. Waked up enough to find a way outa this mess.

"How's this for nice?" I say to her, touching the catfur of the seat beside her leg. Next I'm surprised how quick the cat will yeowl.

"I think he hit my doo-ah," Billy says, his mouth sucked in like a asshole.

"Fershitsake," I say, tramping it. We come up off the right wheels going round a corner. The streetcar is stopped a ways back. Could of hit the fucker headon like that. They should be more careful.

"He was on the wailwoad twacks," Billy says, still all tight. "I saw him cutting acwoss, though, to twenty-fifth stweet."

Highway Mary has her hand on my knee. She ain't far off a rock to hold to.

"Missed it," I say.

"What?" She don't move her hand, squeezing tighter. We look down the length of hood stretched out between my legs.

"Missed the last chance that bugger's going to have at us."

Now if I only can find the road outa town.

We swoop the hill and there's a flashing yellow light ahead.

"Hell, this is still barking up a dead horse's ass."

In case the bugger is cutting up this street, I peel off down the alley. But it's a mistake. The mud flies from the first hole we hit. We skitter out on the big road again, below the yellow light. Big ballpark or something to the left. I turn in.

"Highway Mary, you got any washer left?"

She turns that huge owl's head and gives me a sporting blink. I goddam laugh out loud.

"Help her out, fershitsake, Billy. We ain't got all day."

My real trouble is, the light is getting poor. The sun is already behind the hill.

At least I'm prepared this time. I got them wipers smearing mud before the raindrops fall.

I see, like a flash from Thunder Bird's eye, a crack of light. Little downy curls, like feathers. What a view. What a view! Thunder Bird, I never knew you was a woman, like that!

He lights with a crack behind my head. Again a crack! And still no thunder. Only a steady hiss like rattlesnakes on the ground.

Tires shot out! Fershitsake, we're sitting ducks. I can't even try to drive with Mary blocking my view.

"Sonuvabitch," the bullbellow closes up the side of the car. "Using sonuvabitching women yet."

The voice stamps along the top of my coffin. I don't care to face that final thunder. I'm froze like a goddam prairie chicken. And he sees me, I know. Fly up and be shot; sit here and be shot. I feel sweat lick down my ass like my tongue was tingling through that glass.

"Get outa the car."

I hear the rumble now like distant thunder.

Thunder Bird, I think hopelessly, are you there somewhere?

"No woman's gonna save you. Fucker." He bites it off like the end of the cigar. I get the belly-feeling he likes this sort of thing.

There's maybe one hope left. But my voice has the strangest whinny to it. I act like it's from looking out the window.

"You hurt any woman an' you know what they'll do to you in the pen. Have to keep you in the hole just to save the guys from nutting you."

"Fucker," he bites and spits again. "You ain't gonna make it into any hole again. After what you done to my woman."

Suddenly I ain't ever felt so glum in my life. I look around for something, anything, to hold to. Then that stopped clock on my dash startles me outa the car.

"That's better. I didn't want to mess them nice seats with your brains."

A voice spatters behind me like gunfire.

"Mister, what makes you think he's the one who did it?"

I draw another lively breath. Oh good Christ! I feel the bugger's eyes quit drilling holes in my head.

"How do I know you both didn't, fucker?"

Fershitsake, my fellow husband, say how you know! No, fershitsake, don't bother! Too many streaks of blood spilled already toward the eastern sky.

"Because I'm the one that did it, mister. I did it and I enjoyed it. If you need someone to shoot, take me."

Christ. Oh Christ. But it hurts to breathe so shuddering deep.

Silence. The silence of the grave.

"I'm going back toward the ball park," Many-guns says suddenly. "I don't care which one of you fuckers comes to pay up. Just be sure I got my rod on your woman till I see one a yous coming."

He's gone. I look up at Highway Mary on the hood. I wouldn't want to see his rod on her, like that. I have this wild hope that maybe we can fly again before the wind.

"My fellow husband," I swing round to look at him. His face is moose-gloomy, like before. Now he slips outa the car. I try to catch that sad goose eye coming by. But he doesn't see a thing.

"We'll get married," I say to him in passing. "In a church."

He goes without a word into the shadows.

I'd go myself and wring the fucker's neck. Snap it with one jerk, like a fucking rooster. But I got a wife to think of now. My fellow husband was considerate of that.

Suddenly I'm too drained to fly.

The cops gotta be here soon. Best to skin across them railroad tracks.

I gaze up the length of hood once more, where my prairie chicken squats so lovely.

Jack

I AM THAT I AM
AM I worse than Moses?
I AM

When I step down from the car, I hear the chorus singing over-head. Chirping. The birds are far too sad to be singing. The robins, I think, sound saddest of all. They are mourning the light, tweeting from their perches in the treetips to hold still to the sun. Give us one moment more! Their strain lifts a little at the end, released from breaking hearts.

I AM would be at peace with Himself
His brother could never stand for Him
I AM has to die for Himself

Behind me, it comforts me to think, my brother is safe.

Have pity upon me, have pity upon me, O my brother

The leaves of the trees smell so fresh after the rain. It would be difficult, I expect, to be a tree. Look how the leaves are huddled there against the dark. They shiver so. For who can say that on the morrow the sun will rise again?

O my brother, the hand of I AM has touched me. Pray for me as I do for you

It would be as hard, I expect, to be a man as it would a tree.

To become man

Suddenly it's as if my side is pierced by some thought. I stop between two trees: drape over to ease my pain. The bark beneath my palms is so kindly rough. And now the weight of the world seems drawn out through my feet. You trees: I'm sorry for adding to your burden. Still my heart cannot support this weight; I feel it separate into thick and thin.

Through thick and thin we stuck together, my brother. Now be at peace with yourself

I turn a corner in the high, green wall. Not yet. O then not yet.

So which way to turn? Has He fenced up my way that I cannot pass?

But I see at last where the path is set, this side, in deeper shadows.

Now I know that my — my —

There's something I should remember. But the sound of robins overtakes my thought. I quicken my step toward the corner, bracing as best as can for the rush of what awaits I AM

WEDNESDAY